The White Sibyl

JOANNA LEYLAND

Copyright © 2013 Joanna Leyland

All rights reserved.

ISBN-13:978-1493560448
ISBN-10: 1493560441

To June Everett

1

Lena had surrendered life very gracefully. She awoke early one morning as the first light of dawn was glowing dimly through the shutters and the first muted sounds of birdsong came tentatively from the gardens. She felt incredibly well and strong and happy. She stretched, cautiously at first and then luxuriously; nothing was hurting – no burning tingling in the soles of her feet, no tightness in her swollen knees, no grinding ache in her hips or shoulders – and she smiled with pleasure.

She recognised the benediction for what it was: the strength of the spirit in all its joy and glory as it readied itself to return home. Home, she thought. Yes, indeed. A moment's sadness for those she had to leave brushed her with feather wings. Then she smiled again, and very gently and quietly went on her way.

Tuesday 12th – Wednesday 13th January

The letter was waiting for Jane when she returned to Rome after Christmas in England. It was wedged between an electricity bill and an offer for mail order wine "Especially selected for Jane Harrison! Place your order now and receive wonderful free gift!" She was tired after the journey, immensely happy to be home, and laid the post on the table to look at later. The most important thing was to reconquer her territory, as she thought of it. This took the form of switching on the central heating and all the lights, choosing upbeat music to play, changing the bed and putting on the electric blanket to air the bedclothes, sweeping and dusting. She had poured some wine to celebrate her return and took pleasurable sips whenever she passed the glass. The suitcase, first left just inside the door, she carried to the bed, planning to unpack later, but then remembered her new diary for the New Year, just waiting to be filled in with birthdays and notes to herself.

The search for the diary led to her throwing the clothes to be washed in the laundry basket, and then she came across a novel she had been given at Christmas and sat on the bed reading and leaning on the half-unpacked case. When the phone rang she came back to the present with a start, realised the music had stopped, and hurried to answer, collecting her wine on the way. "*Pronto?*"

"Uh ... I was ... uh ... looking for Jane Harrison," came a tentative male voice.

"This is Jane."

"Jane, ... uh ... this is George. I don't know if you remember me ..."

"George! Of course I remember you – you must be joking! How are you?" She was laughing at the absurdity of George actually believing she could forget him after the events of the previous year. But then, from what she knew of George that was typical of him.

His voice was relieved. Had he really imagined some other dismissive response? "Fine ... uh ... very well. How are you?"

"Great – your timing is perfect. I just got back from England. And George, every time I go I wonder why I bother. All those pasty grumpy faces! Anyway, what about you? What are you up to?"

"I'm ... uh ... here in Rome actually. On my way to Siberia."

"Siberia!" Jane didn't know which news to react to. In Rome or going to Siberia. She chose the latter. "Why Siberia, George?"

"Work – I've got a contract for a new construction project – three months. When I found it was easier to go via Rome, thought I'd ... uh ... stop off for a couple of days."

"That's wonderful! We must get together. Where are you staying?"

"Hotel near the station."

Jane looked swiftly at her watch, just before six o'clock. Her tiredness had passed, the unpacking could wait, and she wasn't working the next day, would not be working until she found another job in fact. She made up her mind.

"George, why don't we get together this evening? Go for beer and pizza? You like pizza, don't you?" A sudden memory flashed into her mind: a summer's day, the pizza place with its red plastic tables in Genzano, and the three of them, George, Gabriel and herself, talking about the golden bough. She almost missed George's reply.

"Yes ... uh ... good. Where shall we meet?"

Jane made some rapid calculations; hotel near station; buses to Trastevere.

"Do you feel like coming down here? There's a family-run place that's good. I can meet you at the bus stop."

"I'll take a cab," said George," if you give me an address."

"Just say Piazza Sonnino. I'll meet you and we'll walk from there. About seven-thirty, OK?"

When she put the phone down, she did so slowly and carefully rather than with her usual clatter, and stood for a moment still looking at it as if it might voice some comment or suggestion. Then, with sudden panic, rushed to make sure the water was hot. It was. Some things at least did work when they supposed to. Now, clean clothes, a shower, it was only a ten-minute walk to Pizza Sonnino, and then perhaps a little more wine and finish emptying her suitcase. She was home now.

Once in the shower, rubbing shampoo thoughtfully into her hair – all her actions had been studiedly calm since the phone call – Jane allowed herself to think about the previous year. At first she only played with bright fragments of memory, moments she had avoided re-living until now:

the slip of paper from the dying man, the professor with the vivid green eyes and enigmatic past ("just a passer-by"), the drive with Gabriel from Rome to Nemi in the black monster he had hired ("I expect the wheels will slip off the edge and we'll roll to the bottom and burst into flames."), and ... that last encounter in the grey shadows of the clearing, the dying rays of the sun slanting and flaring to the west.

She found herself standing immobile, hands still raised to her head, and hurriedly began to rinse away the shampoo. A new year is not enough, she thought distractedly, last year is still too close.

In the Hotel Azeglio Cortina, near the station, George too was making ready to take a shower. The room was a hermetically-sealed box with double-glazed windows and stiff green drapes, so that only a distant hum of traffic was audible. He pulled one of the drapes to one side. The window was streaked with rain and the street below shone a wet black. Rome, but Rome in January. When he had arrived, he had been surprised – then was surprised he felt surprised – by the cold wet gloom, the worst winter for twenty years apparently. The summer before had stayed with him so vividly that he had vaguely expected to find the city still magically held in that time, the streets suffocating and drowsy, the clear sky blindingly blue. Now, in mid-winter, it seemed not only another city but another time. He dropped the curtain back into place, went into the bathroom.

He too was thinking about last year but whereas Jane's memory darted and flashed like a humming-bird, he – the practical, the prosaic – thought of events in sequence and then summarised his findings. Apparently, what had happened, according to Professor Caseman, was that an ancient prophecy had been fulfilled, a battle between good and evil had taken place – as it was bound to – and had been fought and won. By the modern representative of the priest king, the Rex Nemorensis of the sacred wood at Nemi. That the modern representative was a man that George had known and – if not exactly liked – respected was very ... strange; he could think of no better word. And the man, Gabriel, had gone, disappeared at the very moment of victory. George noticed his watch, lying sideways on the basin, and he too speeded up, turning the taps full on.

They arrived in Piazza Sonnino at the same time, hailing each other with pleasure, Jane kissing him loudly on each cheek ("Two for Italy, George!"), then hurried to the pizzeria, talking disconnectedly of his journey, Jane's Christmas holiday, and – of course – the weather; it was better in England at the moment.

The pizza place, one of Jane's favourites, was awash with light and noise. They found a table in one of the three recessed dining areas, away from the main room where a get-out-of-jail party appeared to be in progress; Rome's central prison, Regina Coeli, was also in Trastevere. A short thick-set man, jowly face gleaming with sweat and goodwill, was on his feet at the end of a long table of about twenty people: "And now, let's have a toast to my brother Carmelo, the victim of legal prejudice and judiciary bad faith ..." Cheers, glasses raised, much slapping of backs and more cheers. It was not clear which one was Carmelo.

George and Jane ordered and sat back, momentarily at a loss as to what to talk about; fortunately, their glasses of beer arrived almost immediately.

"So?" Jane said encouragingly; if she waited for George, they could well spend the evening in silence. "Siberia. Isn't it winter there, George?"

"Right," agreed George, relieved that she had taken the lead, "but this is just the first recce – we'll be starting work in the summer."

"Yes, I suppose everything is frozen solid," agreed Jane. They fell silent, and then:

"Did you ... uh ... ever go to see Professor Caseman again?" asked George tentatively.

The waiter arrived with their pizzas, enormous bubbling wagon-wheels of prosciutto, mozzarella, bits of sausage and crispy salami; olive ends bobbed above the oily surface, like survivors of a shipwreck in mid-ocean. They both started cutting and pulling at the pizzas.

"Yes, I ..." Jane paused, put the piece of pizza she had been manoeuvring back onto her plate, and wiped her fingers on the rough paper napkin. She was frowning.

"Yes?" he prompted. The noise of the pizzeria blared and surged, and he did not hear what she said next.

"...?"

"I said, I went a couple of times," repeated Jane, leaning closer. Then she paused again, picked up the piece of pizza and took a couple of bites. "About once a month," she went on finally, "but only three times. I mean ... Sorry, I'm explaining this very badly." She took a gulp of beer, wiped her mouth and smiled helplessly at him.

"What happened?"

She marshalled her thoughts. "Well, the first time was last September. It was still lovely weather and we sat in the garden, had tea, chatted, and she was so pleased to see me. She called me 'dear Jane' and was so interesting and funny. You remember?"

George did. He had a brief memory of smiling green eyes dancing with mischief and a voice saying, "I need strong muscles to carry me, Mr Sutton, and since mine are not, I would ask you to lend me yours." What a game old girl, he thought, as he had at the time.

"Oh, and she was telling me about her university days and her study of ancient Roman religion," said Jane. "Finding Nemi was a complete coincidence apparently – originally she was concentrating on Tivoli, the Temple of Vesta there, and the legends associated with the area. She was so interesting," she repeated, frowning again.

"But ... what about the other times you went?"

Jane again drank more beer, and looked around the room, though it was obvious she saw nothing of her surroundings. Whatever had happened must have been upsetting.

"She changed," she said flatly, looking back at George, and now her eyes were sad. "I went the next month, October – I would have gone more often but it was a nightmare getting there on public transport. I thought she was tired – well, older people do get tired, don't they? – and she was ... vague and querulous. She said the tea was too hot, she complained that her cushion was too hard. It was so … unlike her. I didn't stay long, I didn't want to tire her. I went the next month, and she was the same, worse even. She had aged terribly; I even thought she was going senile." Jane's voice sounded forlorn. It had upset her more than she could have imagined to find – not Professor Caseman but a crotchety old woman. Then, at the end of the third visit, the professor had suddenly flashed her a look of what seemed to be pure spite, and hissed, "And what do you want coming here all the time? I expect you think there'll be something for you in my will." The venom, and the darting, somehow crafty, look the professor gave her, shook Jane to the core. It was the last visit she made.

"Old people," offered George consolingly, now well into his pizza, and looking very greasy and red in the face. "My mother went like that. Dementia. Upsetting. Causes a character change, you know. It's not the real person."

He picked up his beer glass at the end of this telegraphic utterance, feeling very sorry for Jane, who had seen the change at first hand.

"It's just so awful to think of the professor like that," Jane said. "She would have hated the thought, I know." She had tears in her eyes. Little as she had known the professor, she had felt there was a bond between them but it had been broken by old age and its infirmities. She shook herself. *Carpe diem*, she thought. Live for the day, because you just don't know what the future will do. Seize the moment. Enjoy.

"Anyway," she said, forcing her voice to be cheerful,

"what about you, George? How long are you going to be in Siberia?"

"Don't know at the moment," he said, following her lead and leaving the subject of the professor. "Depends on what I find when I get there. Looking at ways to secure one of the gas lines. They're losing too much, seems it's getting tapped off on the way." His talk became technical and Jane, though understanding very little, was relaxed and soothed by the neutral specialist terms. That's the good thing about science, she reflected, it has none of the messiness of human affairs.

The letter – wedged between the electricity bill and the offer for mail order wine – was still there the next morning when Jane remembered the post. The evening with George had been pleasant but with an underlying awkwardness – they had first met in extraordinary circumstances, and had progressed to normality. It wasn't the right way round, thought Jane. They had missed out on the everyday social bits that form relationships.

She was sipping coffee and waiting for her computer to boot up while looking out into her tiny courtyard. The building, an old three-story Roman house, had originally had a much larger courtyard and Jane's flat had been built, probably illegally, on three sides of it. The kitchen formed one 'wing', the miniscule bathroom and corridor-like bedroom the other, while a long living room linked the two; her courtyard, a dim dank place in winter, was all that remained of the original one.

I expect George is on his way to the airport now, she thought, and then noticed the pile of letters and sat at her desk to go through them, the computer humming and blipping its way through its arcane procedures in front of her.

The electricity bill was not as high as expected – just as well, she thought, I really must look for another job. Those bastards ... Then, she saw the heavy white envelope with its embossed heading *Avv. De Angelis, Via Grotticelle, Nemi (RM)*. Nemi. A lawyer's office. The professor? She felt a sudden reluctance to open the letter, sipped more coffee, and wished she still smoked. Open it, you idiot, she ordered herself.

Inside there were two letters, one on heavy cream paper, another inside an envelope with Jane's name on it in spidery, slightly shaky italics. She looked at the main letter first, not so much skimming it as trying to glimpse the meaning behind the ornate Italian legalese. *Gentilissima Signora* ... my sad and painful duty ... the passing away of Professor Caseman ... my office at your disposal.

She burst into tears, blindly groped in the desk drawer and fished out the crumpled cigarette packet with its three musty cigarettes, her 'I dare you' supply. Outside the misty drizzle had turned to heavy rain that drummed insistently on the corrugated-iron roof of the flat. In the courtyard the pot plants and ferns drooped submissively under the downpour, while excess water pooled and streamed and gurgled down into the central drain. I don't like damp, thought Jane, or water either if it comes right down to it. Too invasive, too ... wet. The cigarette – unfortunately – tasted delicious, especially with coffee.

But there was the other letter and, still holding the cigarette, she opened it clumsily and with some difficulty; it appeared to have been gummed down. Inside there was one sheet of thin blue paper, as fine as airmail paper and as translucent as an onion skin. Jane read it as quickly as if she were taking medicine.

My dear, (the professor had written)

You were hurt and puzzled by my behaviour when we last met, and I hope you will forgive me. I had imagined we would see each other again so that I could explain, but the fact you are reading this letter means that cannot happen now.

It is with affection that I remember our first meeting, when you attended my lecture, "The Lesser Goddesses," in Oxford, and I have been so grateful for your friendship and correspondence over the years. I sincerely hope that when you think of me, you will remember your visit last September, when you were kind enough to listen to an old woman reminiscing about her past studies. You always were kind, Jane, kind and imaginative and brave. Keep these qualities, my dear. I know you will use them well.

I have left a keepsake for you at the nursing home. I apologise for asking yet another journey of you, but know that you will not refuse this last request. I wish you all good things, and all happiness, my dear Jane.

Professor Caseman (Lena)

Tears were trickling down Jane's cheeks but she was also aware of enormous relief. With the letter the disappointment and sadness of their last meeting had vanished. That autumn day the journey back to Rome had seemed endless, a muddle of waiting and jolting: waiting for the taxi to Nemi, more waiting for the coach back to Rome that rattled and bumped until the arrival – before Rome – of a thudding headache; more walking and waiting in the city itself to take the metro, airless and crowded, and then two buses back to Trastevere and home. And all the time, the hurt and desolation caused by the professor's words.

But now, she was magically restored. The professor had known how she felt, even asked her forgiveness. It was then that Jane paused, puzzled, stubbed out the cigarette in her saucer, and read the letter again, slowly this time and concentrating on the second paragraph. Her puzzlement grew. What lecture in Oxford? What friendship and correspondence over the years? They had met the previous summer. Perhaps the professor had in fact been senile, had confused Jane with someone else.

Jane closed her eyes, remembered what she had said to George the previous evening, "It was so unlike her," and then looked at the beginning of the letter. "I had imagined we would see each other again so that I could explain." Explain. That meant there was a reason. It had not been the beginnings of dementia or the vicious whim of a sick old woman. There was a reason.

She laid the letter carefully on the desk, oblivious of the computer that glowed its readiness. She angled the table lamp over the fragile paper – as though more physical light would bring more understanding – and sipped at her cooling coffee, trying to clear her mind before reading it again.

This was how she had sat in Silvia's apartment in the ghetto last year, when she and Gabriel had been trying to make sense of the few facts they had. The message left by the dead man, "the artefact is ready. Where is the original?" Nemi, strawberries, Caligula's ships, H.E. Caseman, the professor herself. And now there was this letter – another message – and perhaps a second message hidden beneath the words. The battle they had fought last year had been deadly and dangerous. Jane still had a scar on her cheekbone where Varian had smashed his fist into her face before that final encounter ("A little something to take the heart out of them," the dreadful Mrs Pleiades had said). So, perhaps it was still deadly, still dangerous. The professor, even in a letter left with a lawyer, would have taken no chances, would have been extremely careful, but would have left enough information for Jane to understand.

She picked up the sheet again and glanced out of the window. The rain had eased slightly and the courtyard looked brighter. A smell of soup and roast meat – pork? - drifted from the restaurant next door. Upstairs her neighbour Loretta was clashing pans and shouting at her mother-in-law. I must look at every single thing the professor says, thought Jane, and started studying the letter line by line.

If the professor was what Jane believed her to have been, the first paragraph – the lecture in Oxford, the correspondence over the years – was the professor's way of telling Jane that this was what she must say if asked. *My cover story*, thought Jane, trying for humour, but it did not sound as amusing as she had hoped. Then, "The first time you came to see me last September ... an old woman reminiscing about her past studies." *And I was telling George about the conversation. About Tivoli, the Temple of Vesta, the local legends. The professor wanted me to think of Tivoli and let me know that ancient religion is involved.*

She calls me kind and brave and imaginative. Again she felt tears prickling her eyes. "Keep these qualities, my dear. I know you will use them well." *I must be all of these to do whatever it is she is asking me to do. The fulfilment of another prophesy? Another* – she quailed – *battle?*

Lastly, the keepsake – it could be something important, something that would give her more information, or merely a pretext to return to the nursing home, or both. "Yet another journey ... know that you will not refuse this last request" – Jane had gone to Nemi the previous summer to deliver the dying man's message, and this was equivalent, this was equally important ...

The nursing home. Well, as far as the journey was concerned, she could drive there this time. No more worrying about public transport, and the home had a large car park. Tomorrow even, yes, tomorrow.

2

Thursday 14th January

On the morning that Jane was driving to Nemi, Dott. Salmone, Mayor of Tivoli, was standing in his satisfyingly large office in the municipal building, looking out at the grey winter skies and rain-slick roofs of the town. A small portly man, with the evidence of too many official dinners protruding above – and below - his waistband, he had been attempting to prepare for his eleven-o'clock meeting but, restless, had left his desk to peer down into the gloomy piazza below. With irritation he noticed that one streetlamp *still* showed a fitful glow when all the others had dutifully faded. In Tivoli! The very first city in the whole of Italy to have electric street lighting! He marched to his desk and wrote *Lampione*! on a yellow post-it, slapping it onto the right-hand corner of the desk, which was faded and sticky from past reminders.

He knew why he couldn't settle to anything, and was annoyed with himself for what he considered his 'provincial' reaction – after all, this was not the first time a film would be made in the town. But – and it was a very big "but" – previous films had been documentaries ("The Wonders of Italy", "Hadrian's Vision", "Water as Sculpture", to name but a few), small affairs with gently-spoken presenters and unobtrusive technical staff, whereas this time it was to be a full-scale mystery drama with famous names, stunning locations – all in the area (it was time Tivoli was recognised for the jewel it was) – and a huge budget. It would be altogether different, which was one source of worry, and the time of year was odd too, taking in the last two weeks of January and the first one in February, thus conflicting with preparations for Carnival. Strange – film-makers usually wanted blue skies and sun-drenched scenery for their settings. He rallied. Well, that was their business, and the town itself would benefit enormously; there were few tourists in winter, and consequently little income for local traders. Hoteliers and B&B owners would have unexpected extra business, not to mention local restaurants, local craftsmen, and local shops. It could only be good.

He found himself at the window again, gazing vengefully down at the glowing streetlight, darted back to the post-it and added two more exclamation points to *Lampione!*, then sat down and pulled out the file containing the paperwork and permits pertaining to the shoot.

The pre-production people would be arriving the following week, with actors and main players following later. Miranda Hargreaves was to be the leading lady, she of the fragile blond beauty, and Ed Grayson the tall dark hero. They would be staying in Rome, travelling down to Tivoli on a daily basis, unlike the director, whose name Dott. Salmone could not remember but who had had several box office successes. Commercial, he thought, leafing aimlessly through the various permits, which had all been submitted in perfect order and which had all been approved. Well, if shooting was on schedule, the whole thing should be over well before the 16th February, 'Fat Tuesday', the last day of Carnival before Lent.

Somewhere outside in the grey day, a clock struck ten, and the mayor pushed the file back into the drawer and banged the drawer shut with the decisive air of one who has successfully dealt with the matter. He pulled out the agenda for his eleven-o'clock meeting, transferring his *Lampione*!!! post-it to his notes on Any Other Business.

If the mayor of Tivoli was unsettled and irritable, Avvocato De Angelis, in his much smaller office in Nemi, was a prey to guilt and regret. He was an honourable man, and had of course turned down the initial offer of money without a second thought. Firstly, he did not need it, though the sum was enormous, and secondly he was well aware that lawyers who betrayed their clients' confidence tended to become ever more complacent and morally lax about such matters. He had magnificently and indignantly refused, but the resulting glow was as short-lived as it was pleasant, abruptly extinguished by the arrival of the photographs, the subjects of which were all too recognisable, their actions all too explicit. Just where had the camera been? And the boy – who had looked several years older than the 14 on the photocopy of his birth certificate attached to the photos – had seemed such an angel, such a ... gift. A law student, he had said, at Rome University, and he *had* known enough about the law to be able to show flattering and guileful interest in the lawyer's anecdotes. It must have been planned with much forethought and detail, a deliberate trap for an otherwise irreproachable citizen.

Shaken but ultimately resigned – he had always suspected that, despite his precautions, such a day would arrive – he had done as they demanded. He opened the letter, photocopied the one page, and sent it to a post office box number in Rome. The photographs, together with the negatives, had been sent to him at his office within a few days, and he had destroyed them, shredding and then burning them in the fireplace in his study at home. Finished, done with, a simple business transaction.

Only the feelings of guilt and regret refused to disappear, even seemed to increase in the days following the business transaction. He had – as a good lawyer – made two photocopies of the letter. He put the second copy in his safe at home, reading it again and again in an attempt to understand why this simple last message should be so important. He had met the professor only once, at her request visiting her at the clinic, and he had been charmed by her courtesy and clarity of thought, so unlike his own dear mother, he thought, who clung on to a kind of skittish adolescence, interspersed with bouts of depression. A great lady, the professor, he thought sadly. Unique. And I have betrayed her trust, betrayed her friend as well.

Perhaps I could tell (warn?) the friend, he thought suddenly. He would not have to mention the blackmail, he could say that his office had been broken into, something of that sort, that he felt he could not guarantee the "integrity" of the letter; its private nature might have been compromised. His hand went towards the telephone, hovered and then fell back onto his desk. It had started raining again, he noticed, and from his top-floor office he could see the dense clouds shrouding the mountains above the village; the summit of Monte Cavo, spiky with the antennae of the military base, was quite invisible. And he had to go out, an appointment with the middle-aged children of one of his clients, a ninety-year-old resident in the clinic. They had finally talked the old woman into signing the papers that would simplify their inheritance: she had three parcels of land, each parcel lawfully and equally divided between the three children. Now that the three had decided who would have each parcel, there was only the simple matter of amending the documents to show one owner for each, rather than the potentially litigious three. Avvocato De Angelis thoroughly approved – as a fair man, he deplored legal battles between family members; they might be extremely remunerative for the lawyers involved but they were often poisonous, acrimonious and time-consuming. And while he was at the clinic perhaps he could find out if the professor's friend would be coming to retrieve the keepsake, could arrange to be passing when she came. It was with a much lighter heart that he placed the land documents in his briefcase.

Jane had not originally planned to get a car. Living as she did in the middle of medieval Rome, the thought of endlessly circling the narrow cobbled streets trying to find a parking space seemed on a par with flying endlessly in the circles of the damned. But then a friend, Eleanor, dark, energetic and emphatic, had decided to leave Rome just before Christmas.

"Enough is enough!" she declared, when Jane expressed surprise. "That last Italian guy I went out with was the straw that broke my camel's back. As if it wasn't enough that I popped round and found another woman there, no, not in bed or anything, *worse*." She paused dramatically. Jane could not imagine what *could* be worse, but then, Eleanor had her own scale of judgement. "He introduced us, then buggered off into the bedroom – *saying* he had to make a phone call, but I could hear the silence of him – you know, *listening* to us. Games-playing bastard! There I was trying to make some kind of conversation with this thin, socially-challenged ... idiot. 'What do you do?' I asked – and you know how Italians don't like that – 'Employee,' she bleats – as they do, which means absolutely nothing, though it's usually some kind of unnecessary overpaid clerical work in one of those unproductive over-staffed government ministries." Having pronounced the two "un's" and the two "over"s with vehement disdain, she finally paused to take a breath.

"So?" asked Jane, guiltily aware that she was enjoying Eleanor's drama too much – well, she did tell a good story – and was not perhaps displaying the angry empathy she should. They were sitting in the tourist bar opposite the church of Santa Maria in Trastevere, having coffee and enjoying a cold but sunny day just before the Christmas holidays.

"So," Eleanor said quietly, "suddenly I was just so bored with the sun and the glamour. Glamour! Huh! We still have to wash our knickers and take painkillers for period pains. Even if all this is gorgeous." She gestured at the medieval church and the fountain, mellow and glowing in the morning sun. Jane nodded. Just about everyone's reaction to living in Italy – when they didn't – was the exotic-brochure reaction: Italy was good weather and endless romance. And as for the knickers and period pains:

"Do you still get them as badly?" she asked her friend sympathetically.

"They wipe me out," said Eleanor. "You're lucky, Jane, just sailing through it all every month. You know what it means though, don't you?"

"What?" Jane had no idea what Eleanor was talking about.

"You're obviously some dreadful earth-mother type, and when you *do* get started, you'll be popping twins out at the rate of once of year, and getting long pendulous nipples from the two of them hanging from your boobs!"

Jane started laughing, secretly appalled. "I *really* don't think so, Eleanor. But you're serious – about leaving, I mean?"

"I am. I've started to hate not knowing where the next job's coming from as well," Eleanor said moodily. "No social security, no sinking into the arms of the welfare state." Jane nodded again. Money was an on-going problem with all of them. "And I'm also sick of meeting men of our age," (both Jane and Eleanor were in their early-thirties), "who are not married and you think, 'Great', only to find out that what they're really into is having sex with foreign women but they have some faithful childhood girlfriend in the background who they'll eventually marry to have a 'proper' Italian family with."

She fell silent and picked up her cappuccino. Jane thought of Sergio. Yes, even while they were seeing each other he had disappeared to Naples every weekend, then started vanishing during the week, and then his flatmate, met by chance at a local bar, dropped the bombshell of his impending marriage. "What's she like?" Jane had asked, struck to the heart but still curious. "Depressing, like him," pronounced Mario. "Well, they sound well-matched," said Jane, laughing but secretly planning to go home and get drunk as soon as possible.

"Anyway," said Eleanor, suddenly brisk, "I'm leaving – it's definite – and I'm getting rid of stuff, so do you want Harold? I don't want anything for him if you can just pay the *passaggio di proprietà*."

"What's that?"

"Another bloody tax," explained Eleanor wearily; every aspect of Italy seemed to depress her now. "Just means transfer of ownership. God, they get you every way you turn! Even if I have Harold scrapped, I'll have to pay something."

Jane knew Harold well: a cheerful blue mini, extremely old and extremely basic, he had taken them to the beach at Ostia, to parties on the other side of Rome and restaurants out of Rome – once even to Sorrento, where they had greedily guzzled beer and chips with all the other English holiday-makers. And he was *small*, that was the beauty of him. He could be crammed between larger cars, left on a corner, almost – though not quite – picked up and stowed in a carrier bag if no parking space could be found.

"Yes," she said, suddenly deciding. "I'd love to have Harold, thank you – and I'll look after him."

Eleanor smiled affectionately and patted Jane's arm. "I know you will," she said. "Just keep an eye on the oil. He's a real drinker. Oh, and the battery as well. Now, you'll be coming for my farewell drink, won't you?"

So it was that on the 14th January, with Harold's oil topped up and his tank full of petrol, Jane drove out of Rome on her way to Nemi. Her job-hunting would have to wait. She had enough money for the immediate future, and visiting the nursing-home to collect the keepsake was more important. She had phoned before leaving to check that the *direttrice*, 'the matron' she supposed it would be in English, could receive her at around eleven o'clock. At that hour many of the residents would be in the public rooms having coffee as well; she had sat there with the professor during her second visit.

Though not actually raining the sky lowered and glowered as if promising more watery tantrums. And it always seems much *wetter* than English rain, thought Jane, not for the first time. How can that be? She turned up the heater yet again as she passed the entrance to Ciampino Airport with its guard of black-uniformed *carabinieri*, and remembered that the quickest way to the nursing-home was to the south of the Alban Hills through Genzano. Gabriel flickered in her memory but she sealed him off with, "Now, *he* was a terrible driver."

Outside Genzano the road down to the lake was so steep that swathes of water draining from the slopes fanned out over the tarmac surface, overflowing from the shallow ditches choked with dead leaves and pine needles. The trees lining the road made the already grey day even darker, so dark that she could see her headlights reflected in the wet road. It was with relief – she was driving very slowly and carefully – that she emerged at the bottom, then to follow the road past the Museum of Roman Ships where dim lights gleamed from the enormous windows, past the hidden entrance to the ruins of the Sanctuary of Diana, and start up the hill again to the nursing-home. It was about quarter to eleven when she parked and struggled out, opening her umbrella as she went; the rain had arrived again.

It really does look like a hotel, she thought as she went in through the double doors and deposited the water-limp umbrella in the umbrella stand. Two women were talking behind the reception desk, one obviously a nurse from her uniform and white hospital clogs, the other a slight sallow-skinned girl in a beige jumper who greeted Jane unsmilingly, "*Desidera?*"

Jane explained her visit and was given a curious look by both the nurse and the receptionist, before being directed to the first floor. As she climbed the carpeted stairs, the low murmur of their voices followed her; brilliant light sparkled from the tiered chandelier hanging in the stairwell.

The *direttrice* – the matron – was in her forties, and looked remarkably like Zsa Zsa Gabor at that age, with the same glossy wavy hair, the same dramatic make-up; her figure was full but trim, and her aquamarine suit and palest-of-blue blouse impeccable. Once they were both seated and the formalities exchanged ("Ah, Signorina 'Arrison. I beg you to sit down. Have you come far?", "Just from Rome."), she smiled sympathetically:

"I am so sorry about your friend, Professor Caseman."

""Did she ... suffer?" asked Jane with difficulty.

"No, no, signorina, you must not think so," urged the matron, leaning forward emphatically. "She passed away while she was sleeping – a good death, as we say. She suffered nothing."

"Thank you." Jane was beginning to feel upset again and groped for a handkerchief but was dimly aware that the other woman had crossed to a wall cupboard and taken out a package wrapped in brown paper. She brought it to her desk and laid it in front of Jane. "Your friend wanted you to have this," she said quietly, one hand resting on the package.

"Thank you," said Jane again, looking at the package. "You are very kind," and saw her own name written on it in the same sloping italics as the letter, though the pen strokes were thicker and more decisive.

The matron was still standing, now glancing at her watch, and Jane got to her feet as well, suddenly feeling tired and drained. With an effort she remembered her Italian manners, said she knew that the professor had received the best of care, was so happy that her friend had been in such capable hands, and so grateful for the courtesy she herself had encountered at the clinic. It made it all the easier … Exhausted she stopped but the matron was nodding with approval, obviously charmed by the flowery, appropriately emotional little speech.

"Thank you, signorina. We seek to do our small best here. Now, I am desolate that I cannot personally offer you refreshment – a previous appointment – but perhaps you would like to rest for a little in our lounge? They will be serving coffee now, and I will ensure you are looked after. And, please, stay as long as you like."

Jane thanked her again, and clasped the package to pick it up. It was unexpectedly heavy.

"Goodbye, signorina 'Arrison. I wish you a safe journey," murmured the matron, and Jane found herself outside the heavy door and walking numbly downstairs. It was only when she was halfway down that she realised that she had learnt very little; she had not asked about the professor's health, her last days, whether she had been lucid, whether there had been a funeral or a memorial service, or where the professor was buried even. Had the professor's friend Barbara been informed? Had she perhaps come to Italy for the funeral? Vexed with herself, she paused, felt the dragging tiredness again, and decided to have coffee and sit down before returning upstairs.

The public lounge, again very like that of a hotel, lay through an arch to the right of the reception area. It was warm and brightly lit, so that the gloom of the January day outside was banished, and though the whole building was centrally-heated, the flames of a log fire flickered in a wide fireplace. Chairs and couches had been placed around small tables, and there were already small groups of older people, some obviously with visitors, some just sitting together. Jane made her way gratefully to a large couch in the recess of a bay window. From here the view was of drenched bushes and a corner of the car park; there was nothing to be seen of the sanctuary or the woods above.

A woman in a pink overall came to ask her what she would like – the matron had obviously phoned down – and Jane ordered cappuccino, very hot. As she was waiting she looked at the package, but the place was too public, and she thought about work instead, or rather the lack of it. Bastards, she thought again. Before Christmas the private school where she had been working had ended her contract due to "lack of enrolments," but it had happened almost immediately after Jane had asked whether her series of temporary contracts could not perhaps become one permanent one. She couldn't believe how naïve she had been. Oh, Eleanor, she thought, I know exactly how you felt.

She glanced across the room where the woman in the pink overall was coming back with her cappuccino. A short fair-haired woman sitting a few yards off had stopped her and spoken a few words gesturing in Jane's direction; the woman nodded and came up to place the steaming cup on the table in front of Jane.

"The Signora McCulloch has asked if she may join you. She says she knew your friend – the professor?"

Jane looked across at the woman, who smiled and waved. "Yes, of course," she said slowly. "I would be happy to speak with her."

With his briefcase in one hand and a large black umbrella held over him with the other, Avvocato De Angelis walked briskly round to the tiny lock-up garage where he kept the smaller of his cars, the stylish two-tone Ypsilon with its dove-grey seats. The last time he had used it was before Christmas and the drive down to the nursing home would be an opportunity to check that everything was in good running order. His other car, a Mercedes, was kept at the villa he shared with his mother and their housekeeper, and was only used to chauffeur his mother around and make the occasional trip to Rome to meet with his modest but useful political contacts.

Several people greeted him as he walked the short distance to the lock-up, and he smiled, wished them good morning, raised his briefcase in a half wave. "Such a fine man!" sighed the fat woman under the dripping awning of the greengrocers to her friend as they watched the smartly-dressed figure turn the corner. "So personable! Such a devoted son! If only my Stefano were so good …" She shrugged her shoulders helplessly. De Angelis had helped the family when the same Stefano had "fallen into bad company" and "been taken advantage of", having "no idea" that the packets he regularly delivered from Anzio to Rome had been drugs. As if he *would* get involved in something like that!

The paintwork of the Ypsilon was slightly dimmed after its time in the garage but the rain would wash off the dust, he thought. He placed his briefcase on the passenger seat, noticing that the clasp had slipped open again, backed the car out carefully – there was not much space to turn – and drove sedately towards the tall arch that led to the narrow road down to the lake.

Mrs McCulloch – "Just call me Mamie, sweetie" – had a warm American accent and a rounded maternal bosom. Dressed in a burnt-orange trouser suit and brown roll-neck sweater, she was much younger than the majority of residents, with light ash-blonde hair piled casually on the top of her head, and twinkling eyes that seemed ready for laughter. Jane invited her to have her own coffee brought to the table, and Mamie ensconced herself comfortably in a corner of the sofa, drawing a pair of knitting needles and what looked like a child's sweater from her bag; she knitted slowly and reflectively as they talked.

"Now, I just hope you don't think me too pushy, sweetie – I know you British like to take things slower – but you looked so forlorn, I just had to ask who you were, and then of course, when I knew, I just had to have a word with you." She stopped knitting and looked at Jane questioningly.

"You did the right thing," Jane assured her. "As for being British – well, when you live abroad, you kind of get ... modified," she said laughing. She felt extraordinarily relaxed and at ease with the American woman, and now the sound of the relentless rain outside only enhanced the light and warmth of the room, with its gentle murmur of conversation and the muted crackling of flames from the wood fire; the hot strong coffee had lifted the dragging tiredness and made her feel that the journey had been worthwhile after all. Perhaps she had found an ally, and would be able to learn more of the professor's last days. But somehow it seemed too abrupt, too ... bald to start asking – interrogating – Mamie immediately.

"Have you lived in the clinic long?" she asked politely, draining her coffee cup and sitting back.

Mamie laughed, a laugh that turned into a dry cough, and gestured with her knitting needles. "No, bless you, darlin' – I don't *live* here. Wouldn't be caught dead here. Oh, I'm sorry, sweetie!" and she looked so comically crest-fallen that Jane giggled: "No, no, it's all right." Mamie looked relieved, took up her knitting again. "Well, I go to this kind of place every year for a few months – blood tests, check-ups – kind of like putting your automobile in the shop for a service." Jane laughed again. "And how about you, Jane? Living in Italy, are you?" And before Jane knew it, she was recounting her years in Rome, confiding the many difficulties, including the latest episode, when she had lost her job, and would now have to find a new one. "Then, there was the professor's ..." She suddenly stopped, appalled at the realisation that her next word was going to be "letter." Cover story, she thought frantically, trust no one, then had to stifle a nervous giggle.

"The professor's ...?" murmured Mamie, busy with her needles; a gust of wind sent a sudden splatter of rain against the windowpane, as though a handful of pebbles had been flung against the glass.

"The professor's death," said Jane softly, feeling the hot prickle of something averted sweeping across her skin. "And I made a mess of my meeting with the matron here. I didn't ask her anything about what happened. I was too upset." That sounded right, she decided. "I understand you knew Professor Caseman," she went on, uncomfortably aware that the "I understand" sounded very 'British'. "Can *you* tell me anything, Mamie? I hadn't seen her since last October."

Mamie was nodding, which set her coughing again, and for a few seconds could say nothing. When it passed, she rested against the cushions, her breathing shallow. "Oh, these winter ailments, sweetie." Jane murmured something sympathetic, but found herself leaning away from Mamie; she didn't want to catch a cold at that point in the year. Mamie did not seem to notice the small withdrawal, laid her knitting aside and picked up her coffee cup before going on.

"The professor – a *fine* lady," she sighed, her American accent (perhaps southern?) very pronounced. "I didn't know her well, of course, a few conversations, but a *very* fine lady. Did you study with her, sweetie?"

Avvocato De Angelis was on the first stretch of the road winding down into the valley, staying in low gear and keeping well to the right; so narrow was the road there was no additional space for a proper verge and the craggy face of the cliff was close enough for him to see the rain-wet fronds of small ferns growing in the cracks and fissures. Below him, the crater and its lush vegetation were dark under the grey mist, the waters of the lake opaque and unmoving. He sighed. The car felt a little sluggish – that was the trouble with leaving it in the lock-up for so long, he thought – and he decided he would speed up, test the engine on the next straight.

As he deftly twirled the steering wheel to take the bend he thought he heard a muffled click, but was intent on changing gear and accelerating. The car leapt forward, its sluggishness apparently solved by the surge of power, and the lawyer smiled. It had just needed a little encouragement after all.

Too polite not to respond to Mamie's question, Jane was telling Mamie about her fictional meeting with the professor at a lecture in Oxford. She was wise enough not to embellish and did not even mention the title, "The Lesser Goddesses", which the professor had thoughtfully provided. She was beginning to feel impatient, wanted to get back to any information Mamie might have about the professor, and had a sudden urge to jump to her feet, shake the older woman and demand she tell Jane whatever she knew. She interrupted herself in mid-sentence.

"I'm so sorry," she said, "but ... I really would like to hear how the professor was, whether there was any ... sign that she was about to die?"

On the hillside, a sudden gust of wind briefly buffeted the speeding Ypsilon, and De Angelis leaned forward to see more clearly through the sweep of the windscreen wipers. This rain ... you couldn't be too careful in weather conditions like these. About to change to a lower gear and slow down, he touched the brakes.

Nothing happened. The brake pedal flopped, then twisted to one side as though it was only attached to the rubber mat and had no contact with the main body of the car. There was a frozen moment when the unthinkable became a reality, a second frantic stamping at the useless pedal, and the attempt to steer the car away from the sheer drop on the right. The steering wheel too was loose and useless, and then there was no time for anything else.

The car did not sail out into the valley, engine roaring, to describe a swooping arc through the slanting rain. When there was no longer any purchase for the front wheels, the bonnet quietly tipped down onto the slope, tipped and plunged and then hit a tree stump, slewed sideways and began a sprawling untidy roll that gathered in momentum, snapping off the wing mirrors as it went. The smell of petrol, and then acrid smoke, mingled with the damp air. When the car, now upside down, finally jolted to a bumping spinning halt, there was a second of complete silence. The briefcase had burst open and the papers to simplify the inheritance of the three parcels of land – sensibly, one owner for each parcel, rather than three – lay scattered, some smudged and stained with blood. There was no one to hear the second click, nor see the creeping flames as they hissed and steamed in the sodden bushes. The first anyone knew was when a thunderous explosion tore the car apart and turned the dove-grey seats into molten bubbling streams.

Mamie smoothed her knitting, her pleasant face concerned and worried. She looked beseechingly at Jane. "Well, I don't want to upset you, sweetie, but the professor *was* showing signs of her age. Becoming … a little cranky and – you know how old people can get – kind of suspicious. Perhaps you found the same?"

"Yes," agreed Jane reluctantly, suddenly remembering her last visit. "I did. It was very sad, very … upsetting." She stopped.

"Still," went on Mamie, tapping Jane's hand with her knitting, "She left you a nice present, didn't she?" and she transferred her tapping to the brown-paper package that

Jane had placed on the table. "What is it, sweetie? If you don't mind me asking, that is."

Whether it was the tapping, or whether it was the "nice present", which held unpleasant echoes of Gollum and his 'precious' in *The Lord of the Rings,* Jane would never be able to decide, but her hand went out instinctively and protectively towards the package; she had to stop herself from snatching it up.

"I don't know," she said, turning her gesture of protection into an affectionate pat. She smoothed the rough paper, her fingers lingering on the faint difference in texture where the professor had written her name. "I'm going to wait until I get home."

A booming roar reverberated around the enclosed bowl of the valley, the sound crashing and echoing from slope to slope. The windows rattled in their frames, all conversation stopped and pale shocked faces glanced around fearfully as though the nursing home itself were in danger of collapsing; one little old lady began to whimper but was drowned out by the sudden babble of excited speculation.

Mamie's head swung round – "Well, I'll be ..." – and Jane jumped to her feet but there was nothing to be seen from the window behind the couch. "What do you think that was?" she whispered, finding that she had indeed caught up the package, and was standing with her arms wrapped around it; it was really heavy but she had not even registered the weight in her instinctive gesture of retrieval. "It sounded so ..."

Mamie went back to her knitting, her breathing audible, and then blew out her cheeks. "Probably some kid," she said, wheezing a little, "hot-rodding it down the hill and losing it."

3

Thursday 14th January, contd.

Jane's living room was quiet. She had switched on neither her computer, usually the first thing she did when she came home, nor the stereo, the second. She was sitting at her desk drinking tea and regarding Lena's package.

The journey from Nemi had taken much longer than the trip down. The road by the lake, the only one back to Genzano, had been choked with police and emergency vehicles, and as she waited in the queue of cars, Jane almost regretted not accepting Mamie's invitation to stay for lunch. Across the patchwork of small fields the blue lights of an ambulance flashed intermittently, while the voices of the rescue team shouting out directions and commands seemed to be coming from further away. They must have just arrived for the crashed car was still burning, the flames too intense to be dowsed by the rain. Jane remembered the narrow road from the previous year, and shivered now at the joke Gabriel had made at her worried question ("I expect the wheels will slip off the edge and we'll roll to the bottom and burst into flames.")

And she had not succeeded in seeing the matron again. The sallow girl at reception told Jane that she was now away for the day and would not be back until the evening. All in all Jane had learnt very little, and felt she had only herself to blame. All she knew was that the professor had died in her sleep (the matron), and that she had been "cranky" and "kind of suspicious" (Mamie McCulloch). After the sound of the explosion had effectively interrupted their conversation, Mamie had made no further reference either to the professor or the contents of the package. "But give me your number, sweetie, so I can call if I think of anything," she had said kindly.

And now there was the keepsake to open. She put her tea down and pulled the lumpy brown-paper package nearer. It was wrapped very securely, sealed not only with heavy brown sticky tape and a network of twine but also – a touch Jane had not previously noticed – a flattened blob of sealing wax on the single knot. Jane peered closer, could not immediately recognise the symbol, and peered from another angle; it looked like a leaf. She cut the string, leaving the seal intact, and began to unwind the paper.

What was revealed when she had completed her careful unpacking was a broken statue in pale stone, about eight inches tall, set on a square base. Placing it upright on the desk, Jane could see that it was a seated figure, female from the draped robe that fell in folds to the neatly sandaled feet; the head and part of one shoulder were missing and the figure clasped an ornately-chiselled volume. There was nothing else in the package, no further note or explanation.

That the statue must be another fragment of the message was clear. And now Jane would have to put the fragments together. Tivoli, the Temple of Vesta, the title of the lecture "The Lesser Goddesses", and now the statue, perhaps one of those same goddesses. It all felt like a muddle rather than a challenge, and for a split second Jane was tempted to go no further: she was tired, she was worried about money, and she was depressed by the weather. Tomorrow, she thought; she was just not strong enough to wrestle with the problem that day. I need beer-and-chips therapy, she thought with a glimmer of humour, beer and chips and possibly chocolate as well. Then we'll see.

And that was what she did. Ate chips, drank beer, and – a predictable consequence – started thinking about men – not men in general but past boyfriends and lovers. All nice and all presumably in good faith (with a few exceptions) but all so ... unsuitable. She marvelled that she had chosen one unsuitable man after another when – surely – there had been many others around, those who were not quite so clearly (with hindsight) and unequivocally unsuitable. It was a mystery. There was Ralph, 32 to her 18, and a rotten lover, which was a pity since it was the first time, and it would have been better to have 'given in' to Dave who was into sex rather than love. Yes, he really was into sex, and the foreplay before she heroically pushed him away had been wonderful. "You're a sex bomb," he told her as he drove her home, but she had put off the explosion until true love came along, only to find that the fuse never got lit and deflowering rather than flowering was the order of the day or rather night. Just to mix my metaphors, she thought moodily, eating three chips together and washing them down with a mouthful of beer.

There was the Greek bank robber, not that she had known that at the time, who was dark and brooding and *suffered*, and he had been marvellous at oral sex. When he announced he was getting married (to a nice Greek girl) she found consolation with Tom, who made her laugh and was a great change from all the darkness and suffering. Poor Tom got over their break-up by going round the world and to her amazement she found she had finished it out of boredom and would gladly have gone round the world with him rather than live together as they had been doing. I have no staying power, she thought dismally, I'm completely shallow. "Shallow!" she said aloud, finding self-castigation quite comforting; after all, not everyone can be deep and serious and committed. More chips. More beer.

Oh, she had forgotten Gregory, the 'writer', who carried a notebook round with him and would whip it out (the notebook) if an IDEA came to him. He was working in a pub – and writing – when they met and it was terribly romantic at first; they even lived together until she realised that writers did nothing in the house and that she was only his muse in the sense that she took care of cooking and washing while he roamed the slopes of Parnassus, or Olympus or wherever sodding writers go, she thought bitterly. End of Gregory. End of selected highlights in England.

And Italy? Well, that had been an eye-opener. More unsuitability at every turn but in a much more exotic framework. Antonio, the burnt-out case, forty, divorced, working for Italian television, and with a face straight from the Rome of the Borgias. High straight nose, slanted eyes and sensuous lips, but sexually too rough. Yes, that was the right word, rough. Very little even faked tenderness. He approached sex like painting-by-numbers in reverse – dashing through the details, in this case the loving hand stroking eager skin or the gentle tongue licking a raised hip bone. No, he spent no time on details, but roughly scribbled them in (rough again) because he wanted to get to the blue sky at the top. End of Antonio.

Sergio had been the best sex, and it was while she was going out with him that she met Gabriel. For a moment she hesitated. Get side-tracked with Gabriel or continue her list? She raised her glass to take another gulp of beer only to find it was empty. No, stick with the list, she told herself. More beer, there should still be some in the fridge, then Sergio.

A trifle unsteadily she made her way to the kitchen, poured more beer, and went back to the couch.

Sergio. Tall, an engineer, Neapolitan this time, with warm brown eyes and a moustache – strange, she didn't usually like moustaches – and she remembered sex with him as being warm and wuffly (the moustache?). He had a mole on his chest so that it looked as though he had three nipples and he was thin and wiry. Great sex *and* interesting talk. Seemed completely suitable but was completely detached to go with it. Apparently, he had found true love with a Mexican girl but she had gone back to Mexico, leaving him with a broken heart. And – apparently – that gave him the right to sod other women about. Jane thought of Meg the lawyer in *The Big Chill* describing the men she had known. How did it go? "They're in transition from a monogamous relationship. They need more space, or they're *tired* of space but they can't *commit* and they *want* to commit but they're afraid to get *close*." And then the kicker: "They want to get close and you don't want to get *near* them." Yes, that was about right.

She put the last of the chips into her mouth, suddenly felt greasy from head to toe, and noticed that the beer glass was smeared and cloudy as well. But I do feel better, she thought defiantly, going to wash her hands, and now I'm going to have another cigarette; there are still two in the drawer.

4

The previous October

After the successful outcome of the first battle in the tangled wood above the sanctuary, Lena had not allowed herself to become complacent, though she *had* savoured the victory and shared the news with the other five; five rather than six since, in the months before the encounter at Nemi, Clothilde had abandoned her post at Satricum on the Pontine Plain.

That Clothilde had become increasingly disenchanted with her task had been demonstrated when she began to return to her native New Orleans for a month every year. "It is my only pleasure!" she exclaimed wildly when Lena found out about her absences. "Here in this fascist bourgeois town I have a life of nothing!" She was not referring to Satricum, which was set in open countryside, an abandoned wilderness with only the ruined Temple to the Mater Matuta testifying to its ancient role; no, she was referring to where she actually lived, the 'new' town of Latina nearby, founded at the time of Mussolini and a monument to Fascist ideals. There could not have been in a more uncongenial place for Clothilde, passionate child of the sixties students' riots in Paris. Finally, with a brief truculent phone call she announced she would wait and watch no more, she was going back to the States.

Which had brought Lena to the conclusion that she had shown an error of judgement when she appointed Clothilde to Satricum and Elfriede to Tivoli, though both of them could be said to have the right to be in Tivoli.

The fragment of prophesy Clothilde held was astonishingly complete: "The years will be shortened like months, the months like weeks, the weeks like days, the days like hours, and an hour like a moment." Lena had recognised the quotation as the words spoken by the Tiburtine Sibyl to the Emperor Augustus. Tivoli was clearly indicated. But then, Elfriede's fragment too, with its reference to Cossinia, could only refer to Tivoli as well: Cossinia was a Vestal, whose tomb had been revealed when the river bank collapsed, and found to contain an ivory jointed doll, symbol of the childhood she retained by her adherence to her vows of purity.

And Lena had chosen Elfriede not Clothilde to keep watch there. Elfriede had seemed more dependable, more likely to take her task seriously. And I was correct, Lena was to think ruefully, she did take it more seriously, and that was the problem.

When Elfriede called her in October, a few days after

Jane had made her second visit to the nursing home, Lena's heart sank.

"Professor, it's me," came the slurred voice.

"Hello, dear," said Lena, keeping her own voice light. "How very kind of you to call. How are you?"

"I can't b...!" the rest was an incomprehensible torrent of words; Elfriede sounded not only drunk but excited.

"You'll have to repeat that, dear," Lena said as calmly and encouragingly as possible. She hoped she did not sound patronising, for Elfriede, with the hypersensitive canniness of the drunk, might hear it in her voice and become aggressive. "My hearing, you know," she lied. "Take it slowly, and tell me again."

"Here was ... *eine Uberschemmung* ... *come si dice*?" Elfriede was completely confused. When she was sober both her English and Italian were excellent, and she kept them separate. "*Ein* ... ah, *ja*, a flooding. The river. It covered *das Grab.*"

In her room at the nursing home, Lena sat more upright in her chair; the movement made her wince – her back was very bad that day. Her German was good enough for her to recognise the word for "grave" or "tomb." "Thank you," she said softly. "I understand. Let me phone you back when I've thought about it. No, don't worry, dear." And she gently replaced the receiver.

For a while she sat, her gaze resting unseeingly on the antique chest of drawers that had belonged to her parents, then murmured, "Cum aquae ad Cossiniam lavandam rursus pervenient." When waters rise to bathe afresh

Cossinia. So, she thought, it has begun. Still gazing unseeingly at the chest of drawers, she told herself to be steady, the word from her childhood, when being 'steady' or showing 'steadiness' was her father's advice in the face of difficulty. All at once she felt frail and unwell, and the insidious beginning of fear, like the far-off tramp of enemy troops, was threatening to weaken her resolve. This second battle showed all the signs of being not only far more difficult, but less clear-cut, less ... definitive. In the first, Jane – dear Jane – with her strength and tenacity had made it all possible, and the antagonist, Mrs Pleiades, had been an old enemy, an *expected* enemy. Light and dark, good and evil, had been sharply defined, and defeat or victory had depended simply on that one symbolic encounter.

But now, some monstrous shape seemed to move in the shadows of the future. Lena sensed a vast questing ego that existed only for itself, all the more terrifying in its mindless wanting.

She sighed. Clothilde's defection, which she had accepted with equanimity at the time, now seemed a presage. The loss of one weakened the power of them all; seven was the mystic number, six debilitating if not actively harmful. But there is still Jane, she thought with a surge of hope, we are still seven, for although she has not been trained, she is our innate equal. She has the Venus figurine, the gift that came from the goddess Diana herself; there could be no clearer sign that she has been chosen and has a part to play.

Lean shifted slightly to try and ease her back, then slowly and painfully made her way to the bedside table to take one of her tablets. This was not the time to be undermined by physical discomfort; it could distort any perceptions she might have. Once back in her chair, she settled herself and prepared to pursue her train of thought.

The disappearance of Clothilde, and Elfriede's 'problem'. In themselves these difficulties could have been overcome, but – and here Lena's sense of foreboding deepened – there had then been the appearance of the American woman at the nursing home.

Ostensibly sincere and guileless – and certainly unwell, as Lena's sharp eyes had detected – her efforts to establish an intimacy between Lena and herself had been just a little too obvious. Lena was not flattered by attention nor eager for company, unlike many older people, and though the woman was extremely skilful and tactful in her approach, the mention of a name, which she could not and should not have known, made Lena actively wary. She must take measures to protect both herself and Jane.

At the reception desk, the sallow girl in a beige sweater had also replaced the receiver. She had only understood "river" and "covered." Still, "Anything," they had said. "No matter how small." With a quick glance round the deserted lobby, she picked up the phone again and dialled.

Of all the Vestals, Elfriede had suffered the most from the endless waiting. German, in her sixties, she had been a tour guide before she retired – when drinking meant one glass of white wine to relax after a day's work. But her need to organise and be in control, combined with a tendency towards impatience, had been thwarted by the passivity of her task. As the years passed she gradually began to drink more and more in an attempt to fill the empty days, once even coming to the nursing home to visit Lena in a state of bleary, mumbling confusion. Concerned, Lena realised that Elfriede was unreliable but that there was now no one else to whom the task could be entrusted.

It was at the beginning of October that news first came of a freak surge in the river level upstream from Tivoli; rainfall had been normal so could not be a contributing factor. One hypothesis was that a seismic shift originating near L'Aquila, not in itself an abnormality since the area was prone to earth tremors, had in some way connected with other substrata and caused a tsunami effect beneath the river bed. Experts in the field pooh-poohed the idea but were unable to come up with an alternative explanation.

News travelled fast in the town, and Elfriede, out shopping for the meagre items that would serve her for lunch, first heard of it in the supermarket. The surge was not dangerous but would definitely be visible, and was predicted to arrive at the town around midday. Initially unaware of the significance, she went on with her shopping, head still pounding from the wine she had drunk the evening before, until a stray snippet of conversation seemed to blare out from the parallel aisle. "... seen the waters rise since ..." Elfriede stopped, a tall angular figure in her rumpled brown coat and hand-knitted scarf, the basket containing her four slices of cooked ham and two tomatoes hanging from her arm, hardly able to believe that the long years of waiting were finally over. It was now nearly eleven. She returned to her tiny basement flat to leave her shopping, gulped down two large brandies to calm her nerves, then hurried out again to go to the banks of the River Aniene and the Ponte della Pace.

When she arrived, she saw she was not the only one who had chosen the ultra-modern wooden footbridge with its four concrete piers as the best viewing point; here the river widened into a basin, spanned by the bridge, and both upstream and down could be clearly seen. There was already quite a crowd, with police cars and civil defence vehicles parked on the road above. Sightseers had already been cleared from the bridge itself by various uniforms, for the authorities were taking no chances as to the height of the surge. There was even a fire engine, the purpose of which was unclear, and a group of town councillors, whose purpose might be to give moral support to the populace but who gave the incongruous impression of a welcoming committee.

Elfriede took up her station near the flight of steps leading down to the bridge, then realised that she could not see the tomb; the vegetation was too high. Hurriedly she retraced her steps and reached the long narrow public car park, where more crowds were gathered. There was a festive air to the whole occasion with groups of people eating slices of take-away pizza, smoking, and exchanging reminiscences.

The last great flood in 1826 was well before living memory, but every true *Tiburtino* knew the story of the now-placid river and its turbulent past. Elfriede fought her way to the wall at the front with its view of the river and tomb, ignoring the irritated complaints at her ungainly passage.

"*Eccola! Arriva!*" came the cry just as she found a good spot. Feet shuffled, heads bobbed, and necks were craned upstream; the span of the now-empty bridge waited impassively.

The bulge of water rolled downstream with ponderous slowness as though gently but inexorably pushed from behind; it was much higher than expected – where had all the extra water come from? – and members of the civil defence teams tensed in readiness. Some who were there – Elfriede among them – would later claim that the advancing water paused before the bridge, divided, and swirled carefully around the piers, with hardly a wave or splash, and then once past, came together to flow forward while a tongue of water gathered and rose to lap the weathered travertine base of the tomb. It was then that Elfriede understood that this was indeed the moment she had been waiting for; she made her way through the crowd, intending to go home, have another brandy to celebrate and phone the professor.

5

Friday 15th January

As often happened – Jane had noticed it in herself before, when she had more than one important task outstanding, she picked the one she felt least reluctant about. After her beer-and-chips therapy, with its depressing detour into her past love life, the professor's message and gift still seemed urgent, but also complicated and unreal. She decided to spend the next day job-hunting. It was a good time of year for it, since many schools would be starting up again with new post-Christmas courses, or they might have had staff leaving and needed replacements. I wonder who's got *my* old job, she thought, grimacing. What an idiot I was!

She also justified her procrastination by the thought it was Friday, the last day of the working week, and she would not be able to do anything about work for the next two days. She could phone and arrange interviews for the following week, even go that day if necessary, and then spend the weekend getting to grips with what she should do next about the professor's request. The weather had finally improved as well; no rain fell and pale sunlight illuminated one corner of the small courtyard. If she did have to go and about, at least she wouldn't have to splash around Rome, getting on and off buses – Harold was snugly parked, and she had no intention of needlessly using petrol when public transport was so cheap. She got out her list of schools, fishing out the Yellow Pages from under a pile of papers for extra ideas, and sat at her desk, wishing she had not done this so many times before. Oh, Eleanor, she thought again.

In the valley below Nemi the clearer weather meant that work on the lawyer's crashed car could continue at a faster rate, though still hampered by the viscous mixture of mud and mashed plants churned up by the rescue workers' boots. A television reporter and cameraman had been sent from Rome to cover it, and the item would duly appear in the regional news slot that evening. News channels liked car crashes for they were not only dramatic – particularly when a precipice was involved – but also served as an opportunity to warn against 'killer roads', the danger of speeding in bad weather, and – as the reporter would be told by one of the firemen – the foolishness of carrying "inflammable materials", in this case, cans of petrol, in the boot. Local people were shocked but not overly surprised: how the lawyer had enjoyed dashing around in that smart Ypsilon of his, popping up and down the hill as though walking up and downstairs in his own house! It had only been a matter of time. His poor mother …

In the nursing home it was coffee time in the comforting warmth of the lounge, and Mamie McCulloch was putting the finishing touches to the small sweater she was knitting. Very nice, she was thinking, the two shades of pink and the little bows are just what any little girl would just *die* for. Perhaps a matching scarf as well, crocheted rather than knitted to create a fine difference in texture; she should have her crochet hook with her. She inserted the knitting needles into their holder – the ends were rather sharp – and stowed them away in her knitting bag. Now, the crochet hook ...

In Tivoli Murph, the location manager for the forthcoming blockbuster, was taking a last look round. The heaviest part of his job was finished but he always liked to visit the location when the endless paperwork was over, visualise the various stages and check his notes for any final adjustments. He would be staying on for the first few days after the cast and production team were assembled, but this one day, which he always programmed for every film and which he always spent alone, was in the nature of his own personal wrap. It was a bonus that the day had dawned cold but clear with a brisk breeze blowing from the west that would soon dry the streets.

A rangy bony man, his face seamed and weathered by

countless days spent outdoors, his face bore its habitual expression of thoughtful concentration overlaid with philosophical cynicism; nothing could be taken for granted; Murphy's Law – if something could go wrong, it *would* go wrong – always applied. Well, he countered that with his own Murph's Law: every location was to be considered in the light of what was going to happen there, how it would help, or – more often – how it would hinder, not only the action of the film, but the countless practical details involved in the accommodation and organisation of some hundred odd people.

The main problems were space and accessibility. Built for the horse and cart, these old towns were simply not designed for trucks, bulky equipment and 60-foot trailers. At least the Villa was situated on the edge of the historical centre, with the main road from Rome terminating in a large rectangular piazza only minutes away; they had a permit to cordon off a section as a general loading/unloading point, the two stars' trailers would go where the huge tourist coaches usually stopped (permit obtained), and while the extras would have to park in the public car park on the other side of town, it was not a long walk, and a room at the Villa had been set aside for them so that they wouldn't be cluttering up the set with their lounging, chattering and flirting while they were waiting. Murph didn't like extras, even despised them – all that hanging around so that they could be a faceless figure or a blurry arm.

He had started his review over coffee in a bar on the corner of Piazza Garibaldi, the large rectangular piazza on the edge of town. From there he walked down the main street and off to the left where the stars' trailers would be parked – they would have to be driven in from the other side of town since it was a one-way street – and then doubled back to the Villa; the small sloping piazza outside the entrance would form a good working space as well. As he passed the cash desk inside – by now the two girls knew him and nodded – he saw Anthea, Barney's assistant, in the gift shop, three glossily-illustrated guide books spread on the glass counter before her. She looked up and nodded.

"Hi, Murph. OK?"

"Sure. You?"

Anthea held up one of the guide books, "Barney wanted more background. He's up at the hotel now, reckons there might be some ideas on angles and settings in these."

Murph glanced at the book. "Tourist trash," he pronounced dismissively.

"Yeah, well, you know what Barney says. Trash for the mass is cash for us few." She laughed while Murph nodded dourly; he had worked with Barney before, felt he knew all his sayings.

Anthea bundled the books together, obviously having decided to take all of them. "Hey," she said as she rummaged for money in her purse, "You hear that loopy woman drowned?"

"What loopy woman?"

"You know – no, maybe you weren't here that day – she was outside the hotel, drunk as a skunk, collared Barney as he was going out and started ranting on about water spirits and female principles. Absolutely off the wall – then she got nasty, shouted 'Beware!' and a lot of other stuff. Really gave me the creeps."

"How'd Barney take it?" Murph remembered one of the drivers mentioning the incident a few days back, but he had been intent on scanning a map of Tivoli into the computer to give to the crew, and had not paid much attention.

"The usual – gave her a hundred bucks and said he sure appreciated her telling him." Anthea gathered up the carrier bag with the books, looked at her watch. "Gotta go. See you, Murph."

"Yeah, sure," said Murph, whose eyes had been instinctively scanning the area for possibilities and problems. Now for the rooms downstairs – all the artwork and frescos had been included in the permits and contracts, the legal department had seen to that (once bitten twice shy), and then the gardens with their fountains, waterfalls and pools. How come those little fish in the pools are all black, he wondered suddenly. Should be gold. These were like leeches with fins. Christ, he had hated that shoot in Amazonia!

6

Saturday 16th January

As Elfriede might have said in her tour guide days, Tivoli itself lies at 235 metres above sea level, on a spur of the so-called 'Pre-Apennines'. Traditionally on the route of the annual north-south migration of herds and flocks, from the very beginning its importance was assured by the presence of the Aniene River as it flowed from the mountains towards its confluence with the Tiber. At the foot of the slope, where the river starts its journey across the plain, the district of Tivoli Terme has a quite different character from its hilly counterpart, being famous both internationally for Hadrian's Villa, and locally for its warm sulphurous waters (23°) and the accompanying spa complex, Terme Acque Albule.

Two lakes are the source of the spa waters, *Lago della Regina*, also called *Lago delle Isole Natanti*, the larger and shallower of the two, and *Lago Colonnelle*, smaller but much deeper. The waters themselves are distinctive, being bluish milky-white in colour, and with a strong odour of rotten eggs, explained scientifically by the presence of hydrogen sulphide, and – before their flow was covered by a roofed drain – an unwelcome surprise for first-time visitors.

The inhabitants had initially felt nervous and unsettled when the smell disappeared, and the stone mason working in his dust-filled shed was no exception. As he walked from his workshop to the warehouse, he unconsciously noted that the wind was blowing from west to east. Once it would have attenuated, though not dissipated, the familiar sulphurous smell, but now the air was completely clear. The warehouse, cluttered with stacks of large blocks, panels, joists and off-cuts, was draughty and chilly, the pale sun too weak to warm the shaded interior. He stood for a moment as he tried to recall where he had put the commission – it had been some time ago – then crossed to the far corner. He limped slightly, the result of his left foot being crushed by a falling block.

Methodically, heavy work gloves protecting his hands, he searched through the various items, many of them wrapped in rough sacking to protect the corners. Among other things, there was a small fountain, ordered by a woman from Rome who had paid a deposit then never returned; a stack of floor tiles, leftovers from a bathroom floor; and an urn that had been damaged during sculpture and left there in reserve to carve the small souvenirs sold to tourists in the local shops. He found the commission propped against the wall at the very back, and had to clear a space so that he could manoeuvre a pallet to the base of the block. Once that was in position, he tipped the block, still partially wrapped in sacking, gently onto it, then got the small fork-lift truck to transport the pallet and its load to the corner where he kept his tools; the date of the inscription would have to be completed now.

It must have been three of four years ago that the customer, a German woman, had ordered the headstone. She had specified Travertine, the stone quarried in the area around the lakes of Acque Albule, white – shades went from white to straw-coloured to hazel to dark brown – and unglazed, even when it was explained to her that the white variety was rarer (and so much more expensive), and that the unsealed surface would absorb air pollution and become discoloured. The work on it would cost more as well for the texture of the stone required much patience in the carving of detail, in this case, the inscription. Travertine was pitted with small holes and grooves, the imperfections caused by animal or vegetable matter trapped in the layers as they settled to form the stone. The woman had been impatient, waving aside the explanations that were intended to help her, and the cost had been agreed, the commission executed.

Bending down, tools in hand, he began the delicate task of filling in the second date.

On the same Saturday morning Jane was reviewing her success, or rather, lack of success, on the job-hunting front. It's always the same, she thought, either it's too early or too late; the person you need to speak to isn't there, or they have to see how many enrolments there are and the closing date has been put back again; or if there *is* a job, you find that you wouldn't want to work for them anyway, not unless you were completely desperate, which I am not, at least, not yet. I'm starting to talk like Meg in *The Big Chill* again, she thought, though this time it's work not men.

The day before had been an example: one school she had called, situated near the Vatican, had given her an afternoon appointment. As she waited, she had seen the owner of the school, a large bossy-looking woman with a slanting bosom, with two young teachers in tow who were deferentially hanging on her every word. New to Rome, thought Jane observing them, no qualifications but think they can earn the money to stay here by teaching English ("Well, if we can't get anything else, there's always teaching," she could imagine them saying). Now they were over-awed by the concrete details, had become eager and grateful and willing to learn. She felt her hackles rise, especially as the woman was now fifteen minutes late for *their* appointment but was obviously enjoying pontificating too much to cut it short. I don't need this, thought Jane suddenly. With decision she knocked on the office door and put her head round. Three pairs of surprised eyes regarded her.

"Sorry, I'm afraid I can't wait."

"Oh!" exclaimed the woman, completely taken aback. "Perhaps you'd ... like to make another appointment ...?"

"No, I don't think so," said Jane, feeling a surge of

triumph as she closed the door. She had managed not to add "thank you."

So there she was, with the weekend looming and nothing happening about a job. Was there anything else she could do that day? No, and it was too soon for more chips and beer. So that's that, I'll just have to …

The phone rang. Saved by the bell, thought Jane. It was Stephanie, a nice woman who worked at the same school as Jane had, who had in fact warned Jane against broaching the subject of a permanent contract. They exchanged Christmas news and gossip about mutual friends in Rome, before getting on to the subject of the school:

"They gave you the push then," said Stephanie sympathetically.

"Yes, the bastards," said Jane. "I should have listened to you, Steph. You knew they would do that, didn't you?" Privately thinking that Steph could have been a little more forceful; later Jane found out the school had done it before – and when Steph was there, so she *knew*. "By the by, have you heard of any jobs going anywhere else?"

"Not teaching, no. I've got a medical translation if you want."

"What's it about?"

"Liver parasites in marsupials."

"Oh, my God, no, thanks. Anyway, at the speed I translate medical stuff I'd earn a euro an hour."

Steph laughed, and they rang off after agreeing to get together for lunch, but the call had reminded Jane of the most obvious course of action – ringing round friends and contacts to see if they knew of anything. She was about to start – she had about six or seven people in mind – then realised it would be quicker to email one message, with different beginnings and endings. If she phoned each and every one of them, it would be at least twenty minutes every time if not more; she and Steph had been on the phone for nearly half an hour. She quickly drafted the email, added a bit of her own news, hoped they'd had a good Christmas, and in some cases, suggested lunch sometime. She was finished in forty minutes and making tea, when she remembered her second important task. She *still* had to make a start on the professor's bequest and this time there was no Gabriel. For Heaven's sake, she thought, I'm nostalgic for a man who disappeared into a wood and apparently became some sort of god. Honestly!

She returned to her desk, turned the computer on again – she had switched it off automatically – and started to jot down some notes on a sheet of paper while it was booting up.

Visits:
Sept. - OK   ("reminiscences")
Oct. – querulous

She hesitated then wrote:

Nov – spiteful and hostile

She paused for a moment, chewing at her pen, and then:

Only Sept. meeting valid. Info : Tivoli, Temple of Vesta, legends of area (find out)

She took the professor's letter from the desk drawer and re-read it, then added the few details that seemed relevant to the sheet:

Lesser Goddesses (Oxford?)   keepsake

Again she paused, crossed to the bookshelf where she had placed the broken statue and carried it to the desk. Then, as an afterthought, she went back to get the small clay Venus figurine, the gift from the neo-pagan girl the year before; she kept it in a wooden box on another shelf. This she positioned next to the statue, but almost immediately picked it up again. About three inches long and two wide, with a slight tapering at each end, it sketched the form of a female figure, with exaggerated breasts and a groove where the groin would be. Traces of red in the groove showed that the figure had once been painted. Jane cradled it in the palm of her hand, stroking it gently with the ball of her thumb before laying it aside and regarding the statue.

The statue, left to Jane by Professor Caseman, had belonged to Elfriede Baader, the flawed watcher at Tivoli. A treasured find in a local shop, it was not damaged when she bought it. Over the years it became a symbol and comfort to her, and, in a small way, made up for her disappointment at discovering that the shop, though called *La Sibilla Bianca* and close to the two Roman temples, was merely a gift shop, crammed with tee-shirts, baseball caps, postcards, stone ornaments, wind chimes, stickers, pottery masks, Tivoli ashtrays and plastic dinosaurs – in short, everything a visitor to the town might want to buy as a souvenir.

The discovery that it was "merely a gift shop" did not surprise Elfriede, but it made her realise that unconsciously she had been hoping for some sign, perhaps even some trace of the mythical White Sibyl herself. What she actually found could not have been farther from the vague hope. She instantly disliked the owner of the shop, a thin frizzy-haired woman in a shapeless sack draped around with blue-green scarves, who gave her one sharp glance, and then called out the price in German every time Elfriede picked something up. *"Ein euro!"*, *"Sieben euro"*, *"Zehn euro!"* The cries followed Elfriede around the cluttered alcoves until she chanced on the statue. *"Dreizig euro!"* came the call, but Elfriede was already carrying her prize to the counter.

The statue had stood on a corner table in her small basement flat until the day she came home after drinking several glasses of wine at a local bar, stumbled and crashed into the table. The statue fell and broke neatly into two pieces against the fender of the brick fireplace. When Elfriede woke up and discovered the damage, she was both ashamed and angry with herself. Fully intending to buy the glue to mend it, she kept putting it off, and when she did finally get round to it, she could no longer find the figure's head and shoulder.

It was on impulse that she decided to give the mutilated statue to Professor Caseman. She herself was no longer worthy, and she had begun to have strange dreams that woke her in the early hours of the morning and filled her with foreboding. She planned to confide in the professor, who would perhaps be able to explain the dreams, only to have 'one drink' to help her face the journey that then became five or six drinks. She delivered the statue but her account of her dreams and forebodings – which she had wanted to present in a logical ordered way – somehow escaped her control.

As for Lena, the gift of the statue was providential. She had prepared the letter for Jane to leave with a local lawyer, but had been able to say very little – by that time she was convinced she was being watched; the statue would complete the message. If Jane remembered their conversation about Tivoli, she would have another indication of the path she must take.

From the gift shop in Tivoli, through Elfriede, and Lena and the matron of the nursing home, the statue, though incomplete, had found Jane. As she sat at her desk, she briefly wondered about its history, then glanced at the computer; it was ready. She wrote a final line:

Statue (marble)   Lesser Goddess (?) holding book.

She examined the statue to see if the volume had a title. The part of the cover visible beneath the clasped hands seemed to be composed of intersecting swirls and whorls but there was nothing else. She sighed, read what she had written so far, and then remembered the wrapping paper. It was in the desk drawer and she carefully drew it out to study the seal. A leaf, she had first thought, but now it appeared essentially different, longer, and fatter in the middle. She looked back at her notes. The Temple of Vesta. A flame, she thought, of course, not a leaf, a flame. She sighed again, but this time with satisfaction. Invigorated by her success, she laid the notes aside, moved the figurine and the statue to a corner of the desk, and started logging on. Every so often her eyes strayed to the two figures.

And her computer searches were unexpectedly simple: Google, Wikipedia, Tivoli. And here we are, she thought.

Tivoli, the classical **Tibur**, is an ancient Italian town in Lazio, about 30 km from Rome, at the falls of the Aniene River, where it issues from the Sabine Hills.

She swiftly scanned the first paragraph, which detailed the origins, mythical and historical, of the town, and then started to read more slowly when she came to the second paragraph:

From Etruscan times Tibur, a Sabine city, was the seat of the Tiburtine Sibyl. There are two small temples above the falls, the rotunda traditionally associated with Vesta and the rectangular one with the Sibyl of Tibur, whom Varro calls 'Albunea', the water nymph who was worshipped on the banks of the Anio as a tenth Sibyl added to the nine mentioned by the Greek writers. In the nearby woods, Faunus had a sacred grove.

She ignored the blandishments of Etruscan and Sabine,

paused at <u>Vesta</u> – she would look at it later, she decided, skipped over <u>Varro</u> and went to <u>Albunea</u>. And there she was:

Albunea, the <u>Tiburtine Sibyl</u>, was in <u>Roman mythology</u> a prophetic nymph or Sibyl, a <u>naiad</u> who lived in the <u>sulphuric</u> spring near <u>Tibur</u>, (<u>Tivoli</u>) with a well and a temple. Near it was the oracle of <u>Faunus</u> Fatidicus. <u>Lactantius</u> states that the tenth Sibyl, called Albunea, was worshiped at Tibur, and that her image, holding a book in one hand, was found in the bed of the river Anio.

Bingo! Jane thought.

7

Monday 18th January

Barney Highman ("high by name, high by nature," as he used to say boisterously) was a big teddy-bear of a man, with coarse brown hair and a broad good-natured face only slightly marred by a small mouth. In the film business he was something of a minor legend, since he had first made his money running a cathouse in Nevada, then a string of cathouses, before creating the definitive version, The Pussy Drive, which had made him a fortune.

With the fortune he went into film-making, and here again, a series of successes – more money – assured his status in the industry. Barney Highman was doing what he wanted and didn't mind how much he spent on doing it. The film he was now making at the Cinecittà studios in Rome and on location in Tivoli was a thinly-disguised plagiarism of *The Da Vinci Code,* the title, *The Pope's Protocol,* blatantly appealing to the same audience. "I reckon you can't be too obvious," Barney had said. "Folks are eating up that kind of shit at the moment."

Typically he had arrived in Tivoli earlier than expected; those of the crew who had worked with him before had wisely moved their own schedules forward so as not be caught out. Again, typically, he made sure of his personal comfort by renting the top floor of the Hotel delle Sirene for the duration of the shoot. From the terrace of his suite, which occupied the whole corner of the building, there were spectacular views over a gorge and across to two Roman temples perched on the lip of the precipice opposite. The view was particularly beautiful towards evening when the setting sun, dropping beneath the cloud cover, illuminated the top of the small round temple and its bare rectangular neighbour as shadows softly gathered in the valley's deep cleft. Barney didn't give a shit. His main concern was whether the mini-bar contained Corona Mexican beer as per instructions. "And rustle up some limes!" he told Anthea.

He had made his usual rounds and seen all the section heads, including Murph, the location manager, who was as laconic as ever but whose professional eye was flawless. The fountains in the gardens of the Villa D'Este would be used in several scenes, while interior shots would be limited to the frescoed rooms in the villa. The photographs in the guidebooks Anthea had come up with had given him some ideas too – Barney hadn't bothered with the text – being the kind of stock dramatic views that would fulfil expectations and give class to the whole thing.

As far as PR was concerned, on the Saturday evening Barney had hosted a second 'thank you' dinner at the hotel for the Mayor of Tivoli ("Salmon, eh?" he said when he saw it written down. "Sounds kinda fishy to me!") and the town councillors who had released the various permits. It had been a jolly, protracted affair, with several lovely girls hired for the occasion (appearing as "liaison officers" on subsequent tax returns) to flatter and entertain the locals, who were duly flattered and entertained, some of them privately after the meal as well. Everyone agreed that their host was *"bravissimo"*, *"simpaticissimo"*, and *"non presuntuoso per niente."* In his dealings with others Barney employed the potent triad of sex, sentiment and wonder. "Fucking, feelings and fantasy. That's what folks – and movies – are all about," he was fond of saying.

There had been much hilarity at the mixture of fractured Italian and English they all had to use. ("You like Italy?", *"Io amo Italy!"*) but Barney reckoned they needed more language back-up and got Anthea onto it. Shooting would begin the following Wednesday, the 20th January, and everything had to be in place beforehand. So far everything was fine and dandy.

Jane was unsure what to do next. The previous year, in the weeks before the battle in the sacred wood, all her efforts had been directed towards finding Professor Caseman and delivering the dead man's message; at that point, the professor – Jane still could not think of her as Lena – had known what to do.

This year however, all that Jane understood was that she had to go to Tivoli, and that the task (battle?) was somehow linked to the Vestals and possibly to the White Sibyl. Albunea? she thought distractedly. What kind of name is that? Other fragments jostled together in her mind: the only Roman sibyl, the other nine were Greek; also a water nymph; under the protection of the goddess Venus; her symbol was a book. Jane had decided that Albunea must anyway be a "lesser goddess", and had even found a web site, *The Obscure Goddess Online Directory*, where she – or "She" as the site had it – was described.

So far, so good, but there was nothing else and no one she could ask. She determined that she would take a day-off from job-hunting and drive Harold to Tivoli, if only to have a look round and see if something occurred to her. She would just have to trust that the professor would have had something – or some person – ready to guide her. She wondered if she should take the statue with her, and then smiled at the image of herself wandering round a strange town holding it out to passers-by in the hope one would say, "Of course! You're Jane! Come with me." No, she decided, leave the statue. It's just a recce, as George would say.

The person ready to guide her should have been Elfriede, but she was dead, her commissioned headstone, now complete with the date of 12 / 01 / 2010, waiting for delivery at the stonemason's. Her lawyer wanted it taken to the cemetery before the funeral, and set in place immediately after; there was no point in waiting, even though there was no family to consider.

Only three months had passed since the surge in the Aniene had occurred, three months since the swelling and rising river had covered the only known tomb of a Vestal, Cossinia, before peacefully sinking back. "... (when) ...waters rise to bathe afresh Cossinia"; the sign could not have been clearer nor the fragment more apposite.

And Elfriede had duly phoned the professor, drunk and incoherent and almost beside herself with joy. The waiting was over. The next phase could begin. Only ... Lena did not want to give Elfriede her instructions when the other was so obviously inebriated, and was even reluctant to entrust her with furthering the task. The arrival of the American woman and her attempts at intimacy was an additional factor, and the chance sight of the woman in whispered conversation with the girl at reception had made Lena even more determined to keep her own council. The next antagonist was already in place, was now watching in her turn, and must be given no hint of Lena's plans.

As for Elfriede, she was bereft. The waiting had taken its toll, as witness her drinking, but the sense of anti-climax hard on the heels of success was worse. She had waited, she had been true, and now ...?

Initially she made a heroic effort to cut down on alcohol, substituting wine for brandy, and beer for wine, though she became muddled about which she should be drinking at a particular time of day. When she did not hear from the professor as promised (and the latter had always stressed that any contact must be initiated by herself), she telephoned the clinic – sober this time – only to find the professor vague and reluctant to talk. What was she supposed to do? Was something wrong? Should she go to the nursing home? She dithered for days, which then became weeks, and as her bad dreams continued, nightmares that relentlessly unfolded in dark caverns where the rushing of water threatened rather than soothed, slipped back into her old ways.

Finally, just after Christmas, she phoned the nursing home again, and heard the news that the professor was dead. So bitter was the blow she could neither contemplate the present nor make any coherent plans for the future. She wandered about the town, a haphazard meandering course that took her across the footbridge to Cossinia's tomb, back again over the bridge, up the hill to the winding streets of the medieval quarter, and finally to the ruins of the two temples.

It was there that she paused, sat on the bench above the gorge with her thermos flask of hot coffee and brandy, and stayed there until the flask was empty. It was midday, she should go home, have something to eat, perhaps sleep a little. She heaved herself up, gave the Temple of Vesta a last beseeching look, and had started to walk away when she encountered a group of people coming from the back of the hotel – members of the film crew, though she could not know that.

As the group passed, the sight of the large man in a

bulky sheepskin jacket triggered some kind of buried memory and she was plunged into the dark rushing world of her nightmares; *he* was responsible, *he* was the cause, and *he* was the enemy. She did not know what happened next; when she came to herself, she was standing there alone, dazedly clutching a hundred-dollar bank note, with no idea where it had come from or what she had been doing. She stumbled home, whispering, "I don't know what to do. I don't know what to do."

Elfriede's last evening, the 12th January, was dank and chill, the moisture-laden air – not quite fog, not quite rain – pervading every nook and cranny. It gave a glistening halo to the yellow streetlamps in larger streets and a treacherous sheen to the cobblestones in thin crooked alleys. The few people out and about, padded shapeless bundles, snuggled their chins deeper into coats and scarves, and hurried about their business, thinking longingly of home and hearth, where light and warmth and television would shield them from the knowledge of darkness.

Elfriede decided to go out to have something to eat. The basement flat was cold and cheerless – she had forgotten to buy wood for the fire, and the one working bar of the electric heater intensified the lack of comfort rather than dispelling it. She went to a small trattoria, stirred a plate of spaghetti around in a semblance of eating and indulged in a litre of the local red wine. Coffee and grappa afterwards completed her meal but she felt too restless to return home and wandered out into the now-empty streets and down the hill, drawn again towards the Ponte della Pace and

Cossinia's tomb.

While Jane and George were talking and laughing over beer in Rome, the white tablecloth now satisfyingly smudged with grease and tomato sauce, and the get-out-of-jail party finally and noisily breaking up, in Tivoli Elfriede was walking unsteadily under gently-dripping cypresses towards the steps to the footbridge. At the top she paused to gaze across the slow-moving river towards the cold neon gleam of the station lights on the other side. The sound of her footsteps was muffled in the damp air as she wobbled her way down. At the bottom she paused again, trying to make out the base and plinth of the tomb, but any view was obscured by a dark mass of tall reeds bent waterwards by the wind.

"Elfriede!" called a low friendly voice.

Her frightened half-turn brought her to a bumping crackling halt against an indistinct shape; she had heard no sound behind her, could discern nothing of the shape's features.

"Elfriede," said the voice again, low and caressing, even as her arm was locked behind her, and a hand deftly found her throat beneath her hand-knitted scarf. "How about a drink?"

Ten seconds is all it takes for unconsciousness to intervene when blood flow to the brain is interrupted. By then Elfriede had barely begun an ungainly thrashing of arms and legs to free herself, fingers scrabbling ineffectually at the slick PVC sleeve of her assailant's raincoat; the last thing she heard was the drumming of her heels on the wooden planks of the bridge.

8

Monday 18th – Tuesday 19th January

Later that month, too late for Elfriede, Jane checked her emails on the Monday evening, and found one from Carl Plodinsky, who had indeed suffered at school because of his name. Jane did not know him well. He was a peripheral 'friend', one of the loose network of English teachers, for despite his name Carl had a Canadian mother, which made him "mother tongue" English. Jane had added him to the list of emails, knowing he often heard of government-funded courses for the young unemployed or the police or tourist operators. The message read:

There is a job as PA – aka dogsbody – with film company on location in Tivoli. Only couple of weeks but they pay board and lodging plus salary. Was going to do it myself but offered better one, same company, as guide to one of visiting backers.
    Person to call is Anthea Lee, tel. 340-4400316.
    Good to hear from you - must get together (maybe see you there if

you do the job).   Ciao Carl

For a moment the enormity of it left Jane's mind a blank. Mechanically, she fumbled in the drawer and took the last cigarette from the 'I dare you' pack, found the lighter, lit up, and then slumped back in her chair as she inhaled. The blue smoke briefly swirled in front of the computer screen and – still mechanically – she half rose from her chair to open the window. The clock of the church of Santa Maria in Trastevere struck four; it was already starting to get dark, especially in the dim well of Jane's courtyard. She read the email again:

There is a job as PA – aka dogsbody – with film company on location in Tivoli. Only couple of weeks but they pay board and lodging plus salary. Was going to do it myself but offered better one, same company, as guide to one of visiting backers.
    Person to call is Anthea Lee, tel. 340-4400316.
    Good to hear from you - must get together (maybe see you there if you do the job).   Ciao Carl

So ..., she thought. So ... her mind refused to offer anything else.

And the e-mail shifted Jane's task into another – higher – gear. She realised with dismay that she could no longer procrastinate. The feeling of being absolutely alone in this cold wet January was intensified by the recurring memory of the almost holiday-like atmosphere surrounding the events of the previous August; brochure Italy, she thought wryly. She missed Gabriel with his maddening but practical help, she thought of George on his "recce" somewhere in Siberia (though incongruously she imagined him in his large summer shorts) and would have been grateful to have had his solid presence nearby. There was no one in whom she could confide, not without running the risk of being at best humoured, and at worst, laughed at.

When in doubt, carry on with practical matters, she told herself. She phoned Anthea Lee and they arranged to meet at a hotel in the Via Veneto. Jane had imagined a formal interview in a plush suite or perhaps in the hotel lounge, when she would be interrogated about her experience and asked why she wanted the job. She had in fact spent some time trying to think of possible questions and her (incisive) answers, but it turned out to be all wasted effort. Anthea Lee swooped on her in the hotel foyer, a stick-thin young woman with spiky orange hair, legs encased in fuzzy blue leg-warmers topped with a short leather skirt, sporting a huge orange plastic watch on one bony wrist. The 'interview' took place then and there since Anthea had other things to do. "Gotta sort out a crazy scriptwriter," she explained with a grimace of annoyance. She took Jane's proffered C.V. as though it were an unwanted flier that had been pressed on her in the street, then shoved it under one arm and asked whether Jane could start immediately, the following morning if possible.

Jane barely had time to agree when Althea was scribbling on a yellow pad, ripping off the sheet and thrusting it into Jane's hand. Then she was away, the fuzzy blue leg-warmers whisking purposefully towards the lift, presumably to ferret out the crazy scriptwriter. Jane was left looking dazedly at the scrawled name and address – where she had to report for duty? – and decided to go for coffee – it was nearly eleven o'clock anyway. Hot coffee, re-group, make list, she thought as she made her way from the hotel.

Tivoli's Mayor Salmone was worried. Was it only five days ago that he had been concerned about the *lampione*? It seemed much longer. That had been fixed anyway; from his office window he could see that it had dutifully gone out with the others – or was it still showing a faint rebellious glow? Surely not! He narrowed his eyes to glare at it. If it *was* still trying to shine ...! With a huff of annoyance, knowing that he was avoiding the real problem, he went back to his desk and uncharacteristically threw himself into the chair. Was there no end to the things that could go wrong? He could have understood if it had been an Italian film crew – he would never have given the permits at this time of year if *that* had been the case – but Anglo-Saxons! Well, Americans, but it came to the same thing. *They* could usually be relied upon – almost tiresomely so – to keep to their programmed schedule. It really was too much.

Well, at least signor Highman had telephoned himself. To the mayor, aware of his own importance, that indicated it was a real problem and not just an excuse for inefficient planning. It had been extremely courteous, though the call itself was lengthy, due to the three-way line with an interpreter in the middle. Desolate, unavoidable delay, one of the stars indisposed for a week with a bad chest infection, would do everything possible to speed matters along, etc. etc. One small consolation was that with the exception of a couple of rooms the Villa could be re-opened so at least members of the public would not be disappointed; a new notice would have to be prepared of course, giving warning of the new period of closure. With a feeling of relief he got his post-its from the desk drawer and wrote "*VILLA – avviso*", smoothing it into place on the sticky corner of his desk.

Soothed by the small achievement, he also dwelt on the satisfying memory of Sunday 17th, the feast day of St. Antonio Abate and the day that joyfully ushered in the month of Carnival. Nothing wrong with the planning *there*! Everything had gone like a Swiss watch, he thought complacently, a programme rich in colour and variety. And the weather had been fine. The hot-air balloon over Tivoli showering confetti and messages had been a huge hit, and the offer of rides to the general public later in the day an even bigger one. The sight of the balloon straining against its ropes as passengers were loaded and unloaded in the *Anfiteatro di Bleso* was as fine a blend of history and modernity as could be seen anyway in Italy; everyone had been enthralled and impressed.

In the afternoon, flanked by other dignitaries, he had officiated over the annual ceremony to unveil the Carnival mask, and the accompanying band, jugglers and clowns, not forgetting the majorettes, had done splendidly, handing out popcorn and candyfloss to all and sundry in the time-honoured Carnival tradition. Perhaps the band *had* been slightly off-key, the jugglers a little homely (did two balls count as juggling?) and the majorettes were showing a tendency to become older and plumper but all these were mere details to be swept aside by the sheer exuberance of the occasion and the energetic performance by the *tamburello* players; *they* were good. Now, if only the filming would go forward without mishap.

The post-it caught his eye again. Too bland. He carefully inked over the letters again and added more urgency. It now read: "**VILLA – avviso!!**" Much better.

9

The next morning Jane was driving out of Rome towards Tivoli with her cases on Harold's back seat; his boot was as tiny as the rest of him. She had packed three dictionaries, general English-Italian, technical English-Italian, and Italian-Italian, and had also looked up "filming", "film crew" and "cinematography" on the internet since she had no idea how any of it worked. Perhaps the most useful thing she had come across was a piece headed **A Few Things I Learned From My First Experience As A Television Production Assistant,** which contained such nuggets as "**Transportation (Transpo):** These are the often overweight guys in their late 40's or 50's you see sitting around base camp, eating free food and talking in small circles with other drivers." And: "**Costume:** Friendly, but prone to being anal. Maybe because some of the clothes being bandied about cost thousands of dollars."

Costumes costing "thousands of dollars". That

sounded right. The film, *The Pope's Protocol*, had already received advance publicity and sounded very expensive indeed – big names, international settings, and lots of hype, with promises of "spine-chilling murders", "a labyrinth of deceit" and "shocking secrets revealed".

Fascinating, but Jane wondered how it would work in practice. She fleetingly wished she could have found a teaching job in Rome, something safe and boring and cosy, which would have given her time to travel to Tivoli on a part-time basis. Being in the town itself did not feel cosy at all. The job – not to mention the quest – sounded fraught and difficult and … yes, altogether too much on the spot; Nemi and its battle had been away from Rome, and so, separate, not to mention fast, too fast for her to take in the danger. Or so it seemed in retrospect.

The journey had begun anyway, and at least it had stopped raining, especially since one of Harold's windscreen wipers had started a spasmodic jerking so that it clawed at the glass rather than clearing it. The statue of the White Sibyl and the Venus figurine were stowed in the middle of her case, well-padded by jumpers; their presence comforted Jane, and since there was no one else they would be the ones to accompany her and give her moral support.

The main road fed off to the right through Tivoli Terme, where builders' yards and stone carvers lined the way; Jane briefly glimpsed a brown tourist sign to Hadrian's Villa hanging from a pole, though the villa itself was invisible; and then – finally – the road began a gentle winding climb towards the town of Tivoli on its projecting promontory, and the plain below gradually dropped away.

At around the same time Mamie McCulloch was in her room at the nursing home rather than drinking coffee in the public lounge. She had finished her business in Nemi, and the limousine would soon be arriving. The small sweater – in two shades of pink with the matching crocheted scarf – was carefully wrapped in tissue paper and lay in her carry-all. Her needles, safely sheathed in their holder, lay beside it. She glanced round the room to check she had not missed anything, then crossed to the mirror and pulled her roll-neck sweater down to one side. The purplish patch on her shoulder was coming back, even showing signs of growing larger than before; they had in fact told her that the liquid nitrogen treatment was not definitive.

The stone carver, leaving his local bar, noticed the blue mini with its black roof. He could not see the driver since the angle was wrong, only glimpsed the corner of a large suitcase as the small car disappeared up the hill, further obscured by a rumbling lorry pulling out of a side street.

Maria Grazia, who owned the small travel agency next to the bar, was watching him wistfully through her plate-glass window She had been peeling off old posters and putting up new ones for bargain winter breaks to Sharm El Sheikh (*8 giorni, viaggio aereo, Rehana Resort* ****); it was just the right time of year to advertise Egypt, people were so fed-up with the weather. She wondered what he was looking at, standing there in his rough work clothes in that thoughtful way of his. She stood for a moment, a short girl, slightly plump but with clear pale skin, periwinkle-blue eyes and a mane of dark hair, then poked her head out of the door:

"Eh, Nico, how's it going?"

He turned slowly – all his actions were slow and considered – and then smiled:

"Ciao, Maria Grazia." She waited in vain for some further comment, then remembered he had no taste or talent for small talk. That silence of his, it could be so beguiling, so restful, or … so frustrating. But what a man! She thought longingly of the body beneath the dusty trousers and heavy jacket; the open collar of one of his plaid woollen shirts – what she thought of as his 'American' shirts – showed the white tee-shirt he always wore underneath and threw into relief the dark stubble of beard on his neck and chin. That was right – he never shaved in the morning, only after work in the evening.

"How are you doing these days?" she went on hopefully so that she could continue looking at him.

"Fine." She waited again, and this time he obliged. "Work, the usual," he said. "Fine," he repeated. He made a half-gesture with one hand. "Sorry. Have to go." And he moved off in the direction of his workshop.

She went back into her agency, still holding the poster for Sharm El Sheikh with its bright insets of azure sea, golden sands and luxury hotels ("And all much cheaper than you think!"). So strange, she was thinking, how did we ever ... ? I can't even remember how it started now. And how did it stop? Then, since she was an earthy pragmatic young woman, she grinned. It had been worth it though. "*Scopa come un dio!*" as she had told her friend Cinzia, though Cinzia herself was unimpressed, did not want a man who fucked like a god, just a kind hard-working type with a steady job, someone she could fuss over and have a family with. "*Scopa come un dio*" indeed!

Mamie McCulloch was sitting as comfortably as her swollen legs would allow in the back of the limousine, looking out at the wet green valley of Nemi; the legs of the trouser suit had been generously cut, but even so their silk lining chafed the purplish-red patches and nodules on her skin. The intersection that led to the scene of the car crash was empty now, for the final task of towing away the lawyer's crashed car had been put off due to the rain. She glanced briefly in that direction and sat further back. It would be a short journey so she would not overtire herself, and then, her business in Rome concluded, she would be going to Tivoli, to the Hotel Victoria Terme and her personal guide. What was his name again? – Curt or Carl, something German-sounding, but with a comical Russian surname; Barney would enjoy that.

Finally, business and necessity were coming together: the film, the little girl, and ... the all-important appointment, compared with which the first two weren't worth a hill of beans. As for the future – which would be a short one if this imperative mission in Tivoli failed – it was politic to be in Europe – months of time and a whole ocean away from the States.

For Mamie McCulloch – though they did not know her name – was on the wanted list of six states: Louisiana, Arkansas, Kansas, Texas, New Mexico, and California. They believed her to be male, Caucasian, between 25 and 40, a sociopath and an omnivore, that is, a serial killer who shows no preference as regards gender, age, race or profession. Two of their assumptions were incorrect but they could not be blamed for that since they were going on past experience while Mamie was a case apart. They were also wrong about the number of victims, working on a list of ten over the preceding five years, and had not yet gone further back in time. Crimes potentially related to terrorism took precedence over 'normal' ones and federal computers were backed up "from here to Albuquerque," as one cheerful technician put it. Two of the bodies had never been found either, so that the sequence was interrupted; there was a homeless man who was never reported missing, while the other, a teenage girl, was assumed to have run away from home.

What had linked the crimes was the weapon used, a "thin pointed spike-like object." It followed that she would be called The Spike Killer, sometimes shortened to Spiker or Spike, this last only in the ranks, since higher levels disliked both the levity and the implied familiarity in the name; it sounded as though they were searching for a lost younger brother.

Mamie only took up her knitting about twice a year – when it seemed ... time; it was not inextricably linked to her day-to-day life. The first time the girls saw her busy with her needles, they teased her about it: "Aw, come on, Mame, you're not that old!" To which she good-naturedly replied: "Young ladies, I surely know that, and that is why I am soon going on a short trip. Have myself some rest and relaxation, away from your clacking!" They all laughed; Mamie was a great favourite with all of them.

10

Saturday 30th January

Ten days later the town of Tivoli was becoming used to seeing strange types coming and going and cluttering up the bars and restaurants in the evenings; the local economy was indeed benefiting as the mayor of Tivoli had hoped – more so with the delay caused by the star's chest infection. Apart from the executive group at the Hotel delle Sirene, there were dozens and dozens of the crew installed in small hotels, B&Bs, and even as paying guests in various families. Nothing had ever been seen like it before.

    The *Tiburtini*, while grumbling and keeping a weather eye open for excessive drinking, interference with local girls and other foreign goings-on, were secretly thrilled by having the world of Hollywood on their doorstep. And there was in fact very little they could actually complain about. Barney – for all his apparent good humour and camaraderie – ran a very tight ship indeed; time was money and any shenanigans would only waste that precious commodity.

Shooting would now begin the following Monday, and everything seemed to be on schedule. So much so that an air of impatience began to grow among the troupe. It was fine for the Transpos, "the often overweight guys in their late 40's or 50's you see sitting around base camp, eating free food" that Jane had read about, they took themselves off to Rome or even returned home if it was close enough. It was fine by the bit-players as well, who were quite happy to congregate in someone's room, trying to piece some sense out of their one or two lines in an attempt to decipher what the film was about. They had little success - "His Holiness will see you now" or "The gardens are so *sad* at this time of year!" offered small scope for even the most fevered imaginations.

Having arrived on the Wednesday, Jane was still finding her way around both the town and the job. She knew now that the Gaffer was the chief electrician, rather than someone's bewhiskered grandfather with a clay pipe, that Best Boy was his assistant and not an infant prodigy and that the Key Grip did not actually have to hold on to anything.

Her official job title "Language Consultant" was indeed a code for 'dogsbody' as Carl had said, and a flexible bilingual dogsbody as well. On her first day she had not even seen her digs until the evening. She had been carried off by a frantic technician looking for extra cable, a quest that took them all over town and then down to Tivoli Terme at the bottom of the hill, where a willing but slow builder had finally come up with the right gauge. Luckily, since they had gone in her car, still unpacked, her technical dictionary was to hand.

As for Tivoli itself, she was never sure where she was in relation to everything else; she had to keep checking her map and reminding herself of other points of reference. This is the main street with the road to Rome at the top, the Villa is off to the right, the hospital and river are somewhere down there behind me, my digs are ... No, she couldn't remember, could visualise the street but had a part missing between the centre of town and the road where she was staying. (And the medieval part? Where had that gone to now?). Yet it shouldn't be difficult, the town was not *that* big. It must be the spur of mountain it sat on, she decided, and the strange valley flanked with cliffs that gouged two deep fissures into the hill, Villa Gregoriana it was called. Misleading, since it was a valley.

She had met Barney ("Hey, Janey, glad you could make it. Now don't you go taking any shit from these hicks – we're bringing big money into this place!"), and more or less settled into her B&B, mercifully well-heated for the weather continued cold, wet and grey.

It wasn't easy though. It seemed as though every single member of the crew had been told she was on call for any need for Italian, and – at first eager and willing – she had had to draw the line when asked to go along on a date with one of the local girls; there had been some fraternising despite the official line.

Barney took precedence of course and his messages

were relayed through Althea, who would begin: "Barney reckons ...," the preface to some apparently simple but ultimately convoluted task, or "Barney doesn't reckon ... it'll take long," or ... "it'll be a problem," a patent untruth as it would turn out.

His idea of taking his entourage to the Villa Gregoriana, an idea conceived when he too became infected with the general air of impatience, was a case in point. Anthea: "Barney reckons it would be a good idea to see this – whatsit? – gardens, a gorge, waterfalls? Might be just right for shooting one of the scenes," she said, rushing in one day, skinny arms hugging her enormous diary and clipboard. "Barney doesn't reckon it'll be difficult."

Jane nodded, and then sighed as she watched Anthea trot away. On the Saturday she had planned to do something – she had no idea what – to find the White Sibyl. **Quest for the White Sibyl abandoned for The Pope's Protocol!** she thought, the words wreathed in scarlet banners in her mind. **Will our heroine overcome** – no, scrap that – **Will our intrepid heroine find time to** ... well, even wash her knickers out for a start, she finished. Rather dispiritedly she set off for the tourist office, only to be told that the craggy valley was closed for the winter, though groups could be booked out of season. She cheered up – perhaps one of Barney's declarations ("It shouldn't be a problem") might be true – and trailed off to find the *responsabile* for out-of-season visits, who was based in the town hall, where she had originally thought of going.

But the *responsabile* was away and his stand-in

admitted he didn't know where the master keys were, or even if someone could be found to accompany the group. Phone calls from Althea: "Hey, what's the hold-up? Barney reckons it shouldn't take this long." Another visit to the town hall and an empty office, then a local bar, where she found the stand-in fortifying himself against the cold with coffee and grappa. He greeted her radiantly: the keys had been found, and the appointment was fixed for Saturday 10 a.m. outside the gates. Jane phoned Anthea with the news, and then, worn-out, resolutely switched off her mobile phone. Enough was enough, she was going back to the B&B ("If I can find it") and she really must try and decide what she should do about the White Sibyl. Perhaps after the visit to the Villa Gregoriana on Saturday ... She just hoped that both guide and group would remember the arrangement and also come at the right time.

In that at least she was pleasantly surprised. The stand-in had sent a serious young man with spectacles to be their guide, and the assorted group, about fifteen of them, met him at the gates on the side of the valley opposite the temples. Barney was beaming and massive in a sheepskin jacket and padded trousers, while the others were a mixed bunch of coats, ski pants, jumpers and woolly hats. The day before Jane had gone to see the site, peered through the railings down into the wooded slopes below, and was wearing her most comfortable rubber-soled trainers. It was obvious that some of the others had had no idea what the visit would entail, and the group immediately lost six of its members (four pairs of high-heeled boots, two pairs of designer loafers). Of those who were left Jane recognised Anthea, Jed and Jenny, the production co-ordinator and his female assistant, and lastly a dour man who had given her a map of the town when she first arrived. She had no idea about the others. They seemed to fall into two groups: stylish entourage-type people, and practical casually-dressed technical people. All of them followed Barney and the guide through the gates, then down the first flights of steps to where the main path began.

"Now, ain't this jus' the biz?" boomed Barney, grouping for his ever-present viewfinder and peering through it in all directions, even though little could be seen through the trees at that point. "Wotcher reckon, Murph?"

Murph remained stubbornly mute. He had hoped to be long gone by then but had been talked into staying by Barney ("C'mon, Murph, y' know I can't do without my right-hand man! Location, smocation, y're still needed, guy!"). He noted the rough track coated with a spongy layer of sodden leaves, the dank undergrowth interspersed with mutilated statues and pillars, and could hear the distant roar of cascading water. Involuntarily he glanced about for possibilities and problems. What was this place? It certainly had a feel to it.

As for Jane, she was weak with gratitude that the guide spoke good English. "My name is Enrico," he began, smiling timidly at the clustered group, "and I am happy to be your guide to our beautiful Villa Gregoriana. It was in 1835, after the Aniene River had burst its banks yet again, that Pope Gregory XVI decided to transform this enchanting but extremely dangerous location into a model of integration between art and nature."

He handed round copies of a coloured leaflet, which contained a map of the area. "Here is a small map and you can see how is big the site."

Barney, still looking through his viewfinder, ignored his, Anthea gave hers a cursory glance before tucking it into her diary, while the others looked at theirs with varying degrees of interest. Jane in particular tried to grasp the main features. Enrico, after a nervous glance at Barney, went on:

"We are at the top here – number 1 – and we will take the main route, the blue line. You can see that there are the waterfalls of the River Aniene that comes from the Mount Catillo Tunnels, wanted by Pope Gregory to deviate the river from Tivoli."

"Wanted, eh?" said Barney, looking round and giving a shark-like grin. "No harm in wanting…"

Enrico gave a painful smile, "Ah, my English, yes … thank you. I wanted to say that he … ordered the construction."

Jane suddenly found herself disliking Barney. A bully, she thought. A grinning bully. The velvet of bluff good humour hiding the iron selfishness of big money. All at once she wondered what Gabriel would have made of him. Actually, she could imagine: "He's an *American*, Jane. What do you expect?" Gabriele hated – had hated Americans.

Enrico stumbled on for a few more sentences (the natural grottos, the villa of Manlius Vopiscus) before inviting the group to follow him. Jane was still looking at her map, amazed that such a wild natural area should lie so close beneath the town; it was as though one side of the hill had been clawed away by an enormous paw. And there, just visible through the misty air on the other side of the gorge, were the temples, the round and the rectangular, set so close together that they almost seemed to be touching. Vesta and ... Jane couldn't remember the second one. Was it the Sibyl's or the male god she had read about? She looked at the leaflet. Number 13, Temples of Vesta and Tiburnus. Tiburnus? Not the Sibyl? And there had been another name in Wikipedia as well, one beginning with F.

She suddenly realised the group had disappeared from sight round the first bend, and started after them taking great care where she put her feet. The sound of falling water swelled as she descended.

The group had halted in a long oval clearing in front of a series of shallow arches in the side of the hill. " ... Manlius Vopiscus, one of the so many Romans who possessed the villa in this area," Enrico was saying. "Also other notable personages, as Julius Caesar, the Emperor Hadrian, and ... others." His English seemed to have deteriorated, Jane noticed. Had Barney made fun of him again? She looked down at the map; they had only covered a fraction of the distance.

The route took them deeper and deeper into the valley, the cliffs now rearing above them. Although they did not make the detour to see the huge waterfall issuing from the Catillo tunnels, the sound of falling water thundered dimly in the background.

They finally reached a rough clearing near the bottom of the descent, obviously a central point, for a large free-standing notice board showed a map of the area with their position, the *Radura di Ponte Lupo*; the open space was filled with benches, each with a name; "Avv. Italo Cervigni" read one, and "Donna Luisa Aldobrandini" read another.

"The site is now the property of the Italian Environment Fund," explained Enrico. "The FAI, which means 'you do" in Italian, while the acronym. F-A-I," he carefully spelt out the acronym, "means ..."

"Fuck All Italians, eh?" chuckled Barney; the entourage sniggered.

Enrico flushed a mottled red. *"Fondo ambiente italiano,"* he went on doggedly. "And these benches have been donated by the members, a memorial to themselves or their loved ones and a support to the Fund. This way, please." And he set off from the clearing to the beginning of an even narrower path leading steeply down in brick steps.

Of the things she saw that day, Jane was to remember this part in particular. It was the one detour that they took, which ended at the very bottom of the gorge. Enrico must be very scrupulous, thought Jane. After Barney's tasteless joke, she would have missed it out and got rid of the group as soon as possible.

They had to go down in single file, only a low wall between the path and the empty air beneath. The name *Valle dell'Inferno* had been given to this corner of the gorge, where a minor waterfall came from another tunnel. It looked nothing like hell, being filled with huge fleshy-leaved marsh plants and intersected by sluggish rivulets of water.

The furthermost point of the path ended in the *Grotta delle Sirene*, "The Mermaids' Grotto" read the translation on the sign nearby. Well, yes, it does mean that as well, thought Jane, vaguely dissatisfied. The shadowy cavern, mysterious with the sound of unseen water, was roofed in a stormy sky frozen in stone, but it held nothing of the playful mermaids of popular art. Beautiful and sinister, the arching swirls overhead seemed to threaten to burst into life, crash down in billows and waves that would submerge them all. The group, after some muttering and shuffling and a few trophy snapshots with mobile phones, couldn't wait to leave the place and go back to the central clearing.

And after that, there was still the long climb up the opposite side of the valley. It was a relief finally to reach the top and see a modern-looking snack bar to the side of the rectangular temple. "They have opened for us today," announced Enrico proudly. "Here we can have hot coffee to warm us." The group broke up, some going to the toilets, others making straight for the bar. Anthea was on her mobile, theatrically casting her eyes heavenwards. A fragment detached itself from the rest: "Now, look, Eric, I told you – it's just not on. No, he won't want to reconsider." Snapping the phone shut she went over to Barney. "He's still moaning on about interpretation." "Tell'im he's sold it. What's to discuss?"

Jane found Enrico at the end of the bar sipping lemon tea. He looked wary when he saw her, and the knuckles of his hands around the glass showed white; Barney had done his work well.

"Thank you so much," said Jane in Italian, smiling and holding out her hand. "It was so interesting and you are so well-informed."

"Nothing, a pleasure," he said, relaxing; his knuckles returned to normal as they shook hands.

"Can you tell me more about the temples?" she went on. "I know the round one is similar to the Temple of Vesta in Rome but what about the square one? The leaflet says Tiburnus."

"We do not know," said Enrico regretfully. "There are many theories. Tiburnus was the hero who gave his name to Tivoli, ancient Tibur, but the temple could also be to Hercules, the protecting deity of the city, or the Sibyl. You know the Tiburtine Sibyl?"

"Albunea? Yes. But Tivoli seems to have a lot of mythical figures."

Enrico brightened at this display of knowledge. Here was someone who was interested.

"Yes, yes! In fact!" he agreed excitedly. "There was the hero Tiburnus, then Hercules, then the Sibyl herself, the *prediletta* of Venus ..."

"*Prediletta*"? Jane didn't know the word.

"The favourite," he explained in English, then, smiling shyly "The – how do you say – the darling."

Jane laughed, "The darling of Venus! Yes, wonderful! I didn't know that."

By this time Enrico had completely cheered up. "Then, of course, there was another – Faunus, called Faunus

Fatidicus, he prophesied. His sacred grove was here – the woods beneath the cascades."

Faunus – that was the other name Jane had seen. She was starting to feel that Tivoli was overrun with gods and goddesses; she tried to narrow the field:

"But was he linked to the Sibyl in any way?"

"Only in the sense they both gave prophesies, but Faunus appeared in dreams, while the Sibyl would pronounce in the – let us say – the waking world."

"I see," she said thoughtfully, making a mental note to find out more. "Well, I must go. Thank you again for all your time and knowledge."

He gave a little half-bow. When he straightened up he was holding out a business card. It read, *'Enrico Mattei, operatore turistico'*. "If you have need during your stay ..." he went on.

"Thank you, thank you very much. I'm Jane Harrison."

"Enrico, Enrico Mattei," he said, and they shook hands again. The group had now dispersed, and Jane left the bar, going towards the temples and the view over the treetops in the gorge beneath. The sky had cleared slightly, and a watery sun was endeavouring to break through the clouds.

The rectangular temple, the one nearest the bar, stretched lengthways away from the valley. Its lower corner showed a deep vertical crack with a heap of stones – obviously part of the original wall – forming a bumpy slope underneath; the area had been sealed off with red and white plastic tape tied to wooden staves. There's just too much in Italy, Jane thought fleetingly, there's never enough money to keep up with it all. She walked the short distance to the front of the temple and looked in - it was a mere shell of three walls, the fourth, where she stood, opening onto a bare space containing nothing but a small plinth at the far end. The weathered brickwork may once have been covered with marble or frescos but what remained gave no hint of how the interior had originally appeared. To Jane its very emptiness seemed a rejection; it would tell her nothing. She continued to the round temple, more recognisable with its Corinthian pillars and inner frieze of garlands and animal skulls. Her feet crunched on gravel as she made a circuit of the temple; at the back, hidden from view, she found a bench, the one where Elfriede had sat with her thermos of coffee and brandy. Jane too sat down, almost immediately got up and walked round the temple again, returned to the bare walls of the rectangular temple (the Sibyl? Hercules? Tiburnus? And what about Faunus?), looked down into the valley of Villa Gregoriana, all to no avail. Nothing occurred to her. She looked at her watch – 12.30 – nearly lunchtime. She left the temples and went through the courtyard leading to the street. This must be in or near the medieval part – the street itself was narrow and lined with tall thin houses, grates over their ground-floor windows. *Via della Sibilla* informed a rust-stained street sign.

    She paused when she came to a gap in the buildings on the right. Below her was what looked like the remains of an abandoned factory, then the land fell away and there was an uninterrupted view over the countryside. But which direction? Again she was struck by her inability to orient herself in the town. She had no idea whether she was looking west towards Rome or east towards ... what? The flattened landscape under the grey clouds gave little clue. She felt in her bag for her street map, then with some annoyance (she really *must* get a grip on where everything was!) remembered she had left it on the bedside table. She walked on.

She had gone about twenty yards when a lighted shop window attracted her attention and she looked in. Obviously a gift shop with its cluttered display of souvenirs, but they'll have maps, she thought with sudden inspiration, perhaps even guide books. She pushed open the door, a set of wind chimes giving a mellow ripple to announce her entrance, and stepped inside.

Behind the counter at the far end of the shop sat a woman with pale frizzy hair, apparently reading and sipping at a glass of mineral water; the small green plastic bottle stood on the counter beside her. Jane said, *"Buon giorno"* but the woman, who had glanced up, just nodded and bent her head over her book again. Her features were dappled and shadowed by the glow from a liquid-filled lamp, pale blue with dark blue whorls spiralling lazily upwards.

There was a stand with maps and tourist guides near the door and Jane searched through them, aware that it must be nearing one o'clock, closing time. She immediately discarded the large maps which folded out – she could never find the original creases – and chose a small booklet-type. The books on display were the large paperback tourist

The White Sibyl

guides with red spines that she had seen at Pompeii and Orvieto and she took the one entitled Archaeological Zones of Latium TIVOLI – HADRIAN'S VILLA Subiaco – Aniene Valley

The front cover showed a long oval pool at Hadrian's Villa. The back however had a photograph of the two temples taken from the slopes below, and the photographer had cleverly angled the shot so that the more modern buildings behind the temples were hardly visible.

A church clock was just striking one as she walked to the counter, but she suddenly stopped. At eye-level on a shelf to her right was a plaster replica of the broken statue, the same seated female figure with the same draped robe, the same book with its cover of whorls and swirls. The replica was complete however. She picked it up, studied the head to see if there was some important detail she should notice, but it showed the unremarkable hair and features of a dozen similar portrayals. She looked up to find the woman watching her, and gave an apologetic smile:

"Excuse me – I know you are closing now – I have the same statue, in marble, I think, but it is broken."

"Broken?" said the woman sternly, brows clipping together under the wisps of frizzy hair. Closer she looked much older (in her fifties? sixties?).

"No, I didn't break it myself," said Jane, now flustered and feeling she should justify herself. "It was a gift, a ..." She couldn't remember – if she had ever known – the Italian for 'keepsake'... "I ... inherited it. *Da una cara amica* - from a dear friend. It was broken when I received it."

105

"Ah, you ... inherited it." The woman paused, as Jane had paused. "I see." She seemed in no hurry, but Jane began to fumble in her bag to find her purse.

"German?" the woman queried suddenly, sitting up straight and becoming stern again.

"Pardon?"

"Your friend – she was a German woman?"

"No, no, English, like me," corrected Jane, feeling more and more lost. "I really mustn't disturb you further." She held out a ten-euro note but the woman waved it airily aside, and then gave an air of completion to the gesture by running her hand down the bottle of mineral water.

"What was the name of your friend?" she snapped.

"Professor Caseman. Lena," said Jane, not knowing what to do with the money. "She died just recently. In Nemi. You know, the Castelli?" She could hear her voice becoming choked, did not know why she was volunteering these fragments.

Incredibly the woman was smiling. "Ah." She picked up the bottle of mineral water, held it up against the liquid lamp as if to admire the play of light, blue glow through green plastic, then raised it to eye level and tilted it.

"Look out!" gasped Jane, caught between anger at the smile and confusion at the gesture; the bottle was nowhere near the glass. "It will ..."

Her warning died in her throat. The line of water – instead of splashing over the counter – streamed from the bottle, then stopped in mid-air. The woman was smiling again, eyes mocking as she watched Jane's reaction, then flicked small white fingers at the suspended water.

At the flick the water gathered together into a round mass, another flick and it began to take on a form, at first indistinct, then more and more delineated. Jane, still clutching her money and purchases, felt her whole face balloon into the comic circle of an astonished cartoon character.

The completed form was of a small galloping pony, but it was *moving*, flowing mane flying in the wind, tiny hooves rising and falling, tail outstretched, the whole sculpted in glistening water.

For a few seconds it galloped joyfully on – surely it was running free over sunlit grassy plains – and then quite suddenly dissolved, the water flopping and splattering onto the counter. Jane stared at the woman, who, quite unperturbed, fished out a rag and started to mop up the spreading pool.

"It is the fizzy water," she said in an off-hand way, still mopping. "It does not hold, you see. The bubbles are too rebellious, too … youthful. But still, even they have their place." She smiled slyly, seeming to enjoy Jane's amazement.

"How …" Jane realised she was about to finish with "… did you do that?" and stopped. Her mouth felt quite dry, and she was suddenly terribly thirsty, quite parched in fact. She gazed helplessly at the damp stain left by the rag on the counter.

"We will talk," announced the woman, with a final sweep at the stain.

"Yes," agreed Jane weakly. "I would like that."

The woman closed the shop and set off at a brisk pace up Via della Sibilla without another word, uttering only a spitting growl of annoyance as they passed The Ristorante Sibilla on the left. Jane's thoughts were in a whirl. Is she the White Sibyl? Did she know Professor Caseman? And the German woman? Who is she?

A few minutes' walk took them to an untidy intersection filled with parked cars and then to another narrow street leading uphill in cobbled steps; it was barely wide enough for two people to walk side by side though a trattoria had somehow fitted a railed wooden platform with a couple of tables into a corner formed by two unequal-width buildings. A little further up the hill the woman abruptly stopped, inserted a key into a large wooden door and disappeared up a dim staircase with the speed of the White Rabbit diving into the hole. Jane, like Alice, dived in pursuit.

Two flights of stairs, another door and another key, and they were in a large living room with a table beneath the window opposite. Jane caught a glimpse of three white cats sitting statue-like on the windowsill before they leapt to the floor and formed an unnerving row, for all the world like three soldiers waiting for the order to attack. For a moment three sets of unblinking green eyes regarded the intruder balefully until the woman clicked her tongue and the tableau dissolved.

"In! In!" she ordered impatiently, and Jane ventured further into the room, closing the door. One of the cats immediately padded behind her as if to close off the exit, while the other two positioned themselves on opposite sides of the room so that the three formed a triangle around her. The woman had disappeared again, this time into a small kitchen, to re-emerge holding two glasses and a bottle of water, jerking her head towards the table. Jane sat down. The woman poured two glasses of water, pushed one towards Jane, who drank it gratefully; she really had been parched.

Again the woman seemed in no hurry, had sat down opposite and was now alternatively looking out of the window, then down at her glass, smiling to herself and humming tunelessly. Jane sipped at her own water, wondering whether she should wait for the other to begin, but also wondering whether she was the guest of the local mad woman. But a mad woman who could sculpture a galloping pony out of water? Finally she could wait no longer.

"Excuse me," she began resolutely, "but are you ...?" she hesitated, and then started again. "I am ... a little confused. What should I call you? Albunea?" There, it was said, and she felt just as foolish as she had imagined she would.

The woman laughed scornfully. "Albunea! What am I? Some kind of egg white? Albunea!" She picked up her glass and held it between her palms, fingertips lightly touching above the rim. She had not moved but the water suddenly swirled, then thickened to become opaque and cloudy. Jane quietly put her own glass down.

"*La Sibilla si pronuncia!*" announced the woman, her

eyes – as green as those as her cats – fixed on the now milky swirls. "Past and the present await their promised reunion. The stranger is come to heal and purify. Purify." she repeated. "As must be in this month of Februarius, the time of purification. *La Sibilla si è pronunciata.*" She stopped, the water cleared, and she rose slightly to pour it into a clay pot bright with yellow primroses on the windowsill. There was silence.

"Am I ... the stranger?" asked Jane after a moment.

"Yes."

"And the German woman you asked me about?"

"She was not the one but she bought the statue."

"I'm sorry. I don't understand," said Jane.

"The statue is the object to be used."

"Used? Do you mean in some kind of ceremony?"

"Yes."

Jane had a flash of inspiration. "Was the statue in your shop?"

"Yes, the woman bought it but the Sibyl knew she was not the one."

Jane was finding it difficult, not to mention tiresome, having to guess everything; it was like trying to find the solution to a lateral-thinking problem. "But if the statue is so important, why was it in the shop where anyone could buy it?"

The woman looked at her pityingly. "It *had* to be there of course, ready to be found."

Jane took a deep breath. "So, it was in the shop and the wrong person found it, but now *I* have the statue, so we can

… I don't know … complete the ceremony, … can't we?"

"The thread is broken. The *statue* is broken," snapped the Sibyl. "It must be made whole." She sat back, adding nothing more.

Jane looked about her. The three cats still formed their watching triangle, but now she noticed the rest of the room. It was unremarkable with a small wood-burning stove in the centre of one wall, two faded armchairs complete with antimacassars on either side of it. A polished sideboard, too large for the room, stood against the wall opposite the stove, with an array of ornaments and faded photographs.

Jane looked at the stove, where a comforting glow showed through the glass, and started to think hard. The statue had been in the gift shop, it was sold to a German woman who broke it, then somehow it came into Professor Caseman's possession and was now in hers. If the … Sibyl could be believed, it was now with the right person, herself. She looked up to find the woman watching her, and took a deep breath. "I will try to find the missing part and repair the statue. Can you tell me anything else about the German woman?"

"The Sibyl knew she was not the one!"

"Yes, of course" agreed Jane quickly. "I am sure she … you did, but I need to know how I can find her. If she was a tourist, it will be impossible."

"She was not a tourist. She was a drunk."

"A drunk?"

"Water is the only pure liquid, the only *true* liquid. The woman smelt of drink."

Jane was beginning to feel annoyed. "But how do you *know* she wasn't a tourist?"

"The Sibyl has seen her more times here in the roads of Tibur."

Jane was about to ask, and then remembered Tibur was the ancient name of Tivoli. The Sibyl seemed to be regressing. How on earth does she manage to run a shop? she thought. But anyway … if the woman was living in Tivoli, Enrico Mattei, the young tour guide, might know who she was. Or there would be a record of residents at the town hall.

"I will find her," she said slowly, "try to discover if she still has the missing part. But then what should I do? What is the ceremony?"

There was a momentary pause, then: "The Sibyl does not remember," said the woman, a shade of embarrassment crossing her thin features. The emotion sat oddly on her usual haughty expression.

Jane stared at her in disbelief. "You don't remember!"

The woman recovered her self-possession. "All flows," she said loftily. "The Sibyl too must flow and loss must happen. It will return, even as the rains return to the oceans."

Jane did not know what was the most annoying – the Sibyl talking about herself in the third person, her monosyllabic replies, or her rhetorical flights of fancy. Why couldn't she just say, "Never mind. I'll remember."? She toyed with the idea of giving the woman a good shake, but caught the green gaze of one of the cats. It seemed to be staring at her in warning and all at once she thought longingly of the previous year. She (and Gabriel, she added, I mustn't forget Gabriel) had found Professor Caseman to deliver the dead man's message and the professor had known exactly what to do. In retrospect it had been all too easy. As for this year, how could Jane carry out her task if her only ally was a (mad?) sibyl – if she really was the Sibyl – who didn't even know what the ceremony consisted of? At this point the only thing she could do was to find the German woman, get back the statute's missing part, mend it, and then … hope. Some hope, she thought dismally.

"So it is agreed," said the woman. "The Sibyl will await your news, and prepare for what is to come." She paused, suddenly glanced about her, and then in a low voice, as if fearing to be overheard, "I sense the Other."

Jane felt a sudden chill. She realised that the Sibyl had said "*I* sense the Other." Why had she suddenly dropped 'she'? The change made it personal, and somehow all the more disturbing.

"The Other?" she asked, and she too spoke softly, aware of a flurry of white as the cats ran to huddle together in the far corner.

"While the Sibyl yearns for light and water, the Other craves darkness and filth. She too must sense the time is now. Februarius. The time." A yelping meow from one of the cats underlined her words. Jane shivered, her skin now as cold as it had been hot when she had almost told Mamie McCulloch about the professor's letter; that had been danger averted, this told of danger to come.

"Who ... who is this ... she?" she whispered.

But the Sibyl had straightened up and was toying with her empty glass. "We will speak of it again," she said briskly. "Now is not the time, not the place." She scribbled on a piece of paper. "Telephone number – for when you find the missing part." And the next thing Jane knew she was back on the cobbled steps of the street with no memory of leaving the flat or coming out of the main door.

The piece of paper was still in her hand, and she got out her mobile phone to put the number in. The phone was switched off, and when she did switch it on, it gave the shrill tone of a message. It was from Anthea: **Dinner tonite B's hotel** – **8**.00. Jane looked at it uncomprehendingly – for a second she had no idea who Anthea was – before keying in the Sibyl's phone number. The Sibyl's phone number? Despite everything she smiled, but she put the number under 'Ristorante Sibilla'. Something made her want to hide any revealing reference.

Later, lying limply on her bed – it really had been a trying day – Jane tried to order her thoughts. The first step, as she had promised the Sibyl, was to find out about the German woman, a resident of Tivoli and a drunk apparently. German and a drunk. She wondered whether Tivoli were small enough for everyone to know everyone as was the case in the villages. She pulled her bag from the bedside table and found Enrico Mattei's card. Keying his number into the mobile, she selected fast dial. It was answered after a couple of rings:

"*Pronto.*"

"Enrico, this is Jane, Jane Harrison. We met this morning at Villa Gregoriana?"

"Ah, yes, Signorina Jane. How can I help you?"

Jane took a deep breath. "I was wondering if we could meet for coffee tomorrow morning. I know it's Sunday, but I have some important questions I'd like to ask you. As I said, I'm so sorry to disturb your weekend but it *is* important."

Some of Jane's urgency must have communicated itself to him for he said: "Yes, certainly, no problem. About eleven?"

"Perfect. Where shall we meet?"

"Piazza Garibaldi, you know it?"

"Yes," said Jane with relief; she was still trying to get a fix on the town. "It's the big piazza near Villa D'Este."

"Exactly. The bar on the corner there."

Jane thanked him and rang off. Part of the first step was taken, and if that led nowhere, she could try the town hall. She lay back again, gazing absently at the pastel-tinted picture of two smiling cherubs that adorned the wall beside the wardrobe. Should she try and sleep? What time was it anyway? She glanced at her watch. Coming up to 3.30. There *was* time but …

Mamie McCulloch had arrived but had not as yet gone to Tivoli itself. The intervening visit to Rome to progress her other business had tired her, even though there had been no problems; there never were if you were prepared to pay top dollar. Her lawyers, an international firm that had offices in

London as well as Rome, had seen to the British side of things. They were never involved in actual negotiations of course, having various independent contacts who could be smoothly denied if some questionable affair came to the notice of the authorities. The child would be arriving in a week's time, and her welcoming present, the small sweater in two shades of pink with the matching crocheted scarf, would surely appeal to her. Retards liked bright colours, didn't they?

Tivoli Terme she dismissed as "a dump", which became, "It surely is a sad little place," when she was talking to others. Dirty and dusty from the nearby quarries, littered with rubbish blown by the chill wind, its pavements fouled with dog excrement, it might be very different in its high season as a thermal spa but was lacklustre and bleak at this time of year.

She had taken a superior suite at the Victoria Terme Hotel, the only hotel inside the Acque Abule, the main thermal complex, for she might take advantage of some of the treatments. You never knew. Jedson occupied a single room not far away and was on call if needed. He was her only companion – as she preferred – since he was the only person privy to most, if not all, of her secrets.

Barney had phoned the day she arrived ("Hey, and how's my angel?") with an invitation for Saturday evening, and Jane Harrison would be there. Good. Mamie had told Carl to come along as well. Give Barney someone to pick on. Jedson would drive, and she had already told him to find out where the Cathedral of San Lorenzo was. He had been to

Tivoli before but the appointment had not yet been arranged then.

Jane gave up the idea of taking a nap. Every time she closed her eyes, speeded-up images flashed behind her eyelids – Professor Caseman, the flimsy blue paper of the letter and the rain-soaked journey to the nursing home, the matron who looked like Zsa Zsa Gabor, Mamie McCulloch tapping at the statue, knitting bag folded beside her; there had been that car crash too. And here – the Sibyl and her water sculpture, the green-eyed cats, and ... the mention of "The Other". At this last Jane jumped up, eyed the picture of the cherubs with distaste and went to unhook it from the wall.

Not that she had been unlucky with her lodgings, she mused, quite the opposite. Apparently this particular B&B had not been on the list during the first frantic wave of booking accommodation for the crew, and she had what amounted to a small suite, with bedroom, sitting room including TV (though it didn't work), and bathroom.

She was just looking for a suitable drawer to put the offending cherubs in when her mobile rang. Her heart sank, but when she looked at the display, it was a number she didn't recognise – so not Anthea – and answered it.

"Jane. Ciao, it's Carl. You got the job then?"

"Carl! Hi! Yes, and it really was great of you to tell me about it. I meant to call you," she went on guiltily, remembering he could be touchy on occasion, "but then everything got so busy. You really did save my life."

"No, that's OK – I know what it's like. I've been up to my eyes as well. How's it going anyway?"

Jane sighed, noticed she was still holding the picture and laid it on the bed. "Well, you were right," she said. "Dogsbody about sums it up. But the money's good and with accommodation thrown in … How about you? Didn't you say you were looking after a backer or something?"

"Yeah, actually 'angel investor' is the right expression, so I'm told. And she's great – American woman, very folksy, though probably got a will of iron. Money, you know?"

"Right. Sounds like our director Barney. A matching pair."

"You can say that again. Him and Mamie go way back."

Jane froze, fingers convulsively gripping the small phone. "Mamie? What's her surname?"

"McCulloch. Why? Do you know her?"

"No, yes, or rather, I've met her. It's such a coincidence." But even as she was speaking, she did not believe it. "I'll tell you when I see you."

"I'll be in Tivoli tonight – dinner at the bossman's hotel."

"Yes, I mean, good – I've been invited as well. See you there then? And we can catch up."

She rang off, confused and apprehensive, while the cherubs leered up at her from the counterpane. Coincidence, my arse, she thought. She snatched up the picture and laid it in the bottom of the wardrobe. And I have to decide what to wear. Her mind skittered away from the idea of Mamie

McCulloch to grapple with the more prosaic problem. She began to look through her meagre choice of clothes on the hangers. Perhaps the straight-legged charcoal jeans. Casual stylish. Movie-set stylish?

11

Saturday 30th January, cont.

The Pope's Protocol – unlike *The Da Vinci Code* – was an original film script. Audiences would not be going to see how the book looked on the screen, with the added attraction of Tom Hanks and Sir Ian McKellen. The bit-players' attempts to guess the storyline from their meagre lines was a grassroots reaction to the mystery shrouding the film. Security had been strict, with everyone having to sign a confidentiality contract, undertaking not to reveal in any way, shape or form what the "labyrinth of deceit" and "shocking secrets" really consisted of. Secondary characters had been banned from the set when they were not working. The reactions of those people who did find out varied from laughter to contempt to a vague feeling of unease – could such a thing be possible?

The writer of the script, Eric Moonday, was a fearful

young man, who even as a child had suspected the world was an innately hostile place. His parents, good middle-class Boston Catholics who voted Democrat at every election, had dutifully tried all the usual remedies to help their timid offspring: sports, summer camps, therapy, and even cookies spiked with marijuana. This last attempt only made Eric violently sick and left him convinced that his own parents were trying to poison him. It was something of a relief when they died in a multiple pile-up on the freeway when he was a freshman at college. It gave him the first freedom he had known, and he used it to search for the origins of his unease, a search that ultimately lead to his relieved discovery of conspiracy theories. He delved ever deeper. It was here he would discover the malevolent machinery at the heart of the world.

And he found just the thing, embraced it wholeheartedly and ignored any evidence – which there was – to the contrary. But what should he do with his hard-won knowledge? It had to be shared, the fabric of society was being stretched and torn, western society and democracy itself was in danger.

From here it was a short step to deciding that the cinema was the best medium to put the masses on the alert – hadn't he himself recognised the inherent truth in films such as *Three Days of the Condor*, *The Pelican Brief* and *The Matrix*, not to mention the long-running TV series *X Files*? The script was born and became a dog-eared manuscript in a grimy folder, for he carried it around with him wherever he went; he was sure it was just a matter of the right time, the right place and the right person, and he had to be ready.

His opportunity came when a group of college friends, drunk and happy and expansive, carried him off protesting to The Pussy Drive to "help him loosen up" and "see the good times roll while you can."

That Barney had dropped in on one of his periodic check-ups to make sure all the "pussies" were still the sympathetic working girls they should be was the stuff dreams are made of. Barney's persona at The Drive was that of a good-natured mine host, affably holding court at the glitzy bar, where he chatted to clients and showed a vivid interest in whatever their personal obsession might be – sex was only a part of it, a third if you agreed with Barney's theory of "feelings, fucking and fantasy."

And he listened to Eric Moonday, glimpsed through the stuttered confidences the kind of film that would take the movie-going public by storm. It would out-Da Vinci *The Da Vinci Code*, engender endless controversy, and seriously offend and upset both the Catholic Church and the State of Israel; the free publicity from their thundering denunciations and disgusted denials would ensure huge audiences and even huger profits. He took the dog-eared manuscript, wrote down Eric's contact details, and made a mental note to get his lawyers to look into the legal implications very thoroughly indeed.

The premise of the film was that the Pope was a Jew with a hidden agenda, a premise given added spice by the fact that the current Head of the Church was German, had grown up in Nazi Germany and served in the Hitler Youth.

Out of all the conspiracy theories available Eric had embraced what may be considered the original ancestor, *The Protocols of the Elders of Zion*.

First appearing in tsarist Russia in 1903, the document was carried west by post-Revolution émigrés, later to be adopted and divulged by Henry Ford himself in the United States. "The only statement I care to make about the *Protocols*," said Ford in 1921, "is that they fit in with what is going on. They are 16 years old, and they have fitted the world situation up to this time." The document had by now travelled far beyond its original purpose of scapegoating the Jews and discrediting the Bolsheviks.

The Protocols consist of 24 essays, purporting to be the minutes of a secret meeting of Jews, the Elders of Zion, which sketch out how they plan to dominate the world. Media and finance would be controlled, and traditional social order replaced with one based on mass manipulation. Houghton's 1920 imprint enumerated the titles of the twenty-four as follows:

1. The Basic Doctrine—"Right Lies in Might"
2. Economic War and Disorganization Lead to International Government
3. Methods of Conquest
4. The Destruction of Religion by Materialism
5. Despotism and Modern Progress
6. The Acquisition of Land and the Encouragement of Speculation
7. A Prophecy of a World-wide War

8. The Transitional Government
9. The All-embracing Propaganda
10. Abolition of the Constitution; Rise of the Autocracy
11. The Constitution of Autocracy and Universal Rule
12. The Kingdom of the Press and its Control
13. Turning Public Thought from Essentials to Non-Essentials
14. The Destruction of Religion as a Prelude to the Rise of the Jewish God
15. Utilization of Masonry; Heartless Suppression of Enemies
16. The Nullification of Education
17. The Fate of Lawyers and the Clergy
18. The Organization of Disorder
19. Mutual Understanding Between Rulers and People
20. The Financial Program of Destruction and Construction
21. Domestic Loans and Government Credit
22. The Beneficence of Jewish Rule
23. The Inculcation of Obedience
24. The Jewish Ruler

The text, said to be stolen from a secret Jewish organization in Paris, was edited anonymously and published in different languages. Only ... the original manuscript has never been found, and there is no authorized or standard edition.

Eric Moonday however had found empirical evidence of all twenty-four; for those who chose to see the truth the machinery was exposed in all its ugliness and peril. He ignored the fact that the courts had forced Henry Ford to retract his publication and apologise (which he did, claiming that he had been "duped" by his assistants). He ignored the fact that *The Times* in London had exposed the protocols as a forgery. The truth of the document was self-evident, anything else was a cover-up.

In that case, where did the Church come in? Given that points 4, 14 and 17 refer explicitly to the erosion and suppression of the Christian religion?

Because, like all addicts, Eric had to have more. He believed that the conspiracy had evolved and mutated – it must have. And what could be more reasonable than that the Elders of Zion had achieved the ultimate violation, the ultimate penetration? In the hundred and more years since the protocols had first seen the light, their secret workings had obviously been refined into an ever more insidious form; the Church itself was their prey.

With Barney's interest and subsequent offer, Eric Moonday should have been ecstatic. He had been vindicated, his screenplay accepted and a fat cheque deposited in his bank from the sale of the rights. But it was in this last that Eric felt he had been betrayed. He had taken for granted that the screenplay would stay as he had written it; he had no idea of the workings of the film business, that other writers would be given his work and told to make it into something "more zingy, less draggy, know what I mean?"

Eric's initial meetings with the scriptwriters were a series of unresolved, increasingly acrimonious arguments. As requested, they were aiming for more zingyness, less draggyness by cutting out whole swathes of anti-Jewish rhetoric, adding love interest and inserting tense chases through the shadowy rooms and water-loud gardens of Villa D'Este. Eric on the other hand saw his sacred truth being emasculated and nullified, and became shriller and more contentious; this was not what he had imagined.

By the time he was officially labelled as a liability and a pest, it was too late. Legally he could be ignored and sidelined but in reality he already possessed enough names and phone numbers to continue his one-man crusade – two-man actually since he had found a kindred spirit in the accounts department who kept him informed of the film's progress.

When Eric heard that the cast and crew, including his accounts mole, would be on location in Tivoli, Italy (Tivoli? What had happened to the halls of the beleaguered Vatican? What about the filthy hovels in the old Jewish ghetto in Rome with the candle-lit meetings of hook-nosed conspirators?), he took instant action. The cheque selling his right to the idea and script – his birthright and trust, as he thought of them – was large enough to finance his own journey to Italy, and if phone calls would not divert the film from its sacrilegious course, he would go in person.

After dinner at the Hotel delle Sirene, the scene through the brightly-lit windows resembled a set, the guests moving as though on cue to pre-established patterns. The main room was large and roughly circular, but these particular windows gave onto a recessed bay furnished with plush beige armchairs and occasional coffee-tables. From here the people drinking and chatting in the background were mere extras, shapes and shadows grouping and re-grouping as the evening progressed; upstage were the two people sitting on a couch in the bay, their privacy guarded by the tall outline of a man in the arch connecting the two areas. The two were deep in conversation though nothing could be heard through the closed windows.

"So you're all on schedule?"

"Yup – don't you worry none, Mame – no way I'm goin' to waste your money. Hell, this movie'll double it – if not treble it. Or my name ain't Barney Highman!"

She glanced at him and gave a knowing smile, "Well, if my poor old memory serves me right, it isn't either, Barney."

His roar of laugh was so loud, not only Jedson, stationed in the archway to keep away intruders, but some of the dinner guests in the bar glanced round. "You don't miss a trick, angel, nary a one!" he bellowed boisterously.

"But I surely trust you, Barney, and you know *that's* a fact," she said, patting his knee and lowering her voice. "We've come a long way, you and me." She gave a little wave to Jane, slim and smart in leg-hugging jeans and a grey jacket, who was passing on her way to the bar, but Jane was looking at Jedson and smiling. Now, *that* could be interesting.

Barney was still booming out his big laugh at her jibe, and then took her hand and gave it a smacking theatrical kiss. He leaned back, gave a further appreciative chuckle, and wiped his eyes but his voice too was lowered when he said, "And there's a way to go yet, ain't that right?" His eyes were calculating. "So, what about the girlie, Mame? We on track there?" The crisp note of business had sharpened his tone.

"Next week. Her aunt's bringing her." She absentmindedly touched the chair beside her, but – since the evening was a formal social occasion – she had left her knitting-bag in the car. "And isn't it just a dreadful thing," she went, the southern twang of her voice becoming more pronounced, "to see what a person's own flesh and blood is eager and willing to do for cash dollars? And her a good Christian woman and all."

He whipped round to look at her, and then – when he saw the gleeful malice of her eyes – grinned. Mame was a real card; she could still get him going even after all this time. Through the arch he caught Anthea's eye, waved, and made a "Stay around. I may need you later" gesture. Anthea nodded, and went back to her conversation with Carl, who was gesturing round at the bar and tossing his head.

"And you did real good spotting her, Mame," he said admiringly. "She'll fit right in with the other kittens. First, the cherry auction, and then …"

"Now, Barney, you know I leave all that side of things to you. I'm just happy to help. Always have been, you know that."

"Sure, whatever you say, Mame," he agreed happily.

She gazed absently towards the French windows that looked onto the deserted patio behind the hotel; the lights, large golden globes set on black poles, had been lit in honour of the off-season guests, and were reflected dimly in the wet flagstones. She did not notice the slight movement as Eric Moonday ducked back behind a dripping evergreen, or else she dismissed it as a gust of wind. Her thoughts were focused on the coming appointment – tomorrow evening, and then she would know, would have the means ...

"Ah, and that reminds me," she said, turning to Barney again. He had sprawled back against the couch, surveying the rest of the party through the arch with a self-satisfied, proprietorial air. "Little Jane Harrison getting on alright, is she?" Her hand went to the chair seat again, and a shadow crossed her face to find it still empty. For a moment Barney looked blank, then his face cleared, "Oh, Janey, the Brit, sure. No complaints. Does a good job. But *very* British – know what I mean?"

"Oh, I do, Barney, I surely do."

In the main room Jane was slightly tipsy and enjoying herself much more than she had expected. Barney had not picked on Carl, and consequently neither had the entourage who were present in force. He had only seized on Carl's surname. "Plodinsky, eh! Welcome aboard, Plod, glad my favourite investor's in such good hands!"

As for Mamie McCulloch, she greeted Jane affectionately, and admitted that she had played a part in getting Jane the job "Well, I surely felt sorry for you, sweetie. Why! Those dreadful people, and when you were just asking for a real contract." Jane tried to remember how she had talked to Mamie in the nursing home, wondering if she could manage to recreate the same effect. She knew she had babbled on ingenuously about her own worries (*and* had almost betrayed the professor in the process) and now fell back on politeness, saying stiffly: "You were so kind and I must have been very tiresome indeed, burdening you with my troubles." Mamie patted her hand, and Jane hoped that the small jump she gave would be put down to the famed reserve of the British rather than the very real revulsion she felt; the knitting was not in evidence anyway.

And Carl was a real eye-opener, complimenting her on the tight charcoal-grey jeans and flirting with the waitresses. With a mixture of amusement and affection (this after a few drinks) she noticed he underwent a transformation when he spoke Italian – he was more relaxed, more debonair, tossing his head as if he had a mane of tawny curls rather than the practical brown crew-cut. He doesn't have a bad body either, she mused. His skin's a bit pasty, and surely he shouldn't have spots at his age, but overall … nothing wrong with some kinds of physical contact, she thought, smiling at her glass; it seemed to be empty again. Should she have another? Yes, she thought truculently, off duty, all too much, not going to think about anything. She smiled again as she made her way to the bar, and then suddenly realised – when he smiled back – that Mamie's chauffeur, standing near the arch, must have thought it was for him. So what? she thought, more aggressively still. Off duty is off duty, and *he's* not bad-looking either.

As she waited for her glass of wine, she watched him covertly. Tall, thick fair hair caught back in a pony tail, dressed in the kind of black suit and tie that she associated with C.I.A. agents in American TV dramas. Chauffeur, she had thought, but maybe bodyguard, or both. Not a personal trainer anyway since he isn't wearing sweats. She covered her mouth with one hand, feeling not only another smile but a giggle coming on, and picked up her wine with the other. Through the arch she could see Mamie and Barney talking and laughing together, then saw Mamie's hand go out to feel around the chair seat. She's looking for her knitting, thought Jane suddenly, and for no reason the laughter left her.

"*Tutto bene, Janina cara?*" hailed a voice. It was Carl, still tossing back the invisible mane of curls and now flushed and glassy-eyed. Jane laughed, raising her glass to him.

"Your Italian's great!" she enthused, not really knowing or caring what she was saying. "So, what's happening? What time is it?"

"No, it's early, just after eleven. Why? Have you got a curfew or something?"

"No, no, nothing like that, I've got my own key. But I really am whacked. There's always some bloody thing. I agree with Umberto Eco – only doctors and clandestine lovers should be allowed mobile phones."

"Did he say that?" Carl was regarding her owlishly, the tawny curls at peace for the moment.

"Something like that," she agreed, nodding emphatically. "Anyway, I've really had enough. Want to come back to my place for a drink? I've got beer."

Carl was still owlish, and now wistful as well: "On call. Have to go back with Southern Comfort and Muscles

Incorporated."

Jane found this incredibly amusing and started snorting and hiccupping with laughter. She turned to put her glass down out of harm's way and found herself colliding with a black-suited chest.

"Oh, sorry," she gasped, still laughing, and raised swimming eyes to Jedson's cool blue stare. "Oh, sh ... sugar," she breathed, wondering if he'd heard. He smiled; it was a charming smile that reached his eyes and completely transformed his face.

"I really am sorry," she repeated, suddenly sobering. "I'm a little ... lit-up."

"No problem," he said, with another attractive smile. "Wish I were – and besides, it suits you."

What a beautiful voice, she thought dazedly. He would make the telephone directory sound sexy. My God.

"You about ready, Carl?" the beautiful voice went on. "Miss Mamie's on the move." Behind him Mamie and Barney were coming back into the main room.

"Absolutely," agreed Carl, trying to look alert. "Ready when you are."

"Now, Jane!" exclaimed Mamie coming up to them. "You don't be a stranger, you hear?" She patted Jane on the arm. "Oh, and you have a hair on that lovely jacket of yours." A deft swoop. "There, all gone." Jane – cushioned by drink and tiredness – smiled warmly and clasped the other's hand, thanking her again for her help. "No, it's my pleasure, sweetie. We must have a chat over lunch one day. Jedson here can collect you and bring you to the hotel – if Barney can spare you, that is."

""No problem, Mame!" boomed Barney. "Anything that makes you happy, angel!"

Screened by a trellis of ivy, Eric Moonday, the hidden audience to at least a part of the evening, watched as people took their leave. He brushed the rain from his eyelashes, feeling a chilled shiver run through him; the cheap black baseball cap had been no protection at all and it drooped wet and limp on his soaked hair. It was the first time he had seen the woman talking with Barney and he determined to ask his mole in the accounts department about her. From the body language – and Eric, studying the world with ever-wary eyes, was extremely adept at interpretation – she was the one with influence, not the big man with the engaging grin and larcenous heart. Yes, he must find out more, perhaps she was the manipulator. Perhaps she was even a Jew.

12

Sunday 31st January

The next day Jane woke up with a pounding head and still dressed in her charcoal-grey jeans; she had a vague memory of trying to wriggle out of them while lying on the bed, but then, obviously exhausted by the futile effort, she had fallen asleep. The jacket was hanging neatly from the back of the chair however, so some form of routine had taken over. Just as well Carl didn't come back for a beer, she thought dimly, as she tried to focus on her travelling clock. Ten o'clock, and it was Sunday, so no hurr ….

Ten o'clock. Sunday. Her appointment with Enrico Mattei. Upright in a second, she started pulling at the tight legs of the jeans to draw them down over her feet, and then rolled bonelessly off the bed, her fall cushioned by a fallen pillow. Saved again! she exulted, and started giggling. I must still be drunk, she thought hilariously as she lay on the carpet wrestling with the legs, until finally she freed herself. Pink-faced with effort she crawled round the bed – it seemed easier than standing up – to check the time. Ten past ten. Half an hour to shower and dress, and it was only a ten or fifteen minute walk to the large piazza on the edge of town. She got to her feet, now serious again, and – studiously avoiding all thought of what the meeting could achieve – went to find aspirin and a bath towel.

There were actually two bars, one either side of the beginning of Via Pacifici, the road leading towards Villa D'Este. Across the piazza, formal gardens and a promenade marked the edge of town, with a view of the countryside spread beneath, while over to the right the massive bulk of three pantechnicons belonging to the film company filled one corner. A few people loitered near them, perhaps hoping for a glimpse of Hollywood activity but there was no one in sight except a security guard with a peaked hat who gestured them away. Jane regarded the two bars then saw that Enrico was already standing outside the further one, obviously on the look-out for her. She was amazed since a surreptitious glance at her watch showed it was just before eleven, and something of this must have shown on her face. Their hellos exchanged, he nodded proudly and said in English: "I have the English habit of arrive in time. Is that correct?"

"Habit of arriving," corrected Jane, laughing, not bothering with the "in time". Everything considered maybe it was in time. She realised with a sinking heart that Enrico had decided this was to be English conversation practice; he would expect her to help him with his grammar. Grammar! she thought despairingly, but then again, she *was* interrupting his weekend.

"Shall we go inside?" he said with an interrogative glance, which asked more about the sentence than where they should sit.

"Yes, perfect – both the idea and your grammar!"

The sky had cleared after the previous night's downpour, and the day was bright but cold. From the comfort of the bar it looked warm enough to sit outside but the treetops in the park opposite were ruffled and bent by the chill breeze. Jane insisted on paying "since it was my idea to meet", and got Enrico's lemon tea and her own cappuccino; her headache was giving way to the effects of the aspirin.

Once sitting at a small table, Jane asked Enrico about his job and wracked her brain for other questions so that at least he would feel he was getting proper practice. He happily talked on, making what was obviously a set speech about himself. After a few minutes however he asked how he could help her.

Jane had given much thought to how she would explain her questions, and had even rehearsed some parts in Italian. Like her preparation for the job interview however, it had all been wasted effort.

"A friend of mine died recently," she began. Enrico made a sympathetic sound. "She was elderly so it wasn't a surprise, but even so, it was a shock and very … upsetting." Another sympathetic murmur accompanied by an understanding nod; he really was a nice young man. "She wrote to me before she died." Jane paused. She had considered bringing the letter with her, to produce as a kind of stage prop, but felt it would be needlessly tantalising to wave the letter when she had no intention of letting him read it. To gain time she sipped at her cappuccino, and then slowly put the cup down.

"The thing is – in the letter she expressed concern about a friend of hers, a German woman who was living in Tivoli. She hinted…" At the word Enrico looked blank. "*Accennato*," she offered, and he nodded gratefully, "She hinted that the friend had a drink problem, and asked me whether I could come to Tivoli and visit her. My friend was too frail to travel, you see." She paused, picked up her cup again. "I wrote back saying I would be glad to come, but then I heard my friend was dead. She didn't tell me the name of the woman – she would probably have written again but of course … it was too late." To her own ears it sounded both weak and over-complicated, but Enrico seemed to find nothing amiss. She drank the last of her cappuccino, almost didn't realise he was already answering.

"Yes, I understand," he was saying. "And I know who you mean." She sat up hopefully, but now he picked up his lemon tea and cupped his hands around it; the rising swirls of steam were caught in a fugitive ray of sunlight and briefly made mysterious. He put the glass down again without drinking, and looked at her sadly. "I know you want to respect your friend's wishes but it is now too late for the other lady as well. I am sorry that I must tell you that she is dead."

"Dead?" repeated Jane; she had found the woman only to lose her again. "You mean she was old," she went on, thinking of Professor Caseman, "perhaps in her seventies or eighties?"

Enrico looked even sadder. "No, it was an accident. The drink ..." he looked embarrassed. "As you mentioned yourself, there was hinted a problem with the alcohol."

"What happened?" asked Jane; her lips felt stiff and numb.

"If I remember well, she was supposed to go for a walk by the river." And then, "Is it correct? Supposed to go?"

"She was supposed to have gone," corrected Jane mechanically.

"She was supposed to have gone for a walk," he repeated carefully. "This in the evening. Dark, you know? And she had drunk a lot in a trattoria. An accident – they found her body in the river."

"Do you remember her name?" asked Jane, gathering her wits. "Were there any relatives or friends?"

"I am sorry, I do not know. But you have done what wanted your friend. You can do nothing more."

"What your friend wanted," corrected Jane, very down at heart, then in Italian: "But really, Enrico, my compliments! Your English is wonderful. Thank you so much."

He beamed at her, said in English: "You are *simpaticissima*, Jane. Your English "very nice" is not enough in this case!"

Outside the bar they paused to say their goodbyes,

now more naturally speaking in Italian. They were forced to step back into the entrance when a group of mothers and children rounded the corner. There were two diminutive princesses, a superhero and a vampire, and a baby cowboy in a pushchair, the princesses squabbling over a tiny sequined handbag, the vampire trying to get the superhero's plastic ray gun, and the cowboy mute but with a grumpy scrunched-up face. The three mothers swatted ineffectually at their offspring, and then burst out laughing as they continued their stroll; an anguished wail gave notice that the cowboy had had enough.

"Carnival," said Enrico, gesturing after them. "There are still two weeks but the children like to begin."

"Oh, of course, I'd forgotten," said Jane distractedly; she was wondering if she should phone the Sibyl (phone the Sibyl, she repeated to herself. Email Faunus, she added facetiously, fax Venus), but as yet she had nothing to report and could not face the thought of the woman's cryptic utterances and "The Sibyl says …"

"There are many events," Enrico was saying. "Did you see the hot-air balloon?"

Jane roused herself, made a big effort to sound interested. "No, that must have been before my arrival. Was it fun?"

"It was! And there are many more things, every weekend!" he went on enthusiastically. "Also today there is the first parade to celebrate The King Carnival. Jugglers, magicians, music. Here, I have a programme. If you have time …"

"Thank you," said Jane, accepting the leaflet. "If I have time but ... you know."

Darkness covered the landscape as Mamie McCulloch travelled up the hill to Tivoli with Jedson at the wheel of the limousine that Sunday evening. The bright day had gradually clouded over in the afternoon and now a thin sleet was falling. The Via Tiburtina, following the route of the ancient road from Rome, was clear of its weekday chaos of traffic; many traffic lights flashed intermittent amber to mark a junction rather than flicking through their sequence of green, amber and red to regulate the flow of commuters. On the left a huge quarry for Travertine stone, the sides of its crater chopped into massive shelves and rough-hewn walls, gleamed dimly in the gloom like some alien landscape.

The glass divide was closed, and Mamie tapped on it with one of her knitting needles. Jedson pushed a button and the glass slid back.

"Miss Mamie?"

"So you liked our little Jane, did you, Jedson?" she murmured, her voice warm and intimate. "I couldn't help but notice. And she was looking good in those tight jeans of hers."

"She was, Miss Mamie."

She smiled in the darkness. "Well, you know, Jedson, if you did by chance want a little recreation, I certainly wouldn't stand in your way. Do what thou wilt shall be the whole of the law, as they say."

"Right, Miss Mamie."

"It might even be useful if you follow my drift," she went on softly, toying with her knitting bag, "you cosying up to her."

There was no reply to this, nor did she expect one. She knew that Jedson was most laconic when he was at his sharpest; there was no need to labour the point. When a street lamp illuminated his eyes in the rear-view mirror, she saw he was smiling. No, no need to labour the point at all.

Their destination was Piazza del Duomo, deep in Tivoli's medieval quarter. Jedson did not even attempt to drive straight towards it – too many narrow streets and one-way systems – but circled the town anti-clockwise. From Piazza Garibaldi, where Jane and Enrico Mattei had met that morning, he steered the car to the right up the hill, swinging left past the bulky fortress of Pius II, then down towards the Aniene, where Viale Roma, like a mini-section of ring road, ran alongside the river. Here the traffic was heavier but moving smoothly; the Vestal Cossinia's tomb stood silent and rain-drenched on the opposite bank, invisible from the limousine. Above, the bare slopes of the mountain huddled black against the night sky. Crossing the Ponte Gregoriano, the car swished past the intersection at Via della Sibilla, to take Via San Valerio, and manoeuvre through the arch to the Piazza del Duomo. Here there was enough room for the limousine to park, and it slid to a gentle halt across from the church. The small square was deserted; worshippers at evening mass had long since gone home, though the sound of organ music swelled faintly from somewhere inside.

Mamie stirred and reached for her knitting bag, but the arched portico of the church was empty as well. She glanced at her watch; a couple of minutes early. She sat back, eyes scanning the shadows beyond the arches.

A tapping on the opposite window caused her to start; Jedson's hand had flashed to his jacket. All they could see was a black outline and a gleam of teeth. Mamie got out carefully – the stones were wet and slippery – and followed the figure as it glided away, across the square and past the church; the organ music had stopped.

To the right of the church they passed a squat edifice, the old public wash-house, from which came the mutter of slow-trickling water. The next building was also of stone, surrounded by a high chain-link fence, but the figure extracted a key, opened an all-but-invisible gate in the fence and slipped inside. Mamie followed, glancing at the notice that said *Mensa Ponderaria*. The building's wooden door yielded to another key, and they entered.

Outside in the limousine, Jedson rolled down the window and lit his third cigarette of the day; five were all he allowed himself. His face under the drawn-back blonde hair was beautiful in the half-light, and could anyone have seen his expression, they would have said he was dreaming of some dearly-held love.

In the *Mensa Ponderaria*, darkness reigned, permeated by a dank smell of mould and the stealthy trickle of water, louder here, as though an underground stream crept directly beneath the floor. There was the scrape of a match, then the wavering flame of a candle. In the pallid glow more of the surroundings could be discerned: a vaulted cave of a room, its walls disfigured with leprous patches of moss, with two stone counters against one wall, and inscribed tablets and sections of columns stacked haphazardly on the flagstones; opposite the counters the floor sloped to a shallow well. Swift and sure-footed, the figure crossed to the counters, and lit another flat candle on the uneven surface, saying matter-of-factly: "Mrs McCulloch, please come closer."

The voice was low and feminine, the language English with a lilting French accent. Mamie came to stand beside her as the woman threw back the voluminous cloak to reveal a black satin ball dress slashed with scarlet and scattered with glittering sequins.

"My, and what a *fine* gown you have!" commented Mamie, hiding her surprise.

The woman laughed, a silvery sound that chimed and echoed in the vaulted chamber: "Beautiful, is it not? Fitting. For I am one of the courtiers of our King Carnival, the Lord of the Revels." She gestured down at the iridescent folds, and for a brief unsettling moment the slender fingers seemed to lengthen and curl to form talons. Abruptly Mamie raised her eyes to the woman's face but it was as it had first appeared in the candlelight: large dark eyes, full lips and flawless olive skin, a beautiful face framed by glistening coils of black hair.

"You understand what I want?" questioned Mamie, now wanting to get down to business. "And *soon* …"

"Oh, yes," returned the other, bending to retrieve a large wooden bowl containing some charred fragments of bone and wisps of dried moss. "You were quite clear on the phone. And I had been ... expecting you, so to speak. Now," she went on, "first I must prepare," and, still cradling the bowl, she spat onto the sculptured side of the counter; the spittle clung stickily to a delicately-carved leaf. "I spit on him who forbade the old ways," she murmured, "weakened the Empire and sowed the seeds of its ruin. Augustus, the pious fool, the fearful fool. A curse on him evermore." Her voice had remained low and melodious but the candle flame flared as though responding to the curse, revealing dim frescoed garlands on the walls, and a stone plaque of a figure leaning on a large club. Her preparations concluded, she gently lowered the bowl onto the counter, leaned over it and spat again, this time onto its meagre contents. She straightened, a fantastic carnival figure in the archaic gown and enveloping cloak, hands linked and folded before her, eyes on the bowl. A dark viscous liquid began to form in the dry depths, creeping upwards to cover the fragments. The woman's face was rapt as she began to chant; a scholar of ancient Greek would have understood the archaic tongue:

"Humbly I call on the Snake God, our Lord,
He who lies coiled 'neath the city of Tibur,
His power in thrall to the rushing of waters
But soon to be roused now
His time has returned."

The viscous liquid moved and heaved, swelling and rising until finally stopping a little way below the rim. The woman whirled to face Mamie, who took a step back. The movement had been so swift and so unexpected, and the face opposite appeared subtly different: the forehead more prominent, the jaw thinner and the neck longer and more sinuous. "Do you have the link?" the other asked.

"Surely," said Mamie hurriedly, unsettled but avid, and took out the small envelope containing the hair she had taken from Jane's jacket. "Is one enough?" A slight hissing laugh was the only reply as the envelope was plucked from her hand and the hair tipped carefully into the bowl; the dark liquid sucked it in, moving slightly as though tasting and chewing the hair. Tendrils of greyish-brown vapour began to rise and the opaque surface glowed and then cleared. Pictures began to form.

The first showed a small blue car making its way along a busy road, two figures, a man and a woman, in the background. The driver of the car could not be seen but one of its windscreen wipers jerked and clawed at the glass to clear the rain. The scene faded, to be replaced by Jane's absorbed face; she was looking down, apparently studying the base of a small statue, of which only the carved folds of a robe were visible. The woman looked at Mamie interrogatively:

"Is it her?"

"Oh, yes," said Mamie. "I knew she was involved and this confirms it." Her eyes were fixed on the bowl, where again the scene was dissolving and giving place to a new image. Now the pale face of a child, forehead furrowed but eyes blank, was gazing down from a window set high in ivy-clad walls. Mamie drew a sharp breath, and was about to comment when the child's face dissolved into the furry white head and green eyes of a cat. The cat's eyes narrowed as though aware of an alien presence and its jaws widened in a feral snarl before it disappeared into blackness. Nothing could now be seen.

"What? What does it mean?" asked Mamie urgently.

"A guardian," said the other, "blocking the portal, obscuring the vision. But I know it," she went on, her voice soft but filled with malice, "know who it is protecting." She laughed, another silvery chime, passing one hand over the liquid. Its sluggish movements stilled, and the level began to fall, leaving rings of black slime on the sides of the bowl. Finally, only the charred fragments of bone glistening with greasy residue were left.

"Is that all?" demanded Mamie, voice hard with disappointment and anger. "Of what use is that?"

"We know she is the one," the woman replied tranquilly, again running her hands over the rich material of her skirts. "She has the statue, the object for the ritual awakening. You can do the rest surely?"

"And the child?"

"Ah, the child," allowed the woman in a musing tone. "She is part of another future and one we cannot see."

Mamie considered this, and dismissed it, remembering instead that Jane's address would be on the employee list; she also remembered Jedson. One way or another …

Eric Moonday, crouched at the corner of a house opposite, kept the glow of Jedson's cigarette in sight, watching him but only perceiving him as an adjunct to the woman he was following. When their car had turned under the arch, Eric had stopped his own borrowed car, fearful of getting too close. The time he spent finding a space to cram his tinny vehicle into before proceeding on foot meant that he had not seen the black figure approach the limousine, nor its entry, with Mamie, into the *Mensa Ponderaria*. He only knew that his quarry had disappeared and her tame gorilla was waiting. He leaned patiently against the wall, sure that he could not be seen by the driver of the car.

His accounts mole had told him who the woman was, and of the gossip that surrounded her. Some of it was public record, such as her membership of the Church of Satan, founded by Anton LaVey in San Francisco in the mid-60s. She was listed as one of the people present during a failed drugs raid at LaVey's 'Black House', and rumour had it that she had also been the young woman whose naked body had served as an altar during a much-discussed Black Mass. "Satanism?" queried Eric hungrily. "Anton LaVey?" "A load of bullshit," returned the mole brusquely; *his* interests were centred on White Power, of which he was a member, and the monumental lie of the Holocaust. "Gang of West Coast commie misfits messing about with candles." As a New Yorker he was obviously prejudiced, and Eric was unconvinced.

After her sojourn at the Black House there were years unaccounted for until Mamie and Barney Highman became partners in The Pussy Drive, but Eric had seized on that – it was there that he himself had met Barney, the moneyed manipulator. Mamie McCulloch had originally been the general manager, handling administration and presiding over a little forest of timers, each labelled with the pussy's name and each representing a room and a client. She and Barney had suited each other very well, it seemed, and made a lot of money, so much money that the timers eventually had another guardian, and Mamie disappeared, apparently to enjoy the fruits of her labours and investments. Of these the mole knew nothing – her financial affairs relating to the film were handled by Barney Highman to the extent that it was impossible to separate the two; they were still "thick as thieves". Nothing else came to mind.

Eric had more than enough however to justify his interest in the woman. He was still not clear about what he was actually going to do, only intent on stopping the perversion of his crusade, but he was sure that some opportunity would present itself, and then they would be sorry.

Mamie had not in fact been the young woman used as an altar by Anton LaVey, High Priest of the Church of Satan. She had only been 23 at the time of the satanic baptism of LaVey's three-year-old daughter, reported by *the San Francisco Chronicle* as featuring "a naked 30-year-old priestess draped over the altar, breathing heavily, while Anton LaVey intoned, "Hail Satan!"

However, when the girls at The Pussy Drive got to hear of the story, recounted with relish by Hurricane Hetty, veteran of San Francisco, Mamie did not deny it. "Well, if I did," she replied with a twinkle in her eye, "it is surely my business, young ladies – though would you kindly remember I too had a wonderful body, and one the young fellas just died for!"

Her association with the Church of Satan had only lasted some two years, initially prompted by boredom and the hope of meeting famous people with influence; LaVey boasted affairs with Marilyn Monroe and Jayne Mansfield, and also claimed Sammy Davis Junior as one of his followers. For the rest, it had been part of the sixties, love, peace and harmony on the one side, drugs, sex and self-gratification on the other, and Mamie personally had indeed made some useful contacts even though they were not rich and famous. Later, the details of the Black House, home and 'church' of the movement, made good story-telling, and amused the girls at one of Mamie's weekly tea parties.

"Oh, that big ol' house," said Mamie to her enthralled audience, all wearing the extravagant *My Fair Lady*-type hats and very little else that formed part of the tea-party ritual. "Wasn't really black, more a blackish purple, but it got people going alright. Anton kept a lion too, you know, Togare, and that big ol' beast was quite something, I can tell you. And there was a stuffed werewolf."

Laughter. "Aw, c'mon, Mamie!"

"Well, that's what Anton said," she replied with a sly smile, provoking more laughter. "Didn't save it from the moths though!"

The lion and stuffed werewolf were just a sample of the bizarre details that had aroused waves of media interest in the Church of Satan, the last ripple coming after LaVey's death in 1997, when details of his will included:

- To High Priestess Blanche Barton—Rasputin chair, bed of nails and vintage Gramophone.

- To daughter Zeena Schreck—Vampire boy painting, devil horned cap, Tyrone Power "Nightmare Alley"' movie poster and one-third of LaVey's cremated remains.

- To daughter Karla LaVey—Skull from ritual chamber, Satin Doll pinball machine, coffin and examination table.

- Items of property to be divided by Karla LaVey and Zeena Schreck—autographed Marilyn Monroe calendar, magic mirror with demons and Byzantine phallus.

As for any underlying philosophy, Mamie had done the official reading – LaVey's essays and observations that would later be published as the *Satanic Bible*. She found she was already using what he defined as the "Lesser Magic", the manipulation of others by means of sex, sentiment and wonder, though she had not thought of it as such; Mamie was a natural. The High Priest had also expounded the "Greater Magic"; that too aimed at manipulation, and consisted of three components – destruction, lust and compassion.

It was in this period that she found her secret calling. It is true that there had been other incidents in the past: the puppy and other small animals, the neighbour's child found at the bottom of a disused well, where he had obviously been playing and fallen in, but it was in the Black House of Anton LaVey that the knitting made its first appearance.

First taken up to imitate and toady favour with a close friend of the High Priest, she found she enjoyed the feel of the needles and the wool, the contrast between smooth cold steel and soft fluffy yarn, especially if it was angora. Her first kill came about by chance, a momentary irritation vented in a sudden stabbing, but right first time, as became a natural. With the added bonuses of no witnesses and a victim whose body weight was so slight, it was easy to put her body into a car and dump it in the desert, her future was assured. The Spike Killer had arrived.

13

Monday 1st – Tuesday 2nd February

Jane had had very little to do with the actual shooting of the film and had only been briefly to Villa D'Este; unnecessary visits were discouraged due to the tight security. That Monday however she had been given the job of going round to distribute the wage packets of Italian employees and get their signature of receipt on the accompanying sheets. The list was in alphabetical order, followed by the job title and department, so the first thing she did was to photocopy it and highlight the copy with the different departments in different colours, so that she could make her rounds in some kind of logical order.

This had worked quite well, with the number of wage packets decreasing and the sheets gradually filling up with signatures. Her last group was that of the film extras, who had their greenroom in Villa D'Este, so it was there she proceeded to finish the job.

Showing her pass at the entrance to the Villa, she was directed across the courtyard – another check of her pass – and went downstairs – another check – to a basement room, where a motley collection of priests, nuns and what looked like Louis-XIV courtiers were chatting, doing crosswords or Sudoku, and fiddling with their costumes. Her errand explained, she was hailed with delight, and began the distribution and signing.

"I thought the film was set in the present day," she said to one of the courtiers, a thin man resplendent in satin breeches and an embroidered waistcoat, a heavily-powdered wig under one arm.

"Ah, but there are flashbacks," he explained, giving Jane the wig to hold and scribbling an illegible signature on the list. "Not that we know what it's really about. Isn't that true?" he said, raising his voice to appeal to the others. "We have not the least idea! And how can we act when we have not the least idea!" There was a chorus of disgruntled agreement, as the last person came up to sign, and Jane gazed with amazement at the heavy black robe and thick swarthy skin tones, a lowering face complete with beetling brows and a huge nose. He looked extremely uncomfortable and was sweating through his make-up.

"What is *your* role?" she asked curiously, brushing wig powder off her jacket.

"What the fuck do I know?" he grumbled as he signed, leaving a brown make-up smear on the sheet. "I don't have one line." He scratched at his dishevelled wig. "You know what my script says? *Sidle from the alcove to the window and peer around*! Sidle! Peer! And it is the whole morning I am here." The others laughed and made cat-calls, chanting, "Sidle! Go on – sidle!"

The signature with the smear had been the last, and Jane wished them all *"Buon lavoro!"* and started back upstairs. The security guard on that floor was no longer at his post, and as Jane passed the series of interlinking apartments that formed the first floor, she paused, then, curiosity getting the better of her, went in, the rubber soles of her trainers silent on the stone floors; faint voices could be heard from somewhere in the building.

The rooms themselves were completely deserted, the frescoes covering the walls and ceilings dim and shadowy in the winter light. Jane screwed her eyes up to try to make them out, then saw a light switch and with an air of challenge – she really shouldn't have been there – turned the lights on.

The frescoes covering the walls and ceilings burst into life. As with the mansions of other great families, the ornate decorations included references to its creator, Ippolito D'Este, son of Lucrezia Borgia and Alfonso D'Este. Ippolito's coat of arms was set in one ceiling, an eagle with the motto *Ab insomni non custodita dracone*. Something about a dragon and guarding, Jane thought, but the complete sense was lost to her. The walls showed scenes of Tivoli and the surrounding countryside, sylvan landscapes peopled with gods and heroes, while overhead, the vaulted ceilings held allegories of the virtues the Cardinal had held – if not dear – worthy of public notice. Justice and Strength, Prudence and Temperance were represented, stately figures with grave faces and flowing white robes, admonishing the onlooker to respect and reflect on the spiritual matters of life.

But beneath their solemn presence, peeking round the sides of the calm frescoes of water, hills and woodland, were small grotesque faces, carnival faces that were a reminder of another world. The great ones, for all their solemn admonishment, were held up by grinning imps and knowing workmen, court jesters always present and ready to mock the king.

Jane wandered on, her lists and signatures forgotten, looking and marvelling at what she could only dimly understand, then stepped onto a blue-tiled balcony with views of the gardens below; the land fell steeply away into a long narrow hollow – the gardens – with glimpses of pools and pathways through tall cypresses.

"The Sibyl divined you would be here," said a satisfied voice, and Jane jumped back, heart in mouth. The Sibyl was sitting comfortably on the stone balustrade of the balcony, again dressed in her long flower-child dress and blue-green scarves; she held a milky-coloured bottle cupped between her palms.

"Wh ... what are you doing here?" asked Jane when her breath came back. The woman looked sulky – perhaps Jane should have said, "What is the Sibyl doing here?" – but waved the bottle and said loftily, "Seeking the key to the ritual, here where the flow and rush of waters give power to the seeker."

"Oh, yes, I see," said Jane, thinking, Here we go again. "But how did you get in?" she asked. "Didn't the security guards try to stop you?"

The face under the pale frizzy hair became smug and knowing. "As water finds its way through any crack or crevice, so the Sibyl can enter where she will. And now ..." With a sudden movement she twisted the cork stopper from the bottle she was holding and threw the contents into Jane's face. Jane, caught by surprise with her mouth slightly open, tasted coolness, moss and flowers. "Wh ... why on earth did you ...?" she spluttered, wiping at her eyes with her hand. When she opened them again, it was to see the gardens and fountains with startling clarity, each leaf and frond of the nearby trees etched sharply and individually in breathtaking beauty.

"Come," ordered the Sibyl brusquely, jumping down from the balustrade. "There is no time to lose." Jane followed her, face still damp, drinking in the sights of a world transformed.

They made their way downstairs towards the gardens, Jane cowering back when she saw a technician carrying a bulky hand-held camera. The Sibyl laughed loudly and scornfully, but the man did not seem to hear the sound for he continued on his way without a glance. "Come," she ordered again.

Outside, they crossed the long ceremonial terrace to descend into the gardens themselves. The area outside the snack bar was crowded with people eating and drinking – it must now be the lunch-break – with the usual security guards posted here and there, but no one gave any sign of noticing them and no voice called on them to stop.

Down they went past a small grotto, its walls cloaked with round-leafed ferns, water flowing from the mouth of a stern-faced marble face, though the mouth too was stuffed with ferns. Everywhere the rushing and gushing of waters filled the air, becoming louder and more insistent as they turned right through an arch into a huge courtyard.

In the enclosed space the noise of cascading water was deafening. The hillside of a narrow valley had been sculpted into tiers, the summit a semi-circular outcrop of rocks cradling the enormous original of the small statue Jane possessed – Albunea with her book. The spray from symmetrically placed jets quested towards the sky, and water flowed from the rocks into an enormous bowl brimming over with watery plenty into a circular pool beneath. Behind the pool, arches defined a curved portico, each holding stones urns spouting iridescent peacock tails, while horizontal jets gushed outwards from beneath.

"The Sibyl is honoured here above all other places," said Jane's companion, crossing to the pool and scooping up a handful of water. "Can you not feel it? Feel the power? Feel the passion?"

Jane was gazing awestruck at her surroundings. She could only nod, feeling waves of coolness flow from the waters, their fine mist touching her lips. The Sibyl was no longer at her side, had crossed to step into the pool, where she was splashing her face and neck, seemingly unaware of the cold. She sang as she worked, though the words were inaudible.

Jane could only stand, caught spellbound in the rushing and booming of the waters, her eyes fixed on the seemingly endless variety of water-shapes: the small jets rising vertically at the summit, the peacock tails fanning to fill the moss-covered arches, the huge bowl dimpling and brimming, the random streams that flowed gently from the hillside, the concentric ripples in the final pool.

Exhilarated and charged, she walked forwards as though in a dream, feeling more alive than she had ever felt before, vividly alive and suddenly aroused. Water, she thought feebly, the feminine principle. The thought faded, of no importance, and feeling the light caress of the fine spray on her upturned face, she took it deep into her lungs, her skin glowing and tingling. Thoughts came of warm skin glowing hot, gentle hands cupping her breasts and touching the nipples, lips joined in slow exploratory kisses.

The Sibyl had entered the narrow corridor of the portico, still singing, still harvesting handfuls of water as she walked, her face full of the calm happiness of one who has returned home. As for Jane, she was barely aware of the other, though somehow the Sibyl's song had become a song of the waters themselves, a stream gently chuckling between grassy flower-bright banks. Bewitched and enthralled, she was lost to herself, lost in the pounding roar of cascading waters, her eyes fixed on the peacock tails of water rising

The White Sibyl

and opening and fanning without end as they fell in graceful submission onto fern-wreathed shelves.

Suddenly the Sibyl was wading back through the pool, her frizzy hair pearled with water, her flowing skirts drenched and clinging. She was smiling, green eyes gleaming, as she sat on the stone rim of the pool beside Jane, and then looked at her sharply. Her smile became tender. "You have felt the power," she said softly, "*entered* the power. You too are the *prediletta* of Venus."

She dipped her fingers into the pool, touched Jane's forehead with her index finger. Then, putting her lips close to Jane's ear to be heard above the noise of water: "The stranger must enter the place of power and be recognised," she said. "You have entered, and have been recognised. The first step is taken."

Jane opened her eyes, wordlessly regarding the Sibyl, who was rising and dreamily stroking her drenched skirts. With a final pat she looked around, smiled and took Jane's hand. "Come," she said. "The time of the charm is ending. We must go – and do not forget you must find the part to make whole the statue."

The next day, Tuesday, Jane managed to arrange the morning so that the two sets of the people who wanted her on hand each thought she was with the other. After the appearance of the Sibyl at the Villa D'Este the day before and her own unnerving experience in the "place of power" she had become prey to a growing unease coupled with urgency. Two weeks had passed since she had received Professor Caseman's letter. January had become February, "in this month of Februarius, the time of purification," the Sibyl had said at their first meeting. It had to be soon, a month was nothing, and, as far as she knew, now that filming had started – the star had recovered from her chest infection – her time in the town was limited.

It was on Monday night, lying in bed, that she remembered Enrico Mattei had said the German woman's death had been reported in the local paper. She could go to the offices, and you are so *slow*, she berated herself, you didn't think to ask the *name* of the paper. It happens, she thought resignedly, there must only be one anyway. I can get a copy, find the address of their offices, ask to see the archives for January.

And the Tuesday morning she bought a copy, once again marvelling at Italy's effortless blending of past and present; *Tiburno* the paper was called, after the mythical founder of Tivoli. The address of the offices was on the second page, and she almost groaned aloud – the offices were not in Tivoli but somewhere called Villanova di Guidonia Montecelio. I don't think I can cope with this, she thought despairingly, every step seems to lead to another complication and yet another thing to do. Where the *hell* is Villanova di Guidonia Montecelio?

Still holding the paper, she turned mechanically into the nearest coffee bar, collected a cappuccino from the counter, and sat at one of the small tables. Putting the problem of Villanova di Guidonia Montecelio – wherever it was – from her mind, she idly turned the pages and found that the paper covered various areas: Guidonia (details of a dual carriageway that would relieve congestion on Via Tiburtina), Mentana (photographs of a Carnival event with marriage as the theme, the bride being male and heavily rouged), Fonte Nuova ("The doctors said he was fine and then he died," ran the headline), and Tivoli itself, where apparently the old people's centre was having on-going problems with the central-heating and hoped that the mayor "will give us a new building". Bit of a drastic remedy, Jane thought. Then, a few pages further on, a small article with the heading "*Passeggiata mortale*" caught her eye. She quickly scanned it, and with a mixture of astonishment and overwhelming relief realised she had exactly the information she needed: Elfriede Baader, resident in Via Sant'Antonio, pathologists now confirmed that it was an accidental drowning under the influence of alcohol. Water again, she thought, sitting back, eyes still on the article. It was so small, tucked away in the bottom right-hand corner. Obviously a space-filler. Thank God for that one small space. No trying to squeeze extra time from her work schedule, no extra trip to Villanova di Guidonia Montecelio, its location mercifully of no further interest. She finished her cappuccino, and got out her map of the town. Via Sant'Antonio, not far from her B&B. She looked at her watch. No time now, she would have to deal with the two sets of people, but she could go round to the address early evening. Resolved, she grabbed her bag and set off.

The sight of Jedson coming out of a tobacconist's had

her turning abruptly into a pharmacy but he must have seen her. She was ostensibly browsing when the low voice said:

"Jane. How's it going?" Telephone directory, she thought dazedly, and turned to face him with some article she had clutched in her hand.

"Fine, fine ... thanks," she stammered. "How about you? How's Mamie?"

"Real good." There was a short pause, then:

"Already planning next weekend?" he asked, smiling and nodding down. She followed his gaze, and found she had picked up a lurid red packet of condoms. *Tocco del diavolo* it promised. Jane felt as if her whole body was blushing. How on earth had she come to pick that up? After yesterday too.

"Research," she said shortly, ignoring her red cheeks, then added with sudden inspiration. "One of the technicians ..."

"Oh, those guys," he commented, still smiling. He looked at the label. "What does it mean?"

"Touch of the devil," translated Jane, and then they were both laughing as he took the packet out of her hand to return it to the shelf, and with his hand still on her arm guided her out of the shop. Two local girls standing chatting outside a clothes shop regarded him with awed admiration. Tall and broad-shouldered, still in the CIA black suit, with the blond ponytail and – as Jane now noticed – a diamond stud in his left ear, he was a glamorous sight in Tivoli's weekday streets.

"Glad I ran into you," he went on, bending his head

slightly so that he could look at her. "Miss Mamie wants to invite you down to the hotel for lunch."

"Oh, yes, of course," said Jane hurriedly; so Mamie *had* remembered, "but there's my job and Barney …"

"Barney's no problem. You heard what he said." Jedson was smiling again. The two girls now had their heads together, and the word *bellissimo* floated from their conspiratorial mutterings.

Now caught, Jane had to respond in some way. "Perhaps … I don't know … tomorrow? Look, I really must rush – I've got people to look after."

He began laughing in earnest, "Yeah, I know – two lots, and both telling me you're with the others. Wanted some time-out, did you?" Jane blushed again but felt a twinge of unease: perhaps they hadn't run into each other by chance; he had been coming out of a shop but held nothing in his hand. On the other hand, it *had* been a tobacconist, so …

"Something like that," she admitted. "Anyway …" she tailed off.

"Don't worry, I won't rat on you. So, how about I pick you up about noon tomorrow?"

Jane was looking at her watch to gain time and thinking frantically. Given Mamie's closeness to Barney an invitation from her was like a royal command. Besides, Jane might be able to discover how, if at all, the American woman figured in her quest.

"Thanks. Shall we meet in Piazza Garibaldi, outside town?"

"Sure. About twelve?"

"Yes, fine. I really *must* go Mr ..., sorry, I can't remember your name."

"Jedson."

"Please give Mamie my regards, Mr Jedson, and say I'm looking forward to seeing her tomorrow."

"Just Jedson." The smile was back.

"Sorry?"

"No mister."

"Oh, right ..." Jane turned to go and had to restrain an impulse to break into a run. She did not look back.

At about seven that evening Jane made her way to Via Sant'Antonio, where Elfriede Baader had lived. She had planned to ask a passer-by for the exact address – the paper hadn't given the street number – but a little way up the street, she looked down into the railed entrance to a basement flat below street-level, and saw the red and white plastic tape that denoted a crime scene. It must be here, she thought, not considering that the death had happened at the river and not here at Elfriede Baader's home. The heavy street door above had three plastic buttons with smudgy labels, and she chose *Caponi* on the first floor. A distant buzz when she pressed it was followed by a loud click announcing that the street door had been opened and she pushed her way in, peering up the stairs. Another click and the stairwell light came on, revealing a woman wearing a floral overall leaning out of a first-floor door; a small boy, alert and bright-eyed, clutched at her overall with one hand, a blue plastic elephant in the other.

"*Signora Caponi?*" called Jane, starting to climb the stairs. "*Sì?*" came the reply. "Excuse me, I was looking for someone who knew the Signora Baader. I understand she lived in this building."

The woman took a step back, regarding Jane questioningly. Jane cast about in her mind for some compelling reason for her visit; she had completely forgotten to prepare one.

"I am so sorry to disturb you," she went on, having arrived at the step below the landing, "but my mother was a close friend of the signora and asked me to visit her when I was in Tivoli. I have just discovered she is dead, and I wanted ...." She came to a halt, the wells of inspiration dry, but now the woman was nodding and smiling, "You wanted to take some news to your mother," she said understandingly; Jane had found the compelling reason. "Come in," and she led the way through a narrow hallway into a cluttered kitchen-dining room, where she had obviously been getting dinner ready; a large saucepan bubbled softly on the stove, and the rich scent of meat sauce permeated the air; the theme music of the TV news blared from the dining area. The small boy was staring at Jane and sucking at his plastic elephant.

"Please sit down," said the woman, pulling out a chair at one end of the dining table, and pushing aside cutlery and glasses; she had already laid the table. A white wall-unit held glasses and vases, a set of encyclopaedias, a large TV set and a pile of magazines. "Alfredo, out the way, treasure," she said to the child, gently pushing him to one side. "Let mamma get the signorina some coffee. No, it's no trouble," she said in response to Jane's protests. "Everything is ready here." And she went to get the coffee-pot from the stove, and fill two tiny cups, seating herself in the chair opposite and turning the TV down with the remote-control. Alfredo clambered onto her lap, blue elephant still in one hand.

"What a lovely little boy, and what a fine name, Alfredo," said Jane admiringly. For a few minutes she was regaled with how well he was doing at nursery school, and how all the teachers were full of compliments on his intelligence and social skills. Alfredo took the elephant out of his mouth to gabble proudly "A, B, C, D, E …"

"*Bravo!*" said the two women together, smiling at him, and then at each other. He sat back smugly, and, the niceties concluded, the woman said, "I am very sorry about your mother's friend."

"Thank you," Jane murmured. "To be honest, I haven't actually told her yet. If you could …" She broke off, trusting Signora Caponi would understand but the other woman looked worried and did not meet Jane's eyes. Jane suddenly realised the reason for her hesitancy and said quickly, "I know that Signora Baader had a - how shall I say? - a problem with alcohol."

It was the right approach. Signora Caponi's brow cleared, "Ah, well … She was my tenant. I have a small apartment here in the basement," she added in explanation. "But, that day, you know, I did not see her. Tragic, tragic."

"How did you find out she had … passed on?"

"The next day. The police came – very upsetting, but Alfredo enjoyed himself; they gave him a ride in the car afterwards, didn't they, treasure?" Alfredo made the nah-nah, nah-nah siren noises of an Italian police car. "No," amended Signora Caponi, smiling, "there was no siren, it was very quiet, very ... respectful."

"It must have been a shock for you though," offered Jane. Unlike Gabriel with George the previous year, she had no need to feign interest and sympathy.

"Terrible – and what was worse, when they went downstairs, they found that thieves had chosen that very night to break into her apartment."

"No!" Jane exclaimed, suddenly remembering the red and white tape downstairs. The apartment couldn't have anything to do with the woman's death. She had died at the river. "What were they hoping to find, do you think?"

Signora Caponi shrugged. "Who knows. Money, perhaps. You know, drug addicts. Even here we have problems."

"How awful!"

"Everything turned upside-down." Signora Caponi shifted in her chair, stroked Alfredo's hair. "A terrible mess though we heard nothing – and," she went on, her voice rising, "I had to buy a new lock. Not only - I am *still* waiting for the police to release the apartment. It goes on and on."

"I am so sorry," said Jane. The apartment robbed, her mind whispered, that night, the night she died.

"*Pazienza*," said Signora Caponi, calming down and taking a sip of coffee. "Things will sort themselves out."

There was silence for a moment while the TV muttered on about the latest political scandals.

"You've been very kind," said Jane, casting about for something more she could ask. "I don't really know what else my mother would like to know. Now it's my mother, she thought. How on earth am I going to remember all these lies? Perhaps it would be better to make a note of them. "Was her friend happy here in Tivoli, do you think?" she added.

"Ah," sighed the other, shaking her head sadly, while keeping one eye on Alfredo; he had slithered from her lap and was now rummaging in the wall unit behind the magazines and pulling out a brightly-coloured cardboard box. "I don't know. The alcohol, you know. She was in pension and she had not much to do. And no family. I would like to go to her funeral myself, just so she has someone, but, you know ..." She sighed again, the sigh conveying the weight of family, home and all her other commitments.

"Perhaps I can go?" said Jane, glancing down at Alfredo, who was standing proudly showing her the box. "His treasures," explained the signora, smiling. "He has fossils and other little things." Jane dutifully looked at the contents of the box: a few broken fossils, a tin trumpet, two plastic dinosaurs and ...

"Where did Alfredo get this?" she asked sharply, holding up a fragment of stone depicting a woman's head and one shoulder. It was the missing part of the statue. She saw that Signora Caponi was staring at her, and tried to soften her tone. "I'm sorry to be so abrupt but my mother once described ..." Signora Caponi nodded. "Where did you get this?" she asked her son. "I have never seen it before," she explained to Jane. "Alfredo, tell me, treasure, where did you get this?"

The little boy mumbled something that Jane did not understand. Another question from his mother, who assured him everything was all right, another mumble. "What did he say?" asked Jane. "I didn't understand." "He found it," said the signora, looking slightly ashamed. "In Signora Baader's apartment. I used to do cleaning for her now and then. Alfredo must have ... he is very young and does not understand."

"Oh," said Jane, lamely, turning the head over in her fingers. "Yes, of course, his treasures ..."

The other looked relieved and took a sip of coffee. "I wonder," went on Jane, looking beseechingly at Alfredo, "could I take this ... for my mother? Something to remember the Signora Baader." What if he doesn't want to give it up? she thought in sudden panic. What on earth am I going to do? Could I just make a run for it? After all, it's not theirs.

But he was nodding solemnly, elephant back in his mouth, while his mother hugged him to the floral overall, stroking his hair, and telling him again he was *bravo*.

"Thank you so much, Alfredo," said Jane warmly, weak with relief. "You are really a good boy. And thank you too, signora. My mother will be so grateful."

"The funeral, signorina," Signora Caponi reminded her as they walked to the door of the apartment. "It should be this week. The police will know."

Jane thanked her again as she left, already fumbling in her bag for her cell phone as she started down the stairs. The door above her closed, and before she went out into the street, she fast-dialled the Ristorante della Sibilla. Now that the statue would be whole again, she could only hope that the Sibyl would remember how it had to be used.

14

Wednesday 3rd February

Barney was pleased at how everything was going. He had reinforced the basic idea of *The Da Vinci Code* – a millennium-old secret the Church was desperate to suppress – with the rhythm of *Angels and Demons* – a frantic searching of clues to a loud urgent sound-track (to be added later). The flashbacks were to satisfy the audiences' love of spectacle with period costumes and give some sort of spurious context to the 'great deception', that is, the Pope elect was a Jew, and the conspiracy to put him into that powerful position had been years in the making. The extra who had complained about his instructions to sidle and peer had done his job, had sidled and peered, and then gone home to be plagued by questions from friends and relations, none of which he could answer. In years to come he would rank it as among the worst bit-parts he had ever had.

Barney himself was not interested in the worm's eye view as long as the worm did its job. The schedule was on track, everyone was doing what they should in record time, and there was every possibility that they would make up the lost ten days. He had overestimated in the first place anyway, given that it was Italy, and that it was the fault of the shoot rather than the country was neither here nor there.

If he worried about anything, it was about Mame, who had changed, though he was too involved with the film to analyse the change and try to pin it down to one particular thing. If he had, he would have come up with the fact that she seemed more secretive and more querulous. It had been her idea to visit the location, an event that had only previously happened in his early days as a film-maker, and he knew, vaguely, that she had arrived in Italy well before necessary. Still, Italy was handy for their other business, the acquisition of the British freak for the speciality side of The Pussy Drive – and that should be happening the following week when the "good Christian woman" – he grinned – was bringing her over. Yes, everything on track and hunky-dory.

Mamie herself was more hopeful than she had been for some time. The meeting on Sunday night with the woman who called herself Signora Zauli had progressed matters. When Mamie pressed her, more specific details had emerged: they must have the sacred object, the statue, for Tuesday 16th February, just under two weeks away. Here she had smiled and again smoothed the skirts of her darkly sumptuous gown:

"The 16th is the last day of Carnival," she had said in

her softly modulated tones. "This is the point when our old times briefly touch the new. The portal will be open."

Mamie listened greedily, ignoring the mumbo-jumbo, but retained enough of her habitual sharpness to ask, "And what might you be getting out of it, sweetie? You never did say."

Signora Zauli smiled again, appeared to be studying the scarlet slashes of her gown in the dying light of the candles. When she looked up, Mamie blinked at the lupine expression in the large eyes. "Why, my concerns are of a more ... lasting nature, Mrs McCulloch," she murmured. "Let us say it is a *healing* of another kind." She laughed, the silvery chime tainted by some kind of knowing cynicism. "We will each gain what we want from this."

And Mamie was content. As long as she attained her goal, the rest was of little interest. This world could now offer only palliatives and death, while that other world, the one stagily invoked by Anton LaVey in his Black House, might – after all – be of some use.

The apparent bruising that had appeared on her leg the previous year had quietly announced the onset of the disease – at first she thought she had walked into a piece of furniture without noticing. The bruising became bluish-red lesions however that were swiftly identified. Mamie had Kaposi's Sarcoma associated with AIDS.

Kaposi, a cancerous tumour of the connective tissue, may involve the skin, gastrointestinal tract and other organs, the ugly external lesions having their fatal internal counterparts. It is associated not only with Italian and

African ancestry but also with Jewish. Had Eric Moonday known, he would have crowed in triumphant vindication. "Yes!"

The disease is rare in women but much more aggressive. When AIDS is added, the combination is lethal: a survival rate of between eight and nine months. The unregarded and unmissed homeless man, victim of the Spike Killer, had had his posthumous revenge. At the moment of penetration and death his head had lashed round in pain and denial, his broken teeth closing convulsively on the fleshy earlobe of his murderer. Mamie, outraged and offended by the unexpected attack, had medicated the jagged puncture mark, wore her hair brushed forward until it healed, and thought no more about it. Only later did she connect the disease with the homeless man, and she cursed both him and the compulsion that had forced her to a killing of impulse in the dank alleyway.

Now, knowing that Jane possessed the object necessary for the ceremony that would heal her, Mamie sat in her hotel room and coldly considered ways and means. If they had been in New York, Las Vegas or Chicago, there would have been no problem – a trashed apartment, electrical goods stolen to cover the real theft, bored cops at their tenth burglary of the day, and it was merely another statistic. Here in Italy, in Tivoli, it was another matter; the other break-in had caused enough of a stir as it was. Perhaps ... just perhaps she should draw first on the Greater Magic. If that did not work, she could resort to more traditional methods, whatever the consequences. She stroked her knitting bag, then drew out the steel needles and ran her fingers down their shiny length. It had been so long now, and she was starting to feel restless.

She shook herself, gazed with hatred at the forest of pill bottles on the side table – she should put them away in the bathroom, and then glanced at her watch. Jane would soon be arriving for lunch.

In his draughty warehouse with its blocks and panels, joists and off-cuts, the stonemason was finalising his work on the commissioned headstone. He was using a small paintbrush to free the carved letters of any dust and grit, sometimes running the ball of his thumb gently over the surface to check for any roughness. There was one spot, and he picked up the emery paper to smooth it down, thoughts straying momentarily to the customer.

The woman had been thorough in her arrangements. A lawyer had initially phoned him, crisply introducing himself as representing Elfriede Baader – the name meant nothing at first – and informing him that the headstone would now be required; he would be in contact again when it was time.

And the time had come that morning, with the news that she would be buried the coming Saturday 6th February, at ten in the morning ("I would ask you to be there at that hour"). The stone could then be set into place and their respective duties fulfilled.

"It cannot be placed the same day," the stonemason had quietly pointed out. "The earth must settle or the stone will sink and stand askew."

There was silence as the lawyer digested this, then he said stiffly, "I would ask you to convey the stone there in any event. I wish to see it to assure myself that my client's wishes have been respected. You may then set it later – when you consider it the appropriate time." And so it had been agreed.

A final dust with a soft cloth, and the stone mason got to his feet. He had been sitting on a piece of sacking to complete his work. Now, he stepped back a couple of paces, and studied it.

Tall and slender rather than short and massive, the pale and faintly luminous *lapis tiburtinus*, the travertine stone, gave the headstone an ethereal air. The carved letters of the inscription, highlighted in black, formed a narrow column in the centre. Set beneath, as the woman had specified, not at the top, were the name and dates, with the traditional small photograph in an oval frame, but these personal touches seemed almost an afterthought, as though only the inscription were of any importance. It read:

**Years will be shortened
like months.
Months like weeks.
Weeks like days.
Days like hours
And an hour
like a moment.**

The White Sibyl

Why in English? he thought.

Down the road in the Victoria Terme Hotel, Mamie and Jane were endeavouring to re-create the atmosphere of relaxed goodwill they had shared at their first meeting at the nursing home. Mamie, far better at dissembling, was having much more success than her companion. Jane had half-hoped that Carl would be there, but there was no sign of him, and it was obviously going to be a "just-us-girls-lunch", as Mamie put it.

They had eaten in Mamie's suite, a set menu chosen to combat the miserable weather: hot soup dense with vegetables, followed by roast lamb with potatoes. Jane ate everything except the final tiramisu, and in her nervousness had also drunk quite a lot of the excellent red wine. Mamie had merely picked and toyed with her food, chatting gently about the film ("I can't say too much, of course, but I'm just sure it will be Barney's biggest hit.") and Tivoli itself ("Don't you just *love* these old towns?"). If Jane had been a racier young women, Mamie would have regaled her with anecdotes from The Pussy Drive, but guessed – quite rightly – that Jane had never heard of it, and might even be slightly offended by the idea of what was to sex what Vegas was to gambling. That Jane distrusted her was clear, as was clear that Jane, though part of the "mumbo-jumbo", was a nice ordinary young woman, who probably lived her life in line with vague girl-next-door principles.

"Now, Jane," said Mamie as they were at the coffee

stage. "I have something to confess to you, sweetie, and I just hope and pray you'll forgive my little deception." She was using the intimate folksy tone that worked so well. Jane set down her coffee cup and looked at the American inquiringly and a little blearily.

"You see," Mamie continued, stroking her knitting bag, unaware the gesture made Jane's hackles rise, "I knew more about Professor Caseman than I let on, but at that point I just didn't know whether I could trust you." She paused, took a small spoonful of tiramisu and a sip of coffee, cold blue eyes hidden by the side-swept fringe of ash-blonde hair as she watched for Jane's reaction.

Nothing is more effective with a nice person than the suspicion that she has been deemed untrustworthy, and Jane half-opened her mouth to insist on her good faith, only to close it again. The ploy had worked however, the tables were turned and in some way she was on trial, not Mamie. "What do you mean?" she managed to say.

Mamie appeared to be considering whether she could – even now – be entirely frank, then looked up, gave one of her warm smiles, and settled back to spin her tale.

"Well, I have to go back a little, back to New Orleans a couple of years ago." She paused again. "Ever been to New Orleans, sweetie?"

"No, I haven't visited America at all," Jane replied, smiling apologetically, and wondering what was to come.

Mamie gave another warm smile. "It's a mighty particular place, sweetie. The Big Easy, as it's called. Like New York, it's a real melting-pot. Old French, Spanish,

Haitian, Cuban – they got it all. Famous for jazz and the Mardi Gras. The food as well – Creole cooking. Gumbo, Hush Puppies, red beans and rice. You know, Louis Armstrong signed letters, 'Red beans and ricely yours'? My, they were good! And how I used to love those Gulf oysters," she sighed. "Then, of course there's the Voodoo, Louisiana Voodoo, mind, home-grown. So, down in the French quarter – that's where all the tourists go – there are all these little stores selling candles and amulets, potions and I don't know what else. Real cute." She paused again, and then said with great deliberation: "It was right there – in a small store – that I met a friend of the professor's." Jane sat up with sudden attention. "Yes, I knew all about the professor, but, like I said, I didn't know then if I could trust you."

"What ... what made you change your mind, Mamie?"

"I've watched you, honey, made some en-quiries too. Sorry, sweetie, but I really needed to know before I confided in you. It was too important just to, you know, take you at face value."

A second master stroke. The nice person – though not liking the idea of being doubted and investigated – is now reassured, flattered to be found worthy, and soon to be the recipient of personal – and important – confidences.

"Well, she had her own little store," explained Mamie, taking her time and relaxing into the story. "No, not Voodoo – that was just to give you an idea of the place: it was all candles and herbs rather than amulets and devil-dolls." Mamie laughed. Harmless eccentricity, whimsical dabbling in arty-craftsy remedies and whole food, the laugh implied.

"Clothilde, her name was. Ever heard of her, sweetie?" Her tone had sharpened but Jane, senses dulled by wine, did not notice. "No," she said slowly. "The professor never mentioned anyone called Clothilde. Was she French?"

Mamie relaxed again at Jane's ignorance. It would have been much more hazardous had she known of Clothilde's existence. She became aware she was stroking the knitting bag again and withdrew her hand. "French she was indeed, sweetie, and a real nice woman. We hit it off immediately, became as close as sisters."

"And she was a friend of the professor's?" asked Jane. "Talked about her?"

"All the time, honey, admired that woman to death. And she told me of the … you know … the professor's importance, her being the head of the New Vestals and all."

At this bombshell Jane was speechless, and could only stare at Mamie, who was smiling and nodding in confirmation.

"So, you see, sweetie, I wasn't sincere with you, and I surely do regret it, but Clothilde begged me to be careful. She would have come with me but her sister fell sick, and she just couldn't leave her."

The half-truths finished with, this was an outright lie, but Clothilde, dead and rotting in the airshaft of an abandoned warehouse in the Big Easy, was in no position to protest. As for Jane, her mind was in a whirl. She would have given anything to have the time to assimilate so much new information and make sense of what Mamie was saying. "But you came for the film, didn't you?" she asked, clutching at the one sure straw.

"Oh, that as well, but it was really to see the professor, and a wonderful woman I found her to be, just as Clothilde said. Wonderful, understanding, and" ... a pause ... "ready to help me in just any way she could."

"Help?" repeated Jane, feeling confused and foolish. She too should know all there was to know if she really *were* trustworthy and a true friend of the professor's.

"Let's just order up some more coffee, sweetie. I can see you're all shook up and need a little time. Jedson!" she called; the door opened and Jedson's blond head appeared. "More coffee."

"Yes, Miss Mamie." The door softly closed again, and the two women fell silent.

"Do you mind if I use your bathroom?" asked Jane suddenly, longing to be away and have time – if only a little – to think.

"You just go right ahead, honey," smiled Mamie. "Over there on the right." Jane picked up her bag and made her way a little unsteadily towards the far door. Once inside, she turned the key, and still clutching her bag, leaned limply against the polished wood, trying to fit the pieces together. Mamie had met Clothilde, a friend of Professor Caseman's in New Orleans, and the two had become so close that Clothilde had revealed the professor's other secret life. During Jane's visits to the nursing home, before Lena's feigned senility, the professor had recounted a little of the New Vestals and their guardianship of the knowledge that a final confrontation between good and evil was taking place.

Innately cautious and accustomed to keeping her own council, she had not told Jane that the victory of the true Rex Nemorensis was only the first of three.

Mechanically Jane went to the wash hand basin, clicked on the mirror lights, and gazed at her reflection interrogatively, as though the image could tell her what to do. Her looking-glass self was flushed and upset-looking, hair ruffled, and lips pale. No help there. She rummaged in her bag, found her comb and lipstick and repaired the damage, then, on an afterthought, took out the head of the statue, which she was still carrying. The stone was comforting against her skin, and she cradled the small piece in her fingers as she had once cradled the Venus figurine. "The Sibyl will reflect," the Sibyl had said maddeningly when Jane had phoned her to tell her it was found. "The time is nigh but not yet."

I just hope there *is* time, Jane had thought. Everything is going so *fast*. Oh, professor ... She straightened, then, on impulse quietly opened the door of an ornate cupboard set against one wall. Inside were shelves and shelves filled with bottles and boxes, drugs with menacing scientific names such as Vinblastine and Etoposide, Doxorubicin and Adriamycin, but also dozens of different vitamins, minerals, herb extracts and fish oils. So much for the implied scorn of "arty-craftsy remedies and whole food."

She pulled the handle of the flush and went out again. The coffee had arrived.

"You know you have to ask for American coffee if you don't want those dinky cups of pure tar-oil?" queried

Mamie, smiling. "Yes," said Jane, adding sugar to her cup of excellent filter coffee, and taking a sip. At the taste her eyebrows shot up.

"I just added the teeniest bit of brandy," explained Mamie. "What with the cold day and all. Now," she went on serenely, "where were we?" She had managed to arrange a corner of the knitting bag beneath a fold of her jacket, and could now touch it without the movement being obvious.

"Professor Caseman," prompted Jane, placing the cup carefully onto the table. "She was going to help you." Mamie smiled inwardly as she heard the transformation of her own lie into Jane's acceptance, but knew she would now have to be extremely careful, tread with the utmost delicacy.

"Clothilde – and I really must phone her this evening to let her know I am just fine – told me of the immense power, the immense *spiritual* power, of ... their group. Sorry, sweetie, but I still have a problem with saying it." Jane nodded; she knew the feeling, and even now, after all that had happened, unreality still washed over her at the strangeness of it all. She picked up her cup and took another sip of coffee; it did not seem so strong the second time.

"The fact is," said Mamie, lowering her voice as if admitting to a shameful secret, "I am sick, Jane. Terminally sick, sweetie. Cancer. You see this?" And she drew her blouse back from one shoulder, where livid reddish welts and nodules disfigured the pasty skin. Jane exclaimed in shocked pity at the sight, but Mamie was already pulling the blouse back into place and slumping back; her face was pale, one hand clasping the collar of the blouse, the other apparently gripping the chair beneath her jacket. This time Jane did not even notice for, appalled, she was staring at the other woman in sympathy and horror. "Oh, Mamie, how terrible! I am so very sorry." She did not know what else to say but Mamie was now waving one hand to brush away the sympathy, murmuring: "No, no, it's fine, just fine, honey. I certainly didn't want to tell you like that but I just … couldn't help it." Jane started to demur and Mamie, watching coldly from behind the mask of a pale anguished face, saw what she had been aiming for. The Greater Magic did not lie. Compassion truly was one of the strongest forces in the manipulation of others.

The Sibyl was not in her shop, even though it was well past opening time. She had more important things to do, and besides, it was mid-week, and apart from a couple of out-of-season tourists coming from or going to the temples, potential customers would be few and far between.

She was sitting at home at the large table by the window, the three white cats in an immobile line before her on the chenille table cover. A glass of water and a pile of books were set out, and she was poring over one battered volume with a faded leather cover, turning the pages with great care, pausing now and again to sip some water, read a passage or study a drawing. Her lips moved as she silently read, and her face held the grave stillness of a scholar, the sulkiness, smugness and vagueness completely absent. For a while she browsed and thought, until finally, one slender hand still resting on the open pages of the book, she straightened and focused on the three watchers. They appeared to stiffen to attention and then settle back, an audience given the signal and now ready and willing to listen.

"Februarius, the time of purification and expiation, she said, looking at each of them in turn. Three pairs of green eyes gazed back at her. "Preparation for Spring, the new year of growth yet to come. All were involved. In Rome, the Vestals in their temple held the sacred rites of cleansing. This at mid-month, before the Ides." She rapped her knuckles softly on the table. "And then came Lupercalia." She paused, took a sip of water, then added musingly, "When Caesar, consummate showman, humbly declined the crown of kingship, but it was too late, and besides, not germane to our present purposes. To continue: on the Ides of Februarius, fell Lupercalia, festival of Lupercus Faunus, later ignored but holder of ancient powers. He who kept wolves from ancient flocks, and yes," she said, nodding at the cats, "now we have wolves again."

"To continue: his mating with the dryads formed the forests, source of food and shade for man and beast. At Lupercalia, a sacrifice in his honour – a goat for fertility, a dog to purify, and their mingled blood anointed two fair youths."

She paused again, smoothed the pages of the book as if caressing an animal and the three cats began to purr steadily and rhythmically, eyes half-closed.

"Then – a lottery of love and sensuality. Do you

follow? Two youths, duly anointed with the sacred blood – and two urns. One held the names or signs of girls, the other, the names or signs of boys. One from each, you see. One for one, paired and given leave to love and procreate. Their mating blessed by all the gods of Rome – Mars and Romulus, Lupercus Faunus himself, and also the first great Mothers – Ruma and Rea Silvia, Fauna and Acca Laurentia."

"But I digress. Lupercus Faunus – god of wild nature, savage nature, a Roman Pan with hooves of horn, the part of life that only knows the joy of being." She laughed and the cats opened their eyes. "Oh, that was no good for all those mewling Christ-lovers," she explained. "*They* could have no truck with sex and wildness, so … Lupercus was banished, replaced by Valentine – worshipped on the Ides but nothing below the waist. No wildness now – but hearts and flowers and … chocolates!" she finished witheringly, lips twisted in amused contempt. She gazed out of the window, where one grey cloud had detached itself from the lowering sky and was drifting westwards. Glancing back at the book, she re-read one sentence, murmuring the words aloud: "The third morn after the Ides beholds the naked Luperci, and then, too, the rites of two-horned Faunus." Her face took on a look of intense concentration. "The month is now, the time is near, and it must be the Ides or near the Ides. It cannot be another."

In Tivoli Terme, Jane, still recovering from Mamie's dreadful revelation, was trying – against every instinct – not to feel involved in the older woman's plight. Trust no one, she kept reminding herself, clinging to the memory of Lena's letter. We met at one of the professor's lectures, she repeated to herself. It was called *The Lesser Goddesses*. I must be brave. And what about Elfriede Baader? Dead. Drowned. Should I ask if Mamie has heard of her? But the warm southern drawl droned relentlessly on, its gentle pressure and desperate undertones muddling her thoughts and eroding her resolve. It went on and on – Clothilde had told Mamie not only of the power of the New Vestals, but that there was an object, a small statue with magical properties. It would cure Mamie, let her live. Yes, she knew it was unlikely, a real long shot, but it was – she repeated – her only chance. Clothilde had been convinced, had assured her friend that there really was a possibility. Could Jane help her? Give her the help that the death of Professor Caseman had cruelly denied her? Did she know of this object? Know where it might be? Jane being so close to the professor and all.

Finally she came to a halt, her work done, for Jane could not ignore the plea for help. "Yes, I do know about it," she said at last, looking at her hands and not seeing the sudden flair of triumph in Mamie's small eyes. "But it can't be ... available immediately," she went on. "I think I can get it for you ... by the end of the month."

Jane must know of the importance of the statue, decided Mamie. And she must also know of the date – the 16th – given Signora Zauli. It did not occur to her that Jane knew only one of the two, and was guessing at the second. The end of the month was too late, and, of course Mamie would not wait. Whatever the danger of discovery she would now arrange for the theft of the statue, and if Jane suspected, it was just too bad. Without proof there was nothing she could do.

She patted Jane's hand, told her she was a wonderful girl, and that she, Mamie, would surely show her gratitude. The only thing was, she would ask Jane to keep the illness between themselves. No one else knew, not even Barney, and though he came over as tough he would be devastated, and Mamie wanted to tell him in her own good time. Could Jane do that for a dying woman? "So sorry, sweetie, but it really comes down to that."

And of course Jane, innately kind and compassionate, agreed.

Mamie had been very skilful in her re-working of the Clothilde story. It was true that the two of them had met in the French quarter in New Orleans, true that Clothilde had a small shop dealing in herbs and alternative medicine, and true that Mamie had first heard of Lena from Clothilde herself. It was a sign of Mamie's desperation that she acted on what the Frenchwoman said, for proof of the New Vestals' power was entirely lacking: Clothilde had abandoned her post at Satricum on the Pontine Plain before the victory at Nemi and did not know that the first prophesy had sprung to life.

But Clothilde's scornful rejection of the "pointless watch of the so-called New Vestals" had conversely convinced Mamie of their power. It was Clothilde herself who seemed the charlatan, with her garish African dress and badly-arranged turban, her dangling metal ear-rings and over-dark foundation cream. Having rejected Old Europe and its "petty bourgeois values", she had turned to the Dark Continent, the cradle of all humanity, as she put it, and secretly wished she were black. As the two became friends, her confidences took the form of endless ranting. Her time in Europe had been a waste of time, she had not been appreciated as she should have been, she had been snubbed and ignored – *she* should have been assigned to Tivoli, not that pathetic lush of a German woman, since it was she who had the most complete prophesy. She talked disparagingly about Professor Caseman, identifying her by name, and repeated again and again that *she* should have been in Tivoli, with its sacred groves, and warm springs and powers of healing.

At the word 'healing' Mamie became all attention. And she acted decisively: the same discreet lawyers with their useful contacts – as witness the purchase of the little girl – subsequently earned enormous sums of money by locating Lena and 'tying up loose ends'. Mamie's decision to go to the nursing home herself had really been her only mistake – she had underestimated Professor Caseman, convinced she would find some muddled old woman rather than the sharp intellect and diamond-hard will she encountered. But then Jane had arrived – as Mamie knew she would – and more watching and manoeuvring had led to Tivoli and the final decisive part of Mamie's plan.

Downstairs Jane was crossing the lobby on her way to the glass doors, when a voice hailed her: "Hey, Jane! Over here!" Looking round she eventually identified the source – Carl, slumped on one of the couches, pen in hand and a large diary open on his knees. Despite the upbeat greeting he looked bored and moody. With an effort Jane went over and collapsed beside him, managing a smile. "Carl, hi. I wondered where you'd got to. I've just been having lunch with Mamie."

"I know. I heard. Just us girls, sweetie, sure you understand," mimicked Carl, in a very passable imitation of Mamie's southern drawl. "Now you just have some quality free time." He grimaced by way of comment.

Reluctantly, against her will even, Jane laughed, and with the laughter a huge weight was lifted from her. It was as though some debilitating spell had been neutralised. She exhaled in a long relieved sigh. Outside the glass doors, sheltered from the rain by the roof of the entrance, Jedson was holding his mobile phone to the diamond-studded ear and nodding.

"She is ... something else," Jane agreed, eyes on the tall figure. "And I am *really* drunk First red wine and then a huge slug of brandy in the coffee – but that wasn't my idea, it came like that."

Carl glanced at her. "You OK?" he asked, shutting the diary. He was not usually sensitive to other people but Jane's speech had been slurred and her face was flushed, eyes feverish. Her gaze held entreaty when she looked back at him.

"No, not really. Carl, I ..."

But there was the tall black-suited figure standing in

front of them and looking down. The two on the couch looked up, dwarfed and childlike in comparison, Jane with enormous concentration, Carl with a hint of challenge.

"So, you ready, Jane?" asked Jedson. He merely nodded at her companion, but Carl raised his diary in greeting and grinned. "Mind if I cadge a lift up to Tivoli?" he asked airily. "Got some things to do up in town, and Mamie gave me the afternoon off." The "things" he had mentioned could just as easily been done in Tivoli Terme but, without knowing why, he had suddenly felt it was a good idea to keep Jane company.

"Aw, sorry, Carl," Jedson said smoothly, "but Miss Mamie just phoned. Change of plans and she'd like you to go up."

"Right," said Carl resignedly; Jane would probably be all right. Getting up, he put out a hand to help her from the low couch but Jedson was there before him. For a moment the three formed an untidy triangle as Jane struggled from the deep cushions, one hand imprisoned in Jedson's, the other clinging to the strap of her shoulder bag as Carl held her elbow.

"You sure you're all right?" asked Carl, his uneasiness returning. "Yes, of course," Jane assured him; the impulse to confide had dissipated like smoke. "Just a bit ... lit-up. Lunchtime drinking always kills me."

"OK," he said, turning towards the lift. "Let's get together one evening?"

Outside, an icy sleet was falling. Jedson held open the rear door and Jane half-stepped half-fell into the plush interior. She leaned back against the head-rest and closed her eyes, aware of an enormous lassitude that was actually rather pleasant. Handled Mamie all right, she was thinking, no, don't want to think about her. Later will do. Thank heaven there's no work this afternoon. A sleep, that's what I need. But she felt so ... *good*, so relaxed, carefree even. Opening her eyes she could see the slightly sun-tanned curve of Jedson's jaw. Suntan in February, she thought. Looks good though. And she closed her eyes again.

Jedson, relaxing and allowing himself a cigarette, drove steadily through the slanting rain. He knew exactly where Jane was staying in Tivoli, and at the beginning of the town, again took the circular route: right, up the hill, past the fortress of Pius II on the left, down the slope towards the Aniene, the hospital on the left at the bottom, then into Viale Roma, the mini-section of ring road running alongside the river. The Vestal Cossinia's tomb still stood silent and rain-drenched on the opposite bank, but this time the steep slopes of the bulky mountain above loomed visible against scudding grey clouds. Before he arrived at Ponte Gregoriano however he turned off to the left into a short cul-de-sac that flanked a supermarket with a green and yellow sign. It was here he parked and glanced in the rear mirror. Jane appeared to be sleeping peacefully, a small smile on her lips as if in a happy dream. He smiled himself, snapping open the seat belt and glancing out; the rain had stopped and a brisk breeze had sprung up.

As for Jane, the next thing she knew after getting into the car was Jedson opening the door again, one hand extended. I must have gone to sleep, she thought, looking out, then – recognising where she was – he must know the town very well. He had parked in the narrow cul-de-sac beside the Todis supermarket, where Jane bought supplies of apple juice to keep in her room. The cul-de-sac ended in a flight of stone steps that led upwards through an arch to the road where her B&B was; it was one of the few routes she had been able to learn. The river down at the bottom, the supermarket, and further up the hill the car park, where the film crew had set up base and where Jane's car was parked. I wonder if Harold's battery's OK, she thought fleetingly, clambering from the car and staggering slightly as the cold air gusted over her.

"I'm fine, thanks," she managed to gasp. "Great ... really ... I'll be fine from here. Really. Thanks again." And she half-turned towards the steps.

"Miss Mamie said to see you home," he said calmly, putting his arm about her shoulders and tucking one hand under her arm. "You could slip and fall. Come on." And he started towards the stone steps with Jane walking unresisting at his side.

As they passed under the arch she became aware of the hand beneath her arm, the bent knuckles lightly brushing the side of her breast. He smelt faintly of some musky aftershave that made her nostrils flare, and when she lost her footing on the brick steps, he caught her up, then brushed her hair from her face with a touch that was both maternal and sensual.

She had no awareness of the road to the B&B, but the

main door of the building was open – no need to fumble around for the key – and Jane's landlady Elsa was just emerging with a plastic bag of rubbish in one hand.

"Jane, *cara, tutto bene?*" she called. She liked the young English woman, and had even invited her to a family dinner one evening, a very cheerful occasion when Jane had got a little tipsy and translated English jokes into Italian, some very funny, others incomprehensible to the Italians, who nodded sagely and agreed it was that mystery "the English sense of humour".

Jane tried to say something but the connection between her brain and her mouth seemed to have been severed. She would have liked to tell Elsa that she felt *wonderful* but that her jeans were too tight and she was going to take them off as soon as possible, but she could only gesture feebly in greeting. "She's fine," she heard Jedson's wonderful voice say. "She's fine. Just a little ..." She heard Elsa laugh, presumably at some explanatory gesture. "*Sì, la nostra* Jane ...!" They both shared a laugh, and then there was the dimness of the downstairs hall, the click of the time switch for the lights, and the long flight of stairs to the first floor.

In the street, Elsa suddenly remembered she had forgotten the other bag containing bottles for recycling, and stepped back inside. There it was, propped against the wall. As she bent to retrieve it, she glanced up, to see the two figures – the tall black-suited man and the slender stumbling woman – ascending slowly, step by step, the stone stairs. At the top Jane stumbled, leaned limply against the wall, and the low voice of the man, an attractive mellow murmur, was just audible, as he took possession of her bag to find the key. The door was opened and they passed out of sight, the door noiselessly swinging shut behind them.

In a dim apartment near the old paper mill built over the Temple of Hercules, Signora Zauli smiled to herself and toyed with a necklace bright with rubies. In the cluttered gift shop – now open for afternoon business – the Sibyl paused in her dusting, head suddenly raised, green eyes searching the shadows, while in her empty flat, the three white cats crouched and growled, tails twitching and fur spiked into a stiff brush of aggression.

15

Wednesday 3rd – Thursday 4th February

The sun would officially set at 17.27 that day, but by four-thirty streetlamps were already alight, tinting the clouds over the town a dull orange. Icy draughts gusted through the streets, shadows flickered and trembled, and lighted bars with their gleaming arrays of bottles and colourful displays of sweets did brisk business as chilled shoppers took heart from hot chocolate and local gossip. Everyone agreed that there had never been such a bad winter, and that "all this water" was extremely unusual even for February; there were only two weeks to go before the 16th, and what if King Carnival's bonfire had to be called off?

In Jane's flat, the standard lamp in the living room had been switched on, illuminating her crumpled jacket on the chair by the door and her jumper discarded on a small table. A shaft of light from the lamp banded the bedroom floor, where her too-tight jeans lay in a corner, the rest of her clothes lying somewhere in the shadows.

Jane herself was lost and drowned in sensation. He seemed to want to caress her from head to toe, and she could almost believe that his touch left a trail of fire, like slender tongues of lava seen at night, glowing streaks inching their way down the curves of darkened foothills. The musky tang of aftershave filled her nostrils, and strands of blond hair – now freed from the confines of the ponytail – lightly brushed her skin as he kissed her throat and arms, thighs and ankles.

He was above her, grasping her shoulders and bending to nuzzle her neck, then, with a swift fluid movement was beneath her, clasping her waist to swing her astride him, his fingers sliding to grip her thighs, so that her legs were imprisoned while his thumbs slipped between her legs. "Yes …" she heard herself whisper. "Oh, yes …"

She had no memory of him leaving. When she woke up he was gone, though whether it had been the night before or early that morning she had no way of knowing. All she knew was that she had the worst hangover ever, and when she somehow crawled out of bed, she only just made it to the bathroom before being violently sick.

And it went on and on, horrible retching heaves that left her cold and shaking. The clock showed eight, but after valiantly taking a shower – more spasms and she had to cling to the towel rail to keep her balance – she went back to bed and phoned Anthea: she had some kind of 'flu bug and could not go in, a credible enough story since several people had come down with the same kind of thing. Anthea was brief and business. "OK. Plod can stand in. Let me know, eh?"

"And get well soon to you too," muttered Jane, making a face at the now-silent phone. "Keep warm and don't even think of going out." She burrowed back under the covers, but another spasm hit, and she made for the bathroom again at a stumbling run.

Tivoli itself went about its weekday business. The film crew were busily invisible in the gardens of Villa D'Este, Barney striding about and shouting at a cameraman who was being slow about setting up lighting in the Grotto of Diana. It was only a small space, for Chrissake! How long did he need to get his sorry ass in gear! Also invisible, and also busy were members of the carnival committee, involved in the countless details relating to the arrival of out-of-town groups who would be taking part in the carnival procession. Some had already arrived, and Enrico Mattei, nephew of the mayor on his mother's side (Mattei née Salmone), was also involved; he had been given the job of heading the welcoming committee, which would assist the guests in any way necessary. This was not only because of his family connections but also because he "knew the English, French and Spanish languages," as his uncle had proudly reminded the carnival committee at an initial planning meeting.

Enrico's knowledge of languages was particularly useful. That year – for the first time – the *Carnevale tiburtino* would be a local, national, and international event. Tivoli had its own traditions including the *Zibaldone*; Venice, Viareggio, Acireale, and Ivrea, the four most famous carnivals in Italy, would each be sending five representatives – from Venice stark white masks and sumptuous costumes, from Viareggio miniature reproductions of the satirical masks of politicians and personalities that featured in their parade, from Sicilian Acireale baroque confections of gold and red, and from far-north Ivrea, examples of their robust orange-throwers, who had however promised that they would only carry baskets of oranges and not pelt the crowd as they usually did at home. In addition, Sardinia would send the *Issohadores*, heralds of their festivities, and the *Mamuthones* with their lugubrious black masks and funereal tread.

And that was just Italy. The international elements included Halubje in Croatia, bell-ringers wearing large animal heads, Cadiz in Spain had offered five members of their *coros* with guitars and lutes to play the traditional *Carnival Tango*, French Nice promised "extravagant dresses", and – greatest coup of all – New Orleans, who were actually sending six participants rather than five. There had been a suggestion by one council member to invite Tyrnavos in Greece (he had been there one carnival) but this was vetoed since it turned out that their local celebrations boasted gaudily-painted papier-mâché phalluses, which all the women in the crowd were supposed to touch or kiss. Not in *our* city, the mayor rapped out decisively.

At the B&B Jane passed the day in a feverish doze. Carl phoned to ask how she was, did she need anything? ("No, but thanks so much."); Mamie phoned: "And I really blame myself, sweetie! You just let me know if there's anything at all I can get you – Jedson can deliver it. And you won't forget our little arrangement, will you?" Oh, God, no! was Jane's reaction to the first, though the words she actually said were quite different, and she assured Mamie she would not forget their "little arrangement".

As she closed the call with Mamie she suddenly sat up bolt upright. She had remembered the statue. With an effort, mouth dry, she crossed to the cupboard where she had placed it. Mamie! she was thinking incoherently. She really needs the statue – and I as good as told her I had it! God! All that wine – and the brandy too – Jedson – how could I? – and if it's not there? If it was all a way …?

But when she finally fumbled the cupboard door open, fingers clumsy with haste, the statue was there. She caught it up, scanning it for signs of change or damage, but it was as before. Weakly she let herself slide to the floor, clasping the cool stone between her palms. Her heartbeat began to slow, and she exhaled shakily. It was two separate things, she told herself. Not connected. And why shouldn't I have wonderful wild sex once in a while? Just a fling, a one-night stand. She smoothed the rippling folds of the statue's robe. Must mend it, she thought sleepily. And phone thingy to see if she's remembered anything. So much to do, so little time, she mused drowsily, and, still holding the statue, her head drooping against the cupboard door, she fell asleep.

*

"So I guess you did cosy up to her," cooed Mamie, smiling archly. Though Jedson looked as cool and immaculate as ever she could smell tobacco smoke; he had already smoked his first cigarette of the five, and much earlier than usual. He smiled, rubbing his ear in the country-boy gesture she had so adored when she first came across him. And those overalls – the denim straps hanging from sunburnt shoulders – had sure been cute.

He said nothing however and she reached up to give him a brisk double slap, more a pat in fact, since she did not have much strength; he blinked.

"Well?" she asked sharply. "Has she got the damn thing on not?"

"Yes, Miss Mamie, stashed away in a cupboard. Left it there, but took an imprint of her keys. So, any time you want …"

Mamie smiled again, and this time the pudgy hand reached up to fondle the diamond-studded ear. "You did real good, sweetie. Now listen …"

There was a certain symmetry to events. From Italy, Clothilde, bitter and enraged, had returned to her native New Orleans, there to encounter the one person who would believe in and pursue the power that Old Europe still possessed; from New Orleans, Signora Zauli – last of an ancient family and a forbidden cult – had returned to her origins in Tivoli, there to repossess the powers the city contained.

The gathering of momentum had already claimed three victims: Clothilde betrayed by her anger and duped by an offer of friendship; Avvocato De Angelis, upright and blameless but a loose end to be snipped off; and Elfriede Baader, flawed guardian, who had tried to keep faith but had been killed as casually as a swatted insect.

Jane, believing but unconvinced, could not imagine the future and had not dwelt on where her quest would lead her. As she slumbered on that dark afternoon, rain gently pattering on the small balcony outside the bedroom window, her dreams were placid. She had mended the statue, and once whole, it had come to life, become a woman with serene features and a compassionate smile. The White Sibyl was there too, smiling and clasping Jane's hand in affection and approval. There was no ceremony, no antagonist, no anguish – all was well. Exactly as things should be in a perfect dream.

16

Friday 5th February

It was Friday, and Jane had decided to extend the 'flu. Carl had probably had the time of his life yesterday after his time in Tivoli Terme with Southern Comfort and Muscles Incorporated; she still didn't feel very well anyway.

She phoned Anthea again. "Sorry, Anthea, but I won't be back until Monday." And then, embellishing, "I need to go up to Rome this weekend anyway. Things I have to sort out."

"OK – we've got Plod. See you." Anthea was as brief and businesslike as usual, hanging up in the middle of Jane's thanks. Jane felt only relief at being temporarily away from it all. And she might indeed go home for the weekend. Before that however … She picked up her phone and fast-dialled the Ristorante Sibilla. It was answered after only two rings.

"It's me, Jane," she said, sitting on the edge of the bed. "Have you ... remembered anything? About what to do with the statue, I mean?"

There was what seemed to Jane an offended silence, then, "The Sibyl must complete her search," came the terse reply. Jane rolled her eyes; she had forgotten the third person grammar. "But what about the ceremony?" she asked doggedly. "Do we know when it is, *where* it is?"

"The time is now," came the answer, "Februarius, the time of purification. Purification and purity, so that the year of growth may begin anew."

A sudden thought occurred to Jane. "Purity?" she repeated. "I ... I don't have to be a virgin or anything, do I?" It sounded ridiculous even as she said it, and she felt herself blushing as she suddenly noticed a blond hair caught on the padded headboard. She lifted it off between finger and thumb, was sure she could smell the musky aftershave, and blushed again. The other gave a sudden caw of laughter: "Virgin! What has Venus to do with virginity?" she said scornfully, "and when the time is also that of Faunus. Protect the statue. Now, the Sibyl must have time and peace. Farewell."

"Wait!" said Jane, raising her voice. "Faunus? Can I ask you ...?" But the line was dead, "end of call" flashing briefly on the display. Oh, why was the only person involved a batty sibyl? And who on earth said "Farewell" at the end of a mobile phone conversation? She laid the phone on the bedside table, stood up indecisively, then noticed the guide book on the chest-of-drawers, the one she had bought in the gift shop that day – the day too she had seen a galloping pony sculpted in flowing water.

The book was face down, and a triangle of paper showed above the photograph of the two temples. The notes. She drew out the one sheet of paper. Now ….

Tiburnus, local hero
Hercules
the Sibyl, the *prediletta* – the darling - of Venus
Faunus Fatidicus – prophesied in dreams. Sacred grove in woods under waterfalls in Villa Gregoriana

There he was, fourth on the list. And there was a sacred grove, like Nemi and the Rex Nemorensis. Gabriel, she thought. And they never had got it together. There was just that one time – the evening after the neo-pagan girl had given her the Venus figurine – and they had gone back to Rome, and Jane had drunk too much. But "… I don't want this," she had said, and he had got up to sleep on the couch. Just like that. She sighed, pulled her computer from the bottom of the wardrobe, and laid it on the bed.

While it booted up she glanced out of the window. Another grey day. More clouds. More drizzle. Whatever had happened to brochure Italy? The computer was ready, and she went straight to Google, and keyed in 'Faunus'. Up it came:

Faunus-Wikipedia, the free encyclopaedia

- [Traduci questa pagina]

In ancient Roman religion and myth, **Faunus** was the horned god of the forest, plains and fields; when he made cattle fertile he was called Inuus. ...

Consorts and family - Festivals - Notes - References

en.wikipedia.org/wiki/**Faunus** - Copia cache - Simili

1. **Faunus**

- [Traduci questa pagina]

3 Mar 1997 ... The god of wild nature and fertility, also regarded as the giver of oracles. He was later identified with the Greek Pan ...

There was also a strip of photographs showing Faunus in art, and his imagined appearance was not at all reassuring – half-man, half goat, some images showing him with long curling horns, most with what looked like a leering smile. She averted her gaze, looked down at the next reference:

Da Lupercus Faunus a San Valentino

And she paused. From Lupercus Faunus to Saint Valentine. Well, if Faunus became Saint Valentine, there was the link with February. But what had happened to Faunus Fatidicus, she wondered. They all had so many bloody *names*, no, not names, *aspects*, she supposed. Like Diana at Nemi – a goddess of chastity who also helped women conceive, or did she just look after them? No idea, she concluded, can't remember. Anyway, forget Nemi, concentrate on Tivoli.

She spent the whole morning going backwards and forwards, copying extracts into files, sorting and underlining, trying to put the mass of information into some kind of order. Finally she stopped, went back to what she had copied, and started reading, only to come to an abrupt halt when she saw a detail she had missed before. In Rome, before the Lupercalia, purification rites were carried out by the Vestal Virgins. Sudden associations clicked into place: the Vestals. Professor Caseman. Elfriede Baader. With one thing and another (that's one way of putting it, she thought) she had completely forgotten the funeral. "The police will know," Signora Capone had said. Jane went to look out the old telephone directory she had seen in the pile of tourist information thoughtfully left by the management of the B&B.

17

Saturday 6th February

Appearing around 1903, the word "decompensation" originally meant the inability of an organ, especially the heart, to maintain its function due to an overload caused by disease. Later, it was extended to psychiatry to describe the emotional and behavioural backlash that occurs when an individual consciously or unconsciously **stops** holding themselves together.

Eric Moonday had been decompensating since the rainy Sunday night he had followed the limousine, and the momentum was increasing. To the relief of the accounts mole he had abandoned Tivoli town to haunt Tivoli Terme, where his new quarry, Mamie McCulloch, was staying. Booking a room on the first floor of the same hotel – he was now going through his money at a tremendous rate, what with the hire car as well – he tried to catch glimpses of

Mamie and Jedson in their comings and goings, which proved to be extremely difficult.

Inside the hotel Mamie was never to be seen in the restaurant, and any room service went directly from the kitchen to the suite. As for Jedson, he sometimes had coffee downstairs, or smoked a cigarette on the restaurant patio, but Eric could not be sure that Barney hadn't warned the tame gorilla about Eric's efforts to get the film stopped, and was frightened of being noticed.

He could not carry out continuous surveillance outside the hotel either. Set in its own fenced and walled grounds, it was accessible only through certain entrances, with a wide pavement between the grounds and the main road of Via Tiburtina. There was nowhere to hide, nowhere to take up a watching-post, and at that time of year so few people, apart from the local residents, that hanging around unnoticed was out of the question.

Nevertheless, he had worked out a routine so that he could at least keep watch in the mornings, the most likely time to see them going out. The black limousine was kept in the hotel's underground garage, and so had to exit further along from the main entrance before turning back in again through the gates. And there was a narrow road alongside the hotel grounds, with a bar on the corner. At night Eric parked his car in the narrow road, as near as possible to the main road, and in the morning took up his post inside the bar, to see if the limousine was on the move. That way he had time to get to his own car while the other was circling round, drawing up outside the hotel and leaving with its passengers again. Passengers, because apart from the woman there was also a pale spotty young man who appeared to be some sort of guide, and this was confirmed by the accounts mole.

Eric had duly followed the three on what seemed to be daily tourist trips around the area, except for the day when the woman and the gorilla went to Rome. It could well have been a breakthrough trip – what were they going to Rome for? – but he lost them in the suburbs, and then spent hours trying to find his way back.

There had been one other exception. Staked out at the corner bar, Eric had seen the limousine leave the underground garage, but instead of circling round to the hotel to pick up its passengers it headed for Tivoli. Luckily Eric's car was just outside the bar that day, and he had no problem in following, prudently keeping four or five vehicles behind.

He had seen the gorilla pick up a young woman in the large piazza outside town, followed them back down the hill, and sat in the car until he saw them leave again a few hours later. He too had parked near the supermarket, seen them go up the stone steps under the arch, the young woman swaying and stumbling, and also saw their entry into the house. He had no idea who the young woman was, but took a note of the address, went back to his car and waited, then followed the gorilla back down the hill.

All it took then was a phone call to the increasingly reluctant mole, who was wishing he had never got into the whole thing; Mamie McCulloch was Barney's friend and

The White Sibyl

backer while Eric Moonday was obviously off his head, and of no use to the greater cause of white supremacy. However, Eric now knew who Jane Harrison was, and in his lonely feverish state began to think of her as a potential ally – an opinion based only on the fact she looked like a nice woman.

He then spent the next few days trying to catch a glimpse of her, walking from one end of her road to the other or parking outside the supermarket in case she came through the arch, but his efforts went unrewarded until the Saturday morning. She came past the supermarket and went up the hill towards the large car park. Hurriedly he followed her.

From the opposite direction Murph the location manager was making his way over Ponte Gregoriano to the large car park across from the river, a faded combat cap on the back of his head, a large green canvas holdall slung over one shoulder. Finally he could get out of there. Barney, after plaguing him for days about shooting a scene at Villa Gregoriana, had finally listened to reason. The area was too steep, the paths too narrow, and – the final clincher – it was not on the original schedule, and there was no time to apply for an additional permit. It had been one irritation in a host of minor setbacks. There had been a short circuit on the set that had nearly toasted the leading man, Ed Grayson, who was left with a nasty burn on one ankle, not to mention the disappearance of several important props and the Gaffer falling downstairs. Jinxed, thought Murph. Doesn't smell right. Even Barney had started looking uncharacteristically grim, small mouth shut tight in a discontented line, and Murph reckoned that Barney's sudden interest in the deep wooded valley was the director's way of trying to take control again, switch focus, force things to go the way he wanted. Murph had seen it before, and in the past it had worked.

That Saturday morning was bright and even mild, the air holding a springtime warmth and only a few fluffy white clouds in a pale-blue sky. Another group had arranged a private visit to Villa Gregoriana for there was a large coach parked outside the railings, a trickle of passengers emerging and congregating on the pavement. They were welcome to it, thought Murph. Soon he'd be in Rome, afternoon free as he was flying out that night, so just the time to buy a tourist doll in national costume for Juanita, who had a whole collection of them and was always pestering him to bring her back just one more; crazy about them, the kid was.

He had now crossed the road and entered the car park, impatient to get out of the town and on with his life. His hired jeep was over on the far side, and he wove decisively between the parked cars, holdall hoisted chest-high to keep it out of the way.

But just as he was crossing the last few yards he saw a woman leaning against a small blue car. The car door was open but she just stood there, shoulders drooping. He would have thought no more of it had she not looked up, and he recognised the P.A. taken on as language back-up. Jenny, no, Jane. He raised one hand in greeting, and was about to continue on his way, then saw she looked upset, face pale and worried. Silently cursing – another favourite maxim of his was 'Stay out of it whatever it is' – Murph changed direction and walked up to her. "Jane, isn't it? You OK?" he queried, resisting the impulse to put his holdall down; after all, he wasn't staying.

"Yes," she agreed tentatively, then, recognising him, a look of relief spread over her pale face. "Oh, hello, Murph. I didn't recognise you. It's just dead," she went on, gesturing at the car. "I think it's the battery. I haven't driven him for a few days."

"Humph," said Murph; he well knew the perversity of so-called inanimate objects. As he regarded the small car, he was remembering more about Jane. A pleasant woman, sweet even, though she had shown a wicked sense of humour that time the techs ganged up on her, trying to make her blush with their demands for translations of "Were you born in this dump?", "Do you put out?", "You've got terrific boobs" and suchlike. She had indeed blushed but then got out a pen and paper and scribbled down some Italian sentences, which subsequently turned out to mean "My brains are between my legs", "Go out with me and you'll have the worst time of your life", "My dick is the size of a gherkin" and other choice offerings that had the eventual recipients initially startled and then reduced to helpless laughter.

Nevertheless, it was with reluctance that he now put down the holdall, folded himself into the mini's low-slung seat, and tried the ignition; it was indeed dead as the proverbial dodo. Meanwhile Jane was looking at her watch, clutching her shoulder bag with the other hand.

"No, nothing doing," said Murph, climbing out. "Tell you what, I'll get the jump leads. Oh, Christ!" he exclaimed, now really annoyed. And no way was he going back, he'd just buy new ones.

"What?" asked Jane nervously; the exclamation had made her jump.

"I lent them to one of the guys," he said grimly, looking round threateningly as though the guy in question might magically appear, jump leads in hand, to be shouted at.

"Oh. Oh, dear," said Jane, slumping back against the car. "I ... I really have to get somewhere."

Murph hesitated, looked at her despairing face, and abandoned his plans for immediate departure. "Well, I can give you a lift," he offered, picking up the holdall, "Have to find your own way back though, 'cause I'm leaving, but if that's OK ...?"

"That's great. Thank you so much," said Jane fervently. "Actually it's not that far, just too far to w…"

There was the sudden sound of hurrying footsteps behind them, and a sour odour of unwashed clothes tainted the mild air.

"Hey, wait! I need to talk to you!" Both Jane and Murph turned. Jane, startled rather than frightened, looked round to see who the dishevelled man was talking to, but Murph recognised him. It was the crazy who had been haunting the shoot, and now he was there, shifting from one foot to the other like a little kid needing to go to the bathroom; he smelled bad, and looked worse.

"What? What d'y want?" said Murph gruffly.

"No, not you. Jane, Jane Harrison!"

"I'm … I'm sorry," she started, "but do I know you?"

"Don't talk to him, Jane," warned Murph, moving protectively closer. "He's off his rocker. Now, you leave the girl be!" he said threateningly, turning to Eric and taking a firmer grip on his holdall; he'd bop the crazy if he had to.

The man ignored Murph and fixed his eyes imploringly on Jane. "You got to help me – I know you're nice, a good person, and we can stop them. It's not him, it's her, that McCulloch woman, a filthy Jewess, worse than him but they're in it together! You've seen it – it's … it's not right, they're making it trivial so no one suspects! It … it's everything that's at stake and if they're not stopped …" He stuttered to a halt. Jane had no idea what he was talking about though the mention of Mamie had got her attention; Murph rightly guessed that "it" referred to the film, and, his pleasure at his departure now entirely ruined, lost his temper. "Get out of here, you loser!" he shouted. "And for Christ's sake take a bath!" His voice had carried as far as the people outside the gates of Villa Gregoriana and they were peering over, their expressions a mixture of surprise, curiosity and nervousness, taking in the figures of the young woman, the dishevelled scarecrow and the lanky man with the bulky holdall, who noticed their reactions and gave them a reassuring wave.

"Come on, Jane. Let's get going," Murph said, lowering

his voice and ignoring Eric completely. "I've got the car over here. You got an address for the place or something?"

"Actually it's the cemetery," said Jane, and then smiled faintly as he turned to stare at her. Wordlessly, he shifted the holdall to a more comfortable position, now gripping it as though someone might try to wrest it from his grasp. Christ ...!

Eric watched them go, mouth half-open to utter words he could not say, hands dangling uselessly as his sides, overwhelmed by the enormity of the peril and his own futile efforts. No, he had to try, had to make one last effort; he broke into a shambling run to reach his own car parked near the supermarket.

"Who is that man?" Jane asked as they drove off. "How did he know my name?"

Murph sighed, and changed gear, "Like I said – a crazy. Wrote the original script for the film and didn't like the changes."

"What changes?" Perhaps she would now find out what the film was about.

"Sorry – confidentiality agreement. If you don't know, I can't tell you."

"Oh, yes, of course, sorry," she murmured. She sat trying to remember what the man had said.

"It's not him," he had said. Barney? And then he called Mamie "a filthy Jewess". Jewess? What did that have to do with anything? The man must be mad. Jewess, she thought again, and then remembered the extra in the green room, the one with the heavy black robe, swarthy skin and huge nose.

It had not registered at the time but of course, he had been a caricature, Shylock as played to audiences in Victorian England. But the film was called *The Pope's Protocol*, so … Oh, God, who cares? she thought wearily, feeling tired and ill. Wasn't there enough without teasing her brain about the film?

The cemetery wasn't far but there was the one-way system; Jedson would have known. Having missed the turn-off to the left, which was hidden in a junction of five roads with ambiguous traffic lights, Murph had to circle round again, up towards the fortress of Pius V, down towards the river again, and off to the right, where a suburb of shops and apartment buildings prosaically heralded modern Tivoli. And it was here – as they arrived at the junction for the second time and turned off – that Eric Moonday, breathing a prayer of gratitude and clenching the steering-wheel in sweaty hands, caught up with them.

The large car park outside the cemetery doubled as a bus terminus, and a couple of the large blue coaches that plied between the outlying villages were drawn up at the far end. Murph circled round and stopped about fifty yards from the entrance, an unimposing hole in the wall with a security camera mounted to one side; the top of a small mausoleum poked above the wall.

"OK here?" asked Murph, eyes fixed on the rear-view mirror, ready for the off. Jane gathered up her bag and slithered down. "Thanks so much, Murph. And … all the best," she added.

"Yeah, you too. Take it easy, eh? Don't …" He stopped.

Jane half-turned to look at him interrogatively. "Don't?" she asked.

"No, nothing. It's just a job, right? No need to …" he came to a halt again, with no idea what impulse had prompted him to begin, but Jane was nodding. "Thanks, Murph." She suddenly smiled, an urchin's grin that lit up her face. "I love the jeep! See you" and she walked towards the gates, while Murph gunned the engine and took off. Jane's figure, last glimpsed in the rear-view mirror, looked small and thin in the yawning expanse of car park. Stay out of it, he thought, swerving out of the car park to get the hell out of there.

The cemetery consisted of two distinct areas. To the right, on the slope of a foothill, was the typical Italian necropolis, the marble family chapels and tombs giving the impression of a miniature Roman town; the downhill section, at the same level as the car park, was invisible, but above the boundary wall the tops of enormous cypresses, so huge they belonged to some Jurassic landscape, vied for space and air.

Jane paused for a moment to shade her eyes and look at them. She felt sluggish and slightly nauseous, with a nagging throb behind her eyes, the after-effects of the alcohol and 'wonderful wild sex'. Jedson had given her a love bite as well – at least, she supposed it was a love bite though the inflamed bruise looked more like the sting of a jellyfish than anything else. Her overall memory now – though she kept telling herself she had been drunk at the time – was of darkness and violence. The smooth suntanned skin had been rubbery beneath her fingers, and the large hands too eager, too ... hungry in their giving of pleasure. He had been 'all over her', as her mother might have said, and her memory gave an image of herself as a clockwork toy wound up again and again to jerk and flail. She shivered, rubbed her forehead, then looked at her watch. She was definitely late, and she made for the entrance and the *Ufficio custode*, a small modern building constructed of smoked glass and wrought iron security grills. If there was no one there, she would now have a real problem trying to find the grave on her own. The cemetery looked much bigger from the inside, with long aisles lined with tombs stretching into the distance under the shade of the giant trees.

There was a battered truck outside the office however, where a workman was securing some kind of trolley to the truck bed, watched by a small clerical type wearing fawn slacks and a checked jacket.

"She must have shelled out a lot to get that space," the clerical type was saying, gesturing with his cigarette. The workman nodded, and then straightened as his eyes became aware of Jane's approach. Incongruously, he had a grass stalk in one corner of his mouth. Jane was about to speak but the clerical type was off again. "Not to mention *your* work. That stone must have cost a good bit ..." The workman ignored the implied question, took the stalk from his mouth and gestured with it. "You have a client."

"Dead or alive?" joked the man turning. "Ah, alive. Much better so. Signorina?"

Jane repeated the story she had invented for Signora

Caponi: Elfriede Baader had been her mother's friend, Jane happened to be in Tivoli, was going to look the friend up, and then discovered she had passed away. Was there the funeral? She knew she was late, problems with her car, but could they perhaps tell her where to find the grave? The workman had turned away to finish loading, finally lifting the truck's tail-gate into place and banging home the bolts with the heel of his hand.

The clerical type, now serious and a little abashed, muttered condolences. Of course, no problem, it was at the far end, he told her, gesturing down the length of one of the long aisles. In the distance, where the overshadowing cypresses ended, sunlight gleamed on marble and stone. A lovely spot, he went on, very beautiful, very tranquil. And if the signorina wanted to take a souvenir snap – for her mother, that is – that was no problem. Jane, grappling with the notion of photographing a grave, murmured her thanks, and was turning to go when the clerical type piped up again: "Nico will give you a lift, won't you, Nico? It's a fair walk."

The other nodded, walked round the truck to open the passenger door, and then returned to climb up behind the wheel. Jane thanked the clerical type again, made her own way round, and, after two attempts, managed to heave herself up; it was higher even than the jeep. She sank back thankfully, already longing to get the visit over and done with and go back to bed. She didn't even know now why she had felt it important to come here. Better to go back to bed, and perhaps she should stop at a pharmacy as well, see if they had anything ... The truck grated into life, rolled slowly towards the distant sunlight.

Apart from wishing the visit was over, Jane was weakly thankful that she had a lift. Though slow, the truck was going much faster than she could have walked, and now she had time to take in the grid-layout of the cemetery, the aisles stretching to left and right, with their huge box-like tombs, small mausoleums, and ornately carved crosses. So close they were she could see the photographs of the dead, some in black-and-white, some in what she thought of as 'early Technicolor'. Most of the deceased were smiling, others, from an earlier age, posed formally and sedately; one tomb, glimpsed briefly to the left, obviously belonged to a child for toys and a teddy-bear had been left as well as flowers.

Finally the truck emerged into the sunlight and turned right. Here, the road described a circle, with paths leading off like the spokes of a wheel. The workman brought the truck to a halt and switched off the engine; silence fell and birdsong could be heard above the faint rumble of traffic from the main road.

"I'll show you where it is," he said; the grass stalk had disappeared. Perhaps he's eaten it, thought Jane, her mind fastening on the one small detail. He leaned across to open the truck door – instinctively she shrank back – then opened his own door. As he walked round to help her down, she suddenly saw he limped.

"Have you … hurt your leg?" she asked impulsively as she managed to slide down before he got there. He stopped, one hand resting on the bonnet of the truck. "Foot," he said.

"Work accident – but a long time ago."

"I'm … sorry," she said, wishing she had not asked such a personal question, but he just shrugged. "It's not important." He stood there waiting, a relaxed still figure in his plaid shirt and heavy work trousers. "This way."

The grave was immediately inside the cemetery wall at the end of the path. The hole had not yet been filled in and there was a mound of water-logged earth to one side, both hole and mound partially obscured by a cover of artificial plastic grass; it had obviously been used countless times before since it was worn and showed blotches of both fresh and dried mud. Had anyone come to the funeral? Jane was thinking.

"Did anyone come?" she asked the workman. "Any friends or …?" She wanted to say "mourners" but had no idea what the Italian word was.

"A priest. And her lawyer."

A trill of birdsong came from the cemetery wall, and they both glanced up to where a blackbird perched, head cocked to one side, surveying them with bright inquisitive eyes. It was then that Jane noticed the headstone leaning against the wall; it had been carefully placed on sacking on a wooden pallet to keep it clear of the muddy ground. She looked at the inscription, lips moving slightly as she read the words:

**Years will be shortened
like months.
Months like weeks.**

**Weeks like days.
Days like hours
And an hour
like a moment.**

An hour like a moment, she repeated. She went closer, bent to look at the small photograph. A thin plain face, earnest but hopeful. The dates showed that Elfriede Baader had been in her late sixties when she died but she looked very young; it must be an old photograph.

Another trill of birdsong broke her reverie. What else should she do? There was nothing here. Elfriede had bought the statue, broken it, must have sent it to Professor Caseman, and the professor had left it for Jane. To lead her to Tivoli and the White Sibyl. Was there anything else? Only … with an effort she rummaged in her bag, found her diary and a pen, and copied down the inscription and dates on an old receipt, before reluctantly turning to go; the workman was still there.

"It is a very fine headstone," she said hesitantly, and then with sudden inspiration, "Did you make it?"

He nodded again. "It is very beautiful," she added, "very … unusual. Delicate even."

Now he looked at her with more attention, and she too saw him clearly for the first time. Coarse dark hair hacked short, slanted eyes, and what she thought of as 'devil's eyebrows', black, slashing rather than arching upwards; he hadn't shaved either.

Suddenly the nausea returned with double force, a

stabbing needle of pain lancing through her temples, a wave of coldness draining the strength from her limbs. She took an uncertain step forwards, gave the workman a tremulous apologetic smile. Surely she couldn't be fainting?

But the surrounding tombs and crosses tipped and lurched, then started to gyrate in a bizarre whirling merry-go-round. She averted her eyes, half-turned towards the delicate headstone, and for a second Elfriede Baader's earnest young eyes held her own. What did she want? What could Jane do for her?

Then there was nothing more. She pitched forward, blind and deaf to the last warning trill and whir of wings as the blackbird took flight. She did not feel the arms that caught her as she fell, did not even know she had been saved.

As Murph had noticed, Barney was indeed uncharacteristically grim. The series of injuries and technical hitches had finally got to him, and the place itself was getting to him as well. His original decision to shoot the film in the darkest months of the year had seemed a stroke of genius at the time. The sub-text was that Italy was not a land of blue skies, golden sunlight, and fascinating history but one of bad weather, dangerous foreigners, and the corruption within a decaying Church. "Show 'em the underbelly of all the crap!" was how Barney expressed it.

And he had succeeded beyond all expectations – many of the actors vowed they would never set foot in Italy again, while others were aware of a creeping depression they put down to tiredness. The only exceptions were the Italian members of the crew, who viewed their co-workers as just another group of invaders, nothing compared to the Normans, Moors, French, Spanish and Germans who had tramped through the country over the millennia and then gone again – as these would.

Early that Saturday morning Barney and the rest of the crew were at Villa D'Este, outside the coffee bar and cafeteria on the long terrace beneath the villa. Coffee and breakfast had been served inside, and the shooting schedule, work sheets and script changes distributed. The scene in the enclosed courtyard of the fountain surmounted by the statue of the Sibyl had to be re-shot – yesterday's rushes had been terrible, the booming of the waters masking the dialogue so that the actors appeared to be mouthing and grimacing grotesquely. "Absolute shit!" was Barney's judgement. Neither could the background shots be used, for every frame was flawed by a wavy smudge darting from left to right; the canister of film must have been defective.

So it was that everyone was called late Friday night for a re-shoot on Saturday – a disappointment since Barney had magnanimously proclaimed a free weekend. They were so close to the final wrap and Barney had hoped to get the scene in the can, but everyone was so demotivated that he had brought out his tried-and-tested response to setbacks: pretend it wasn't happening, everything was on track and hunky-dory.

But the bad rushes made him nervous. It was a key

scene, when the American professor of the History of the Catholic Church (the actor Ed Grayson and Barney's equivalent of the Tom Hanks character) revealed the true nature of the new pope to the Vatican archivist (Miranda Hargreaves), niece of a captain in the Swiss Guard. The two stars, having motored from Rome at dawn, were sitting grumpily outside the bar, heavy overcoats over their costumes, and looking over the new scripts that Barney had just given them.

"But I don't *say* anything," protested Miranda Hargreaves, glancing up. She looked cold and pinched, and her blond hair was starting to frizz in the damp air. "What happened to all the dialogue?"

"Yeah, right," chimed in Ed Grayson. "How can anyone make sense of it when there's nothing to hear?" He bent down, rubbing irritably at his burnt ankle; it was healing very slowly.

"Now, Miranda, honey!" boomed Barney, all smiles and confidence. "Ed, my man! If you just look at the next part, you'll see we switched the dialogue down to the what-d'y'-call-it." He snapped his fingers. "The Grotto of Diana," supplied Anthea briskly, not looking up from her diary. "Right. There," said Barney, taking out a cigar and lighting it. "Where it's quiet – see, angel, see, Ed?" His voice was coaxing and soothing. He was always good with stars, not for him the Hitchcock "Actors are cattle" approach. "Just take another look, huh? And you!" he suddenly yelled at the make-up artist, who started guiltily: "Sort Miranda's hair out! She's supposed to look cool and collected, not a damn bottle brush!" He went back to scrawling notes on his shooting schedule, while the two stars studied their scripts. Miranda was frowning slightly, while Ed slumped back, the plain-glass spectacles of his role dangling from one hand. Another problem with yesterday's scene was that the glasses had misted over from the fine spray in the courtyard, giving his strong handsome face a vague watery look; he would be holding not wearing them in the re-write.

They had to admit however that Barney had solved the problem very neatly. Unwilling to sacrifice the monumental background of the cascading waters – despite the underbelly approach, he was first and foremost a film-maker – he had placed the actors further back so that only their figures were to be seen, shot from a low angle so that the layers of the fountain loomed menacingly above them (cameras being set in position in the courtyard). Their role here was simply to mime the idea of "We can't talk here." "Where then?" "Down in the Grotto of Diana away from prying eyes." There would also be shots from behind the pool (cameraman on hand with plastic-swathed camera), so that as the professor and the archivist hurried from the courtyard they would be 'watched' from that angle through the peacock fans of water. The actual revelation of the professor's appalling discovery would then take place in the peace and quiet of the Grotto (lighting guys there setting up), backlit so that the crumbling mosaics were also in evidence.

If Barney had one regret it was he had let Murph go; he *needed* Murph as a sounding board but the dour location manager must have headed out Friday night. When Anthea called Murph's on-set mobile she got the admin. office, who told her the phone was already back with them plus all the other paperwork. Job signed off and paid for, and it was anybody's guess where Murph was now – probably on his way home to Mexico, where he spent his off-work time. Still, Plod, summoned from Tivoli Terme to stand in for Jane, had turned out swell, more forceful than Jane, more ready for a crack, refreshingly direct with Barney himself, more a guy's guy in fact. Barney had even brought him along to the shoot that morning, and there he was, giving Miranda Hargreaves a coffee, making himself useful, not just standing around waiting for instructions. Barney *liked* that.

"Hey, Plod!" he yelled on a sudden thought. "Get y' ass down to the grotto-place and check to see if that old trouper the Gaffer needs anything."

"On my way, Barney," called Carl, sketching a salute and making for the steps. He was hugely enjoying himself after the days of Mamie's folksy company and Jedson's irritating cool. He had originally switched jobs, from language back-up to investor's babysitter, thinking it would lead to more important contacts, but he had completely misjudged the situation. However, now he had the chance to make good, and if Jane were ill for just a few more days …

18

Sunday 7th February

Mamie had been glad to get shot of Carl, did not care if he never re-appeared. He had been bossy (with her!), traipsed her round sights she had no desire to see, including an expanse of heaped stones nearby, supposedly the remains of some Roman emperor's villa, and – the greatest sin of all – been relentlessly cheerful the whole time. It is true she had managed to dim him down some ("You know, sweetie, there are so many *good* acne preparations these days – or is yours the *nervous* kind?") but he had been unexpectedly resilient and bounced back. More than once her fingers had positively *itched* to grab at her knitting bag, and she had started another small sweater, this one in bright yellow decorated with green bobbles, so that at least she had the smooth steel in her hands and the calming click of needles in her ears.

On Saturday evening she had called Barney, who was in high spirits after a successful day's shoot at the monumental fountain. The problems had been ironed out, the rushes were good, and there were now only a couple of scenes to complete; they should have a wrap before the following weekend.

"So, y' see, Mame, it's all coming together," he bellowed joyously. "Day off tomorrow, so why don't y' come up for lunch? Nothing big, just the two of us, hey?" He lowered his voice. My, but Barney could be so *obvious* at times! "You can fill me on the other thing. You been in touch with … uh … London, right?"

"I absolutely have, Barney," she assured him, ignoring a prickle of irritation. "And you have just read my mind. Why, I was going to suggest you come down here, but a drive up would be real nice." As she put the phone down, she was thinking hard; she needed to get the copy of Jane's keys from Jedson.

The day was fine enough to eat outside, and a table had been set on the balcony of Barney's suite. It already held a bottle of red wine, squares of cheese, olives, bread and some small triangles of toast covered with pâté; it was to be a local lunch that day. Barney was standing outside, hands in pockets, gazing moodily down into the wooded valley of Villa Gregoriana. A scene there would have been something, but – hell! – after all the problems maybe it had turned out for the best. He heard footsteps and turned round with a huge smile; him and Mame hadn't got together since the first evening at the hotel, and it was good to see her. She was looking a bit thin. "Hey, there. You OK, angel?" he asked as Jedson pulled out the chair for her to sit down.

"I'm good, Barney," she assured him a trifle breathlessly, settling back; she was wearing one of her pants suits, topped with a shawl and a silk scarf tucked high up round her neck. "My, and isn't it so pretty here?" She settled her knitting bag beside her, and then the two waited until the black-suited figure had disappeared into the suite.

"Now, you just tell me about the shoot, Barney," she said warmly. "It's real good news you're about done." And Barney regaled her with gossip from the set: how the Gaffer, after his fall, had insisted on being carried in to oversee the scene in the grotto – a real trouper; Miranda had been a bit pettish – after the initial feeding frenzy the media had all gone back to Rome – so he had arranged for some fans to mob her for autographs one morning ("You surely are *thoughtful*, Barney."); the PR guy had been pleading for more details about the film to jazz up the press releases, and now had a couple of carefully selected stills to weave some magic with. All in all, good news, and now, what about the London thing?

Mamie pursed her lips: "The aunt wants more money, Barney," she said tersely, now all business.

"Jeez, Mame! We already went way over our original figure!"

She smiled, not a pleasant smile, and smoothed the tapestry material of the knitting bag. "Well, I guess we didn't reckon with her conscience – must have grown a mite."

"So," he queried, "what d'y think?"

"What I think," she said with great deliberation, "is that maybe Jedson would like a trip to London, he could have a talk with her, kind of explain that a deal is surely a deal."

Now it was Barney who pursed his lips. "You reckon?" he asked doubtfully.

Mamie had an impulse so strong she could almost *taste* it - to pull out one of her needles and ram it up into his throat, just under the fleshy jaw there, angled upwards towards the big red ear. My, wouldn't *his* eyes pop out with surprise before he went crashing down like a felled redwood. Tim-ber! She pulled herself together. This was *Barney*.

"Nothing *heavy*, Barney sweetie," she murmured reassuringly, now folding her hands primly in her lap. "Nothing ... untoward. But Jedson does have a *presence*, you know."

"Sure, sure," he agreed hastily. "Just ... England, that's all. Back home, no problem, but those Brits are weird, no sense of proportion."

"Jedson is just *fine*, Barney," she urged him breathily, and he saw she had one of her knowing smiles; she had already figured it out. "He's their *escort*, don't you see? We were worried about her *managing*, what with the girlie and the luggage and all. Jedson is there to *help*, and I don't think he need even *mention* money."

By the time she had finished this persuasive speech Barney was grinning. Mame had indeed figured it out.

"Yeah. Don't know about you, Mame, but I've had the shit worried out of me, just thinking of them all alone," he said, now laughing outright; the big sound boomed out across the quiet valley below, and two pigeons which had been drowsing on the roof took off with a frightened flap of wings.

Her smile deepened, then her expression grew serious, and her hands sought out the knitting bag. "Oh, and talking of Brits, Barney, I'm afraid I have some very *bad* news for you. I really didn't want to tell you, but then ... it's *not* the kind of thing one can just *ignore*."

"What's that?" he asked sharply. "Any bother with the hotel? You just ..."

"No, no, nothing like that. It's about that British girl, Jane."

"Oh, yeah, off sick just now."

"Well, I invited her down to eat just a few days ago, and I'm sorry to say she *took* something of mine, *stole* it, Barney. Would you believe it?" She stopped, shaking her head in mock sorrow, though her small eyes were calculating.

"Call the cops, Mame," he said instantly. "And I'll fire her ass. Got Plod on the job now, and he's working out fine. No problem. What d'she take anyway?"

"It was when I was up in Rome on the London business. I came across one of those real cute little antique shops." He looked bored. Old stuff was OK in films but ... "No, I *re-alise* that's it's not your thing, Barney, but I came across a darling little statue – about so high" She sketched the height, some eight inches, with her pudgy hands. "It was *just* the thing for one of our speciality rooms. You know – the one with the choice of artistic dildos?"

Barney started laughing again. "You sure are creative, Mame!" He became serious. "But like I said, you call the cops, I'll fire her ass. No problem."

Mamie conjured up a very fair imitation of concern. "The thing is, Barney, I don't want any *unpleasantness*. She's a nice enough girl. Maybe had a moment's *temptation*, or maybe ... you know ... maybe she can't *help* herself."

"You're too forgiving, Mame."

"No, no," she waved away the suggestion. "But I was thinking. The film is about done, and if she's off sick, she doesn't need to come back, does she? That's what you can tell her. No fuss, and you just pay her off, Barney."

"And the whatsit she took?"

"Well, that was in the rest room, Barney, and she must have slipped it into that big shoulder bag of hers when she popped in there. *But* - she must have taken things out to hide it way down, and then forgot her keys on the side there." She produced two keys, laid them on the table. "You just ask that nice boy Carl to go and get it when she's not there. Tell him it's a prop she was looking after and that it's needed. No fuss, Barney, that's the thing. I'm sure she's just *mortified* now."

Perhaps she had embellished a shade too much but Barney hadn't noticed. "Don't you want to send the boy wonder?"

She gave a tinkling laugh. "Oh, Jedson was so

disappointed – had a little *thing* for her, so it's best we leave him out of it. Anyway, he'll be on his way to London now, won't he?"

When Jane woke up she was no longer in the cemetery – that was obvious – neither was she in hospital for there were no hospital noises, nor any smell of disinfectant or floor polish. Slowly she opened her eyes and saw that she was not at the B&B either. Not two feet away two vivid green eyes were regarding her intently.

"Finally!" exclaimed the Sibyl with an explosive huff of breath. "Here, drink this," and she put a small bottle into Jane's hand, similar to the one she had produced at Villa D'Este. It was not water but tasted like some distillation of flowers, moss, and leaves, cool as a draught from an underground spring. As Jane sipped it, she began to feel stronger and more awake. The nausea and nagging headache were gone, and for the first time in days she felt rested and well. And she was hungry too.

"Better?" snapped the Sibyl, and then, not waiting for an answer. "Drink it all, and then come to the living-room." And without another word she disappeared through the door.

Now, Jane pulled herself into a sitting position and looked around. It seemed to be a small box room containing only the narrow truckle bed where she lay covered by a blue blanket, a shelf of books and a vinyl armchair with spindly legs. The Sibyl's spare room? she thought wonderingly. But how …?

She obediently drained the bottle and disentangled herself from the blanket. Her shoes were set neatly under the bed, and as she bent to put them on, she felt a slight pulling at the skin of her neck. She reached up and her fingers encountered some sort of dressing over the love-bite; she blushed. Wild, wonderful sex, she thought wryly. Still … she got up, taking the bottle with her, and resolutely opened the door.

It was indeed the apartment in Via Platone Tiburtino, with the wood-burning stove glowing behind its smoke-dimmed glass, the two shabby armchairs, one with Jane's shoulder bag hanging from the back, the old-fashioned sideboard, and large table by the window. The morning sunlight had gone and the window framed a billowing cloudscape of grey and white shot through with silver. The wide sill was covered with clay pots of primroses, and the three white cats were sitting on the table, each stretched out with front paws neatly together, like three small lions on an ancient coat-of-arms. They looked up as Jane entered the room, but this time did not run to the door, nor form a watching triangle around her, merely looked and blinked.

"Here, by the fire," ordered the Sibyl, suddenly turning and disappearing into the box room; she re-emerged with the blanket, arranged it over the chair and pushed Jane down with the bossy briskness of a nanny. "There!" she said. "Now, something to eat …" And off she went again, this time into the small kitchen. After some banging and clattering, she came back with a tray and placed it on Jane's lap, before seating herself in the chair opposite. The tray held a large cup of bean and bacon soup – which smelled delicious – and chunks of the local bread.

"How did I get here?" asked Jane. At least she hadn't had to say "Where am I?" she thought. Was it even the same day? She began to eat; the soup tasted delicious as well.

"My son brought you here of course," said the other matter-of-factly.

"Son!" exclaimed Jane, almost upsetting the tray and so astonished she did not even notice the sudden personal "my"; her last memory was the cemetery. "Do you mean the man at the gate? Or the workman? Is he your son?"

"Stonemason," corrected the Sibyl sharply. "Craftsman. Workman indeed!" Her family pride had obviously been offended.

"I'm sorry," Jane murmured. Son! She couldn't get over it. "I didn't know ... I didn't ..." in confusion she took refuge in sipping at the soup.

"... imagine?" finished the other, and now she was smiling, a secret knowing smile that hinted at remembered passion. "And why not? Is not the Sibyl the *prediletta*, the darling, of Venus?" The third person had appeared again. "When he saw you had been poisoned ..."

"Poisoned!" Again Jane was speechless. The Sibyl was dropping bombshells as casually as scattering rose petals on a counterpane, and from her face there was more to come. "*Latet anguis*," she intoned as if it explained everything, then, "The serpent ever lies in wait."

Jane's hand went instinctively to the dressing at her

throat; she had thought it resembled a sting.

"No, not that," said the Sibyl impatiently. "The male to whom you gave yourself so thoughtlessly is a minion, nothing more. A parasite taking nourishment from the Other but in itself a nullity." She gave an abrupt little nod, while Jane could only look at her wordlessly. How had she known?

"Now listen," she continued, green eyes glowing with reflected light from the fire. "The time is nigh – the 16th, the place, the Sibyl's Temple on the hill. You have the statue safe?"

Jane did not immediately answer, intent on trying to assimilate so much new information. The 16th. That was … ten days away, if today was still today; she really must ask. And the Sibyl's Temple? Which one was that? If the round one was to Vesta, it must be the …

"The statue!" insisted the other. "You have it safe?"

"Please … just wait a moment," Jane pleaded. "Is today still …" she hesitated, "Saturday?"

"Sunday. Sunday afternoon."

"Sunday!" She had lost twenty-four hours – no wonder she was hungry – and now she was doing nothing but repeat everything being said to her. She ate more soup and bread, and the Sibyl waited, though her eyes snapped with annoyance. Today was Sunday, the … 7th in that case, which meant only nine days left. Something else occurred to her:

"And is the Sibyl's Temple the rectangular one? Above Villa Gregoriana?"

"Of course! Where else would it be?" The Sibyl was

offended again. It was like being near an unpredictable firecracker that kept spluttering and cracking into life. "Now, is the statue safe?" she demanded again.

"Yes, but ..."

"But what!" The Sibyl had jumped to her feet and was glaring accusingly.

"No, it's just that I haven't mended it yet," admitted Jane. "The main part is at home – at the B&B, I mean, but the broken piece is here." Carefully placing the tray on the floor, she unhooked the shoulder bag from the back of the chair and felt inside. The head was there, wrapped in paper tissues, as she had wrapped the Venus figurine the previous year. "I just kept forgetting to do it," she explained feebly.

The Sibyl took it from her, freed it of its wrapping and held it up to look at it, now smiling with pleasure. "I will keep this, and you must bring me the other part."

"Yes," agreed Jane meekly. "I'll go now." She started to get up – she wanted to be alone as well, to sort everything out in her mind – but the Sibyl was shaking her head:

"Tomorrow," she said. "You still have the poison in your veins. Rest and get well." And then, ruining the apparent solicitude: "There can be no mistake. You must be strong for what is to come. Now, go, sleep."

19

Monday 8th – Tuesday 9th February

On Monday Jane was pronounced "still under the influence" – drink driving, she thought bemusedly – and she would spend another two days confined to bed, sleeping, being woken up to drink more of the cool distillation, and eating. The only contact she had with the outside world was on Monday morning when she phoned Anthea to say she would be back at work as soon as possible. Anthea had not made a fuss, merely said. "Don't bother – we've nearly finished so you're not needed. Room's paid for till Saturday but you can just leave when you want. Oh, and don't forget to call in at admin – sign off and all that. OK?"

Jane started to thank her but Anthea had already hung up – completely normal, and Jane thought nothing of it, she was actually glad that she was free of work commitments. Now she knew the date of the ceremony was the 16th

February she would ask her landlady if she could stay on, pay the difference herself; with the time of year and the film finishing the apartment would probably be free anyway.

There was also time to question the Sibyl more closely; Jane still did not know if she had another name. Some of the information she had already read about – all the pages and pages she had copied from Internet – so at least she was not completely submerged in new names and multiple legends. The Sibyl, when on the subject of the past, moved through her material with the agility of a fish in its native element, but she had still not answered the main question, the only question that Jane wanted answered:

"But what about the *ceremony*?" she asked. "What happens? What do I have to *do*?" She was remembering Nemi and the battle in the wood above the sanctuary – and she was also remembering the fear, then the sadness and loss that had followed their victory.

"Not your concern," snapped the Sibyl, "but you must be there." She *had* remembered the ceremony, hadn't she?

No further details were forthcoming however and so Jane concentrated on the immediate future, that was, get well, go home, collect the statue from the cupboard in her room and deliver it to the Sibyl, who would make it whole again.

It was fortunate that Jane did not know that the statue had already been stolen, and now stood on the round polished table in the drawing room of Signora Zauli's apartment.

Outside, the evening wind whined and moaned, even stirring the long velvet curtains as it forced its way through every crack and cranny of the warped window-frames. The room was a vast dark cavern, dimly illuminated by sparsely-placed lamps, but for all its size it was hot, too hot even for Mamie, as though the floor itself rested on a platform of fire.

Seated opposite her hostess, Mamie watched complacently as the other carefully freed the statue from its cotton wrapping. *Now* they were set! Easy as pie, and twice as tasty.

But when finally the statue was revealed, Signora Zauli recoiled, head thrown back with such force that the pale column of her neck arched and stretched. Suddenly she was standing, the movement so fast and fluid that her body seemed to have reared upwards with no need of support from her legs.

"But this is useless!" Her voice was a furious hiss; her long white fingers curled and clenched about the statue as if she would willingly crush it to dust.

"Why? You wanted the damn thing, and here it is!" Mamie's southern drawl had completely disappeared, and her voice held the rough hectoring of a bar-room brawl; one of her hands had dug into the folds of her knitting bag.

"It is broken, you foolish woman! Broken, it has no power! *Now* do you understand?" Signora Zauli's expression was venomous, her eyes gleaming black through narrowed eyelids, and had Mamie been made of softer stuff, she would have quailed before their gaze. As it was, she first glared back, and then gradually the full extent of the disaster began to dawn; she half-rose, the white smudge of her face briefly mirrored in the table's gleaming surface, then sank back. She had withdrawn her hand from the bag, and was now twisting and worrying at the bag's tapestry material. "And now ...?" she whispered.

But Signora Zauli was no longer there. She had replaced the statue on the table, and was walking the length of the dark cavern – from the massive door with its serpentine carvings to the wine-red velvet curtains, from the wine-red velvet curtains to the gleaming table, from the gleaming table to weave between formal brocaded armchairs, heavy foot-rests and marble statues. Her figure glided from dark to light to dark as she passed between the lamps, her elongated shadow sliding across the walls and high frescoed ceiling. As she paced, she murmured, murmured and crooned, at one point pausing to caress a sculpture of a dragon large as a mastiff. Mamie watched, scratched her neck, looked at the broken statue with loathing, and waited. Finally, the other returned and sank gracefully onto another chair; she was smiling.

"It is near," she said slowly. "It is not lost." She sighed – but with satisfaction and now her eyes were soft and languid: "The vision did not lie, merely ... played with the truth, showed us the base of the statue, and withheld the head." Now she laughed outright, indulgently, as if admiring a clever game. Mamie looked at her in baffled anger, and then felt the cool steel of her needles beneath her fingers; her hand had crept into the knitting bag again, and again she withdrew it. *After*, she told herself, *after*. Her list was growing. Only the promise of *after* was now stopping her. "So what now, sweetie?" she asked, the warm southern tones back in evidence. "You have a *plan*, I'm sure."

The other was toying with her lustrous coils of hair, still faintly smiling, her expression far away. She cast a knowing glance at her companion. "Oh, yes, Mrs McCulloch. I have. Though it entails more effort, and more effort must be rewarded, as I'm sure you understand."

"That's just *fine*, sweetie. And you'll let me *know*? Soon?"

When the American woman had gone, Signora Zauli was still smiling, though now the smile was a painted mask she had forgotten to take off. She did not care about the money, had asked for it out of contempt. Americans, they really believed that their money-god was all-powerful when *real* power ... she looked towards the windows, listened. Nothing. Only the wind. It had dropped slightly, and now merely sighed and whimpered, its sound coming faintly through the thin window-panes. A good night for what she had to do, this time without the McCulloch woman's distracting presence. Later she would go out, return to the *Mensa Ponderaria*. Her smile deepened, became natural. How apt. That small ancient building, still miraculously intact after two millennia, had once housed the official weights and measures of the Roman Empire. The centres of the stone counters had been hollowed out into a line of cavities, each cavity a different size, each size corresponding to a bronze bowl, each bowl representing an exact measure. Trade, commerce, and ... money.

She laughed. Apt indeed! They too had worshipped money, praying to Hercules to aid them in their affairs. Hercules. God of trade, but often portrayed with a serpent, emblematic of the two he had killed in his child's cradle.

And as the early Christians had hidden their worship in the sign of the fish, so had followers of the old religion, the shunned religion, hidden their master in the symbol of another. The Mensa Ponderaria, repository of weights and measure, was also the repository of that ancient hidden power.

20

Wednesday 10th – Thursday 11th February

It was with a light heart that Jane left the apartment in Via Platone Tiburtino on the Wednesday morning. The wind that had rushed and sighed for much of the night had swept the sky clean and cloud-free, and though shaded corners still shone damp, the road was dry. She felt well and rested, and hopeful for the first time in days – not only would there be an end to what seemed an endless upsetting muddle, but finally she would be able to carry out Professor Caseman's last wishes. Then, she would see; she would have to find another job but that could wait until she returned to Rome; her mind refused to dwell on the intervening time. All she had to do now was to take the statue to the gift shop later that morning and give it to the Sibyl. Then it was a matter of waiting until the following Tuesday.

She reached the bottom of the steep alleyway and

paused. If she turned right the B&B was only ten minutes away; obliquely to the left was the road to Ponte Gregoriano with the Hotel delle Sirene on the other side, while directly left, its beginning tucked between narrow houses, Via della Sibilla slanted down towards the two temples. On impulse she walked that way; she wanted to look at the Sibyl's temple again.

She passed the closed gift shop – the Sibyl had shooed her from the apartment early, saying she had "matters to attend to" – and found the opening to the courtyard leading to the temples. Again she was struck at how close the houses were, only a few yards away, the ancient and more recent separated by an iron fence and an open strip of gravel. The glass door to the modern building of the snack bar and tourist office was open, though there were no customers in sight.

She stood in front of the rectangular shell of the Sibyl's Temple. How gaunt it looked, how empty, merely a three-sided roofless box – nothing like the wooded clearing where last year's battle had taken place. She turned and walked between the temples to the terrace overlooking the valley of Villa Gregoriana. Here, behind the Temple of Vesta, where the strip of gravel was wider, the bench was empty of visitors. Jane crossed to the railing. The sun was rising over the mountains above the cemetery, invisible from this viewpoint, and she thought back to the weekend: how ill she had felt that day in the car park, Murph's fortuitous arrival, the wild young man who had accosted them (and where did he fit in if he fitted in at all?). Then there had been the cemetery itself, the clerical type and the workman, no, *stonemason*. The Sibyl's *son*? How and where? They looked nothing like each other – the one with pale frizzy hair and vivid green eyes, the other stocky, dark, with slanting (brown?) eyes and black slashing eyebrows. Curiouser and curiouser, she thought. "He saw you had been poisoned." Which must have been sometime after (during?) the lunch with Mamie and the afternoon with … Her mind shied and veered. Thank heavens she wouldn't be seeing him again, at least, she hoped not. That hairless rubbery skin … Instinctively her hand rose to touch the dressing on her neck hidden under her jacket collar. She hadn't even looked at it, didn't want to. The stonemason on the other hand (did he have a name?) was swarthy, his skin natural (weather-beaten? No, that was for old sailors). Well, anyway, he had helped her, made sure she was safe. In the instant before she fainted she had a dim memory of reaching out to him, just after that last whirling vision of the delicate headstone. **Years will be shortened like months. Months like weeks. Weeks like days. Days like hours, and an hour like a moment.** So short, but encapsulating the passing of time, time rushing forwards but also backwards to the briefest of flashes.

"Miss Harrison?" queried a soft voice beside her; Jane had heard no sound of footsteps on the gravel underfoot.

Startled, she half-turned to find a young woman beside her. No, not young, that was the first impression given by the skilfully-applied make-up and shining black hair. The woman stood there, dressed in shades of evening: a dark grey raincoat that glinted as though interwoven with silk, a wide purple scarf about her shoulders with a heavy brooch nestling in its folds, and suede boots of an even deeper purple; one white hand tipped with blood-red nails held the scarf high about her neck as though she were cold.

"Yes?" said Jane. "Sorry. Do we know each other? I've met so many people on the film set perhaps …." She trailed off, knowing full well she would have remembered such a striking face.

"You may call me Signora Zauli," replied the other, "though it is of little importance. I see you were looking at the temple." She smiled. "Perhaps you were wondering about the ceremony? About the statue? Thinking about *repairing* it perhaps. Since you know that broken it has no power."

Jane stared at her. The shining threads of the raincoat danced and glittered, the top of the heavy brooch – a jewelled circlet Jane now saw – momentarily reared from the folds of the scarf.

"Who are you? What … what are you talking about?" Even to her own ears she sounded unconvincing, the words a feeble ploy to gain time.

The woman's smile held a tinge of contempt. "Come now, Miss Harrison, let us not waste time. We both know that a ceremony of power is to be enacted on the 16th, that the statue is essential to its completion, and that our mutual friend Mrs McCulloch is also concerned, in her case, as a matter of life and death."

"I don't understand," said Jane helplessly. "What …?"

"You will not find the statue when you return to your apartment," stated the woman crisply. "I have it." And now she smiled in triumph, dark eyes flaring and glowing.

Jane's fingers had tightened on the strap of her shoulder bag. Thank heavens she had left the head of the statue with the Sibyl ....

The woman's gaze was calculating as it rested on the shoulder bag. "But you no longer have the missing part – a great pity, otherwise you could give it to me now and there is an end to the matter." Her voice was musing as she went on: "The statue is useless without the head, as equally, the head alone is useless. We have a common problem, Miss Harrison."

Jane had gathered her scattered wits. She had no doubt that "Signora Zauli" was telling the truth. She would not find the statue in the cupboard, and the statue broken could not be used.

"So, what do you suggest?" she said, her tone as crisp as the other's had been.

There was no immediate reply. Signora Zauli was looking out over the still valley, calm in the morning sunlight. Then, slowly, "We both have an interest in the completion of the ceremony. And since neither will relinquish their part, it follows that we must celebrate the rites together. Neither can trust the other so we must meet here at the temple, each bringing a part."

Jane nodded. She would have to go back to Via Platone Tiburtino, tell the Sibyl. What had Signora Zauli said? "You no longer have the missing part – a great pity, otherwise I would take it now." Her skin crawled. She must return now, warn the Sibyl. What if the other tried to take it by force?

For the first time the smile left the other's face. If she had read Jane's mind, her findings gave her no pleasure: "Tell your ... friend of our meeting, tell her to come with you to the temple at ten on the evening of the 16th. With the missing part." And with that she turned, strolled away, and disappeared round the corner of the Sibyl's Temple.

For a moment Jane stood, struggling yet again with uncertainty and fear, and then she sprinted to the corner of the temple, no clear thought of what she would say if she did catch up with the woman.

But the strip of gravel and the area in front of the snack bar were empty. The only person in sight was a girl in overalls half-heartedly raking dead leaves from a narrow flowerbed. She looked up when she heard Jane's approach, then went back to her raking. Jane looked again at the bare rectangular shell. Could the ceremony be completed in that way, by two opposing forces? Good and evil uniting? Gripping the strap of her shoulder bag more tightly now, she hurried away. She did not see the scarecrow figure of Eric Moonday peering through the plate-glass window of the snack bar.

The way back seemed much longer – the courtyard, the narrow length of Via della Sibilla – the gift shop still closed – past the restaurant, into and across the intersection, right up the steep alleyway to the front door – open – and up the stairs.

But when she pounded on the door of the apartment

there was no answer. For minutes it seemed it remained stubbornly closed, and then – finally – opened a crack, and the Sibyl's annoyed face peered out. "Later!" she ordered, closing the door. Jane knocked again, torn between urgency and embarrassment at the noise she was making; the knocking reverberated through the stairwell. Any time now someone will come out and complain, she thought frantically, all sense of proportion gone. Oh, *why* doesn't she answer!

Just then the door opened again and the Sibyl was there. She made no move to let Jane enter however and remained barring the opening; over her shoulder Jane could see a large green bowl set on the table by the window, the three white cats grouped around it. "Please listen," she said, now whispering, and rubbing her hand; it was sore and throbbing after all the knocking. "A woman approached me. She said her name was Signora Zauli, she …. "

"That is not her name," retorted the other.

"But who is she? She said she has the statue, and … and … I believe her. She wants us to go to the temple on Tuesday at ten carry out the … ceremony together."

The green eyes narrowed, but the Sibyl merely gave an abrupt nod. "So, we will go."

"But you didn't answer my question. Who is she?"

The door began to close. "As there is the White Sibyl, so there is the Black," came the words. "It is written. Go now. Return at nine on Tuesday. Be *ready*," and Jane was left standing and staring in defeat at the pitted wood of the door. Enrico Mattei was sitting in a coffee bar, the same bar in

The White Sibyl

Piazza Garibaldi on the edge of town where he had met Jane, sipping his usual lemon tea and perusing the carnival programme. With only days left before the final evening and its ceremonial burning of King Carnival, he was feeling increasingly pressured. The out-of-towners had taken up most of his time – pleasurably as far as the Italian groups went, for they kindly spoke standard Italian to him; Enrico, for all his knowledge of languages could understand little of Venetian, Sicilian or Sardinian dialects. The Spanish *coros* too had been both co-operative and out-going, even making the rounds of the restaurants in Tivoli one evening to play their *Carnival Tango* – a huge success. And the French contingent – though slightly over-conscious of the glamour of their native city Nice – had been fine. No, it was the Croatian and American groups which had taxed his energies. None of the Croatian bell-ringers spoke English or Italian, and though they had brought a manager/translator, every suggestion, explanation or problem had to be first translated, then discussed by the five, before a group reaction was forthcoming and some arrangement made; it was a lengthy process, especially since two of the bell-ringers seemed to be embroiled in an on-going personal feud that involved disagreeing with whatever the other had said.

As for the Americans from New Orleans, they spoke English so *fast*. Not only that but they would suddenly lapse into a sort of patois that bore no resemblance to the French Enrico had studied. The only exception was the extra sixth member of the group, a beautiful woman of uncertain age who spoke a slow lilting English very easy to understand. At first Enrico had been enchanted by both her accent and the languid gaze of her dark eyes, but that was before he overheard her reading aloud the English translation of the carnival programme to the others, the translation he himself had done.

"And they have make-uppers." she had murmured slowly, tapping at the sheet with one long red nail. "And animators. And – how sweet – a competition for the best masked baby."

Enrico had gone away and dolefully regarded the programme. He wished now he had asked Jane Harrison, the nice English woman, to check his translation, but it had seemed so easy at the time, just he had been busy and dashed it off. Of course he should have known that *truccatrici* were 'make-up artists', and *animatori* were 'entertainers'; he just hadn't thought. But what was wrong with 'masked babies' for *bambini mascherati*? That seemed right.

He sipped at his tea and looked at the remaining days. This was Thursday, and there were events planned for later that day, then Friday, Saturday, Sunday, and finally, Tuesday 16th. He opened his diary, a mammoth leather affair bulging with bits of paper, to make sure he had marked when he was on duty. He wasn't needed for the exhibition of martial arts that afternoon, nor for the judging of the *bambini mascherati* in the evening. Tomorrow, Friday – he checked the programme, which read:

Serata di gala in maschera con musica e spettacolo jazz dal vivo presso il ristorante LA SIBILLA nel centro storico Castrovetere, ingresso con prevendita.

On a sudden thought he compared it with his English translation. "Masked gala evening with live music and jazz at the La Sibilla restaurant in the Castrovetere historical centre." That was OK, and then … "*Cazzo!*" he muttered when he saw what followed: "entrance with pre-selling". What had he been thinking of? Of *course* he knew it should be "booking required". Well, he *had* booked for the New Orleans group to go. They had wanted to hear the jazz, and also agreed to wear their costumes, so at least that was done. Then he would be accompanying them to translate – his heart quailed – and generally make sure they enjoyed themselves. Oh, and make sure they had *caffé americano* rather than espresso after the meal. *Cazzo*, he whispered again into his tea.

Jane too was looking at a translation of Italian into English, but whereas Enrico was frowning, Jane was smiling, charmed by the enthusiastic – though erroneous – rendering, and mentally translating it back into Italian, where it was much more at home.

After her abortive attempt to talk to the Sibyl – and why *had* she refused to let Jane enter, had even refused to discuss what they should do? – Jane went back to the B&B, feeling restless and at odds with herself and the world. She hesitated before opening the door of her rooms, but inside everything was in order. Only, when she hurried to the cupboard and threw the door open, the statue was gone. It was no surprise – she had not expected to find it there – but even so her depression deepened. She wandered aimlessly about the sitting room, picked up a tattered magazine, put it down again, and then – almost a physical effort she felt so drained – went to get her computer from the bottom of the wardrobe. Well, if the Sibyl wanted to treat her so ambiguously, on the one hand like some kind of indispensable element to the ceremony ("the stranger"), on the other excluded from any real knowledge, she would just find out for herself. She went straight to the Google site, this time searching for "Carnival", and one of the first references on the page started:

<u>History of Carnival Origin: Farewell to Meat in Italy or Dionysia ...</u>

This was more like it, and she settled back to read:

How is wonderful magical holiday come from and where its sources? Of course, nothing born in an empty place, and no single opinion on these questions.
It is known that holidays was celebrated in the pre-Christian time and had many common with present carnivals: In the Rome it was heathen holidays, named the Saturnalia and initiated to the Saturn, god of grain, vegetation and wine. The general idea of the feast consists to invert the ordinary motion of life in time. During two weeks all class boundaries was erased by nonpublic law of festival: the rich and poor was equalized in rights, children headed families, slaves could sit freely with theirs masters at the table and demand from them a subordination, and for reason do not spoil the merriment - everybody hid their faces behind masks.

Also, a pseudo-king was chosen at the time of the holiday and in the end of Saturnalias he must be to die by any ways: to be burned, hanged and etc. After Christianity became popularity, all heathen feasts were forgotten.

And only thousands years later, in the Venice of Italy, it was created merry and motley holiday, which was celebrated every year before the beginning of the traditional Christian fasting of Lent, at that period Catholics do not eat the meat.

By the time she had finished her depression had lifted – the style was so jolly, so … frisky. She returned to the top and read it again slowly. "How is wonderful magical holiday come from?" the article chirped. "Nothing born in an empty place," it philosophised confidingly. "And for reason do not spoil the merriment - everybody hid their faces behind masks," it explained ungrammatically but quite clearly. It was only "The general idea of the feast consists to invert the ordinary motion of life in time" that she did not understand. The ordinary motion of life in time? It made no sense the second time round either.

She created a file and copied over the extract, smiling again as her eyes rested on "it was created merry and motley holiday." Merry and motley holiday. Well, why not? It had a ring to it. She went back to the Google page, and another heading caught her eye:

Carnival - Origins of the Carnival season

Here, the English was correct and even scholarly.

It is sometimes said that this festival came from Saturnalia, Saturn's festival, and Lupercalia [1]. In the later Roman period, these festivals were characterized by wanton raillery and unbridled freedom, and were in a manner a temporary subversion of civil order. Historians think that this spirit was transmitted to the Carnival.

Ah, something she recognised – this page mentioned Lupercalia, the festival of Faunus Lupercus, the Roman Pan. There at last was the connection between February and Faunus on the one hand and Carnival on the other, the 16th February in particular. She went back to compare the two articles, noticed with amusement that the "merry and motley holiday" of the first article was described as "wanton raillery and unbridled freedom" in the second, while "all class boundaries was erased" became "a temporary subversion of civil order." The second article went on to quote the theory that the festival marked the beginning of spring and was intended to scare evil spirits away. She sat back and thought. February was the month of purification, Lupercalia was celebrated in honour of Faunus, and was an openly sexual festival; she remembered the photographs of Faunus in art with his horns and leering smile, not reassuring at all. But then again those were more recent interpretations, because while Faunus stood for wildness and unbridled freedom – to borrow a phrase from the second article – he was prepared for by the Vestal Virgins and their rites of purification.

There had been something else too, in the frisky article. She checked. There it was: "Also, a pseudo-king was chosen at the time of the holiday and in the end of Saturnalias he must be to die by any ways: to be burned, hanged and etc."

So, the freedom and licence of the holiday – the

pleasures of the flesh – followed by the symbolic destruction of the flesh in the person of the 'pseudo-king'. Clearing away the old to make way for the new.

King, she thought. Another king. Like the Rex Nemorensis, the King of the Woods. She sat back, her earlier good humour evaporating like smoke. But what did it all mean now, she wondered. What was going to happen the following Tuesday?

21

Friday 12th – Sunday 14th February

"Why, and aren't you just the *cutest* thing!" exclaimed Mamie happily, one gloved hand waving the small sweater she had made at the nursing home in Nemi, the one in two shades of pink with the bows and matching scarf. "Look here at what I've brought you, sweetie. Now, isn't this just *fine*, and won't it look just *perfect* with that lovely blond hair of yours?"

The child, the 'freak', had been brought to Tivoli itself, for although Tivoli Terme was quieter and more out of the way, those very qualities made it more likely that she would be noticed and remembered should there be any problems. Tivoli on the other hand was teeming with strangers, and now that the film crew were packing up, any comings or goings would go unnoticed in the general confusion; she could be anybody's child.

She and the aunt, thoughtfully accompanied by an ever-present Jedson, had been installed in a suite at the Hotel delle Sirene, one of the smaller suites, far below Barney's luxurious penthouse. Mamie had come up to meet them, and the three were sitting in the suite's reception-room. The aunt, a thin angular woman with limp hair scraped into a lopsided bun, an expression of distaste on her face, was sitting bolt-upright, clutching her handbag before her, as though on a train filled with thieves and prostitutes on its way to an unpleasant destination. Beside her on the couch, the child, blond hair plaited into two stiff pigtails – obviously the aunt's handiwork – sat doll-like, her back straight against the cushions, her thin legs sticking out at angles; she looked much younger than ten.

"Now, sweetie, you just call me Auntie Mame," Mamie went on, feverish and exultant at how well everything was going, though her hands were so *hot* in the gloves. "Me and your other auntie here go *way* back, isn't that right, Doreen, honey?"

The aunt's expression of distaste deepened but she nodded in confirmation: "That's right," she pronounced stiffly. The child regarded Mamie blankly, looked at the small sweater, then transferred her gaze to the ceiling as though searching for something. She seemed to find what she was looking for in the pink mouldings, for she now regarded her aunt, and said expressionlessly but clearly: "Something is rotten in the state of Denmark." Her gaze then returned to its study of the ceiling.

"What's that, sweetie?" asked Mamie, perplexed, the

sweater still half-raised.

The aunt's lips tightened. "Mowenna … Mowenna!" she said, giving the child's arm a shake.

A few seconds elapsed before the child replied: "Madam, I am here, what is your will?" though all the while studying the ceiling.

"Go and look out of the window." Again there was an eerie pause, then the child replied with a kind of mournful sigh: "I must hence to wait."

"Yes, go on." The two women watched as the child clambered down from the sofa and went to the windows, which even here had a view of the ravine of Villa Gregoriana and the two temples.

"Well, I never …" said Mamie looking after her; she laid the sweater across the back of the chair, and sat down.

"Well, Miss McCulloch. No, she can't hear us," she added as Mamie shot her a warning look. "As I told you, Mowenna is a … prodigy." She pronounced the word as if she were saying something filthy. "She knows a great many of Shakespeare's plays." Her gaze became malicious. "Shakespeare – you know? Our famous writer?"

"Of *course*, Doreen, sweetie," agreed Mamie, glancing round for her knitting bag; she had left it by the door, which was really too far away. With some effort she got up to fetch it, which also gave her time to hide her annoyance and compose her features into a more amiable expression. "*Everyone* knows Shakespeare, honey. Even across the *Atlantic* we've heard of *him*. We Americans just *adore* all that tradition and *history* you British have! And it's just *marvellous* that the little one is *part* of it all."

"Be that as it may," returned the aunt dismissively. "I did explain all this, but it seems …"

"Where shall we dine?" interrupted a voice from the window; Mowenna's gaze was now steadily on her aunt.

"What was that, sweetie?" queried Mamie, suddenly aware of her needles between her fingers in the depths of the tapestry bag; she stroked them placatingly before withdrawing her hand. "I didn't quite catch it."

"Mowenna wants to know when we're having dinner," the aunt explained. "Soon now," she called. "You be a good girl now." The child looked at her for a moment, then turned back to the window.

"She says what she wants to say," went on the aunt, "but always using words from Shakespeare's plays. I thought you knew that."

"Yes, I surely remember now, Doreen," said Mamie, all smiles now that she had fondled her beloved needles. "A prodigy *indeed*. I'm a mite surprised there hasn't been more … *interest* shown in her. Professors, people like that." Her voice held a gentle question.

"Oh, they wanted to," said the aunt triumphantly, "but I couldn't allow that, of course." Her lips pursed virtuously. "Too much attention is bad for children. Seen and not heard, *we* were always taught, but no one seems to worry about that these days." Now she smiled spitefully; she had thwarted them. "They wanted to do a study on her, record her answers, find out which plays she knows, all wicked rubbish and no good to anyone."

"But she understands *normal* English, doesn't she, Doreen?" asked Mamie softly, beginning to wonder if Jedson's presence had been enough; the aunt seemed too sure of herself – did she think she was under divine protection, or was she just incredibly stupid? "I don't recall that learning the whole of frigging *Shakespeare* was part of the deal."

For the first time the aunt looked frightened. She had suddenly remembered the black-suited chaperone who had appeared so unexpectedly in London. "Oh, no," she said quickly. "She understands what's said to her – but then she finds something from one of the plays to answer with."

"And that's the creepy silence before she says something?" said Mamie. "Delayed reaction, is it, Doreen? Shuffling through that weird computer of a retarded brain of hers?"

"Yes," whispered the aunt, completely cowed by both the words and the venom with which they had been uttered.

"Well, I never …" sighed Mamie, now all admiration and Southern charm. "She surely is a *prodigy*, sweetie! Now, why don't you just call room service and get her something to eat?"

"And what about my … my compensation?" asked the other, timidly but stubbornly. "I have to get back, I have commitments, church commitments that need …"

"Of *course*, sweetie! But you know you agreed to stay a couple of days to get the little one settled in, don't you? And you don't worry your head about a *thing*. You need just anything at *all*, Jedson's *right* outside the door."

Once Mamie was outside the door herself, she nodded to Jedson in confirmation, then leaned against the wall, stroking her knitting bag; it really *wasn't* the same wearing gloves. "I do declare, Jedson, honey, the world would be a *much* better place without that woman," she confided fretfully, and the hand stroking the bag moved faster. "It makes one wonder about the *fairness* of everything. Still, after …" she paused, eyes darting and overly bright, "… after we've finished here – and it's only a few days now – everything will be just *fine*."

Not prone to introspection but always one for networking, Carl was wondering if he should telephone Jane. His wish had been granted, she had not come back to work and he had been able to carry on as though the job had always been his and one he was born to.

It had not done him much good however. The last scenes were shot on Thursday, so that he had only had six days to make his mark, and not everyone was as happy as Barney about the change; the technicians who had teased Jane with the translation of the embarrassing sentences for example had been grumpy. They had enjoyed her retaliation, and one of them – the one who got the sentence "My dick is the size of a gherkin" – had even wanted to – well, perhaps not thank her, but say something nice. It must have been fate that Maria Grazia, the recipient of the sentence, not only spoke good English but was also worldly and well-travelled, not only owned a travel agency but also a wicked sense of humour. "I like gherkins," she said, laughing, and then came the explanations, and more laughter, and an invitation to dinner; they were still seeing each other.

Carl knew nothing of all this however. When he totted up the pros and cons of his time in Tivoli, it did not amount to very much: he would be able to update his C.V. with "personal assistant to film backer" and "language consultant to international film crew", and he had earned a useful amount of money (but also an annoying nickname), nothing that could actually be called concrete prospects or real opportunities. He was now regretting that he had chosen this job and turned down the offer of doing the course for young unemployed Italians funded by the Lazio region. They might not call him the next time there was a state-funded course – whoever had been taken on might have got in tight with the *responsabili* and gained a toe-hold in that very lucrative sector of English language teaching.

So he was wondering whether Jane was still in Tivoli, and whether he should phone her. The last time he had seen her was at Tivoli Terme when she had gone off with Muscles Incorporated after lunch with Southern Comfort. After that, there was just the errand to collect the prop, and when he returned with the keys and the prop, Anthea had said that Jane wouldn't be coming back and he was to stand in.

And now it was over. He had already called in at the admin. office, a trailer set up in a corner of the large car-park near the river, and was now setting off to walk back up to the centre of town, a route that would take him past the

Hotel delle Sirene and over the Ponte Gregoriano. All he had to do now was to get a bus back down to Tivoli Terme to pack – and *that* had been a hassle, not having a place to stay in Tivoli but making the journey every day; without a car too – and he would also look at the timetable to see when the next coach left Tivoli Terme for Rome; he should be back in the city – it was now 3.15 – by about six or seven. Not that late.

As he was going past the Hotel delle Sirene, he saw Mamie's dumpy figure, made dumpier by her layers of pants suit and shawl, just coming out of the hotel. She had spotted him, and she waved, gesturing at him to come over. Reluctantly he went.

"Why, Plod, sweetie, you still here?" The Southern drawl was breathy, and her face looked shiny and flushed. "I thought you'd be *long* gone by now," she said, one hand clinging to his jacket sleeve, the other pinning the knitting bag to her side. She was also wearing gloves though the day was fairly mild. Probably the eczema thing she had; Carl had noticed it one day when she had stretched out her hand to get her knitting needles out of the bag.

"I'm just off, Mamie. Back to Rome," he explained. "Thanks for everything, I …"

"No, thank *you*, sweetie," she replied enthusiastically, the gloved hand pawing at his arm. "I couldn't have asked for a better guide – so well-informed, so …. *professional*. You surely are going to go *far*, young man!"

Carl began to thank her again, wishing she would let go of him, but she swept on: "And you being so interested in the past, and all that *history*, I just want to show you something. This fine hotel is right over the gully there, and I just *know* you'll be fascinated to see the view from up here. Now, you just come with me."

Carl wanted to get back to Tivoli Terme, but it occurred to him that he might be able to get a lift back down with Mamie, and he could take the opportunity to ask if he could name her as a reference; "personal assistant to film backer" could be bulked up into something much more substantial, and it wouldn't do any harm to humour her.

They entered the hotel together, Mamie leading the way towards the stairs. Earlier, when she had walked away from the lower suite and gone towards the lift, she had noticed a small dim corridor leading off into the depths of the hotel. Ever inquisitive, she had what she called "just a *teensy* peek." It was a short corridor, ending in a window overlooking the valley, a half-open door revealing a dusty storeroom; it was a very nice room, a very *quiet* room.

Barney didn't want to meet the freak. He left all that kind of thing to Mame – she was more of a people person. Up in his penthouse apartment he was busy with the last bits and pieces, papers to be signed, reports to be read from the various heads of department, phone calls to be made on the follow-up, and all that stuff. They had had the final wrap party the night before, again in the hotel, and Barney had also invited the Mayor of Tivoli, a last sweetener to make up for the extra time they had taken over the shoot. The mayor had been sweetened, though mentioning the ensuing problems with Tivoli's hoteliers, and Barney, genial and generous with success, had said: "No problem – I'll tell accounts to pay the bills until the 17th – then, the hotel guys are covered. And if they do have last-minute bookings, it'll be all extra. Know what I mean?" And he winked. The exchange was conducted through Enrico, and Barney, affable and expansive, made no more sarcastic comments; the film was in the can.

Later, standing in his suite, a cigar in one hand, a bottle of Corona beer in the other, Barney was going over what was to be done: he would be going up to Rome the following day, and jetting back to the States – not soon enough for him, he had really done a number on himself as regards Italy. And Mame was staying on for a few days, wanted to finish some kind of health and beauty treatment down at Tivoli Terme, would then be joining him at The Pussy Drive with the girlie in a week's time. As for *The Pope's Protocol*, post-production would be done back on home ground in the States, so after The Pussy Drive ... "Hey, Anthea!" he yelled. "Gemme Jace on the phone, willya? Gotta fix a date to get moving on the rough cut."

As he waited, he took a slug of beer, balanced the cigar on the edge of a coffee table, and picked up the piece of paper on the other side of the table. It was the carnival programme that the mayor had pressed on him, "if, by chance, you would like to assist at the Carnival parade." Shit, no ... he crumpled the programme up without even looking at it, and lobbed it towards the waste bin, where it bounced off the rim and landed in a corner. "Hey! You got him yet, Anth? C'mon! Get y'ass in gear there!" Smoke from the forgotten cigar curled towards the ceiling.

If Barney had even glanced at the sheet, he would have seen that – while he was heading for Rome, then New York then Nevada – the Tivoli carnival would be celebrating its final big day before the climax of the 16th.

SUNDAY 14/02/2010
14,30: Exhibition of dance, music and theatre by the Beats Accadamy in Piazza Garibaldi
15,00: Make-uppers, wandering masked animators, magic performances in the streets of the city
15,30: Allegorical parade of the King Carnevale float and masked groups with folk bands and Majorettes
19,00: Prize-giving with the authorities present.
19,30: Proclamation of the most beautiful mask of the Carnevale with the sum of popular votes and the votes of the technical jury in Piazza Garibaldi, with the prize of a weekend in Venice for two in a prestigious hotel.

Jane did look at the programme, pressed on her by her thoughtful landlady at breakfast, and decided to go that afternoon. She had been calling the Sibyl at least three times a day since her futile knocking at the heavy door, but each time the message appeared that she was "unreachable." Jane had gone to the gift shop as well, only to find it closed, a cardboard notice dangling inside the window to the effect that it would re-open on the 17th. Apparently the Sibyl had decided to dedicate herself to her preparations, whatever they might be. Jane could only fervently hope that everything would somehow work out.

So, it was now just a matter of waiting until she had to "return at nine on Tuesday" and "be *ready*," so Jane felt she might as well fill in the time to see the Tivoli carnival, which featured its own pseudo-king, *Lo Zibaldone*, the centrepiece of the parade that afternoon.

Fortunately, the day was grey and cloudy rather than pouring with rain. At this point people were grateful for small mercies, and could only hope their luck would hold for the evening of the 16th, the evening when King Carnival would be consigned to the flames of the ceremonial bonfire; it really had been a terrible winter.

Despite her worries Jane's spirits lifted as she walked up the steep street to the centre of town. It was already gloomy in the narrow alleys and side-streets but nearer Piazza del Plebiscito, a large piazza where the fruit and vegetable market was held, the shops were open for holiday business, windows brightly glowing, and doors hospitably wide, gusts of warm air rushing out to do battle with the surrounding cold. There were clothes shops with cashmere sweaters and leather jackets, their elegance and mellow warmth emphasised by cunningly-placed spotlights, general stores with displays of costumes and masks, acrylic wigs and gaudy noise-makers, and tobacconists with displays of plump red hearts, fancy chocolates and pink furry rabbits with *ti amo* on their chests.

As for the carnival events, the make-up artists were

already in the piazza, crouched behind folding tables full of paints and lipsticks, and doing a roaring trade in producing endless versions of Spider Man and Miss Italy on small excited faces. There were jugglers performing in one of the side roads, and a couple of men on stilts waddling stiffly through the crowd, dipping and bowing as they went; on a far corner the enthralled audience of a puppet show watched Punchinello, the Italian Punch, beating a wooden *carabiniere* about the head with his own truncheon, and there was a living statue representing the Statue of Liberty with torch upheld, though no one was very interested – why watch lack of movement when there was so much else going on?

The *Tiburtini* – on this last Sunday before Carnival ended and penitentiary Lent began –were determined to enjoy themselves. The children, dressed up in their carnival costumes, clutched electric-coloured balloons in the shape of Mickey Mouse, more Spider Men, and even sharks twisting and turning on the end of the string. The adults' faces were wreathed in smiles above their heavy coats, while teenagers strolled in twos hand in hand or in groups laughing and calling out to each other.

As Jane walked along, she smelt popcorn and coffee, wood smoke and roasting meat, all happily meeting and mingling and dissipating in an atmosphere reminiscent of a medieval fair. Merry and motley holiday, she thought smiling. Looking around, she saw that more and more people were flowing into the piazza from all directions. And the parade? Where did it start and finish? It must be passing there anyway; council workers, bulky in florescent jackets, were hooking ropes onto short metal supports to clear a way, shooing away interested children who wanted to help.

Jane found herself wanting to celebrate as well, take part in some way, and went into the larger of the two bars, where she ordered a hot chocolate with whipped cream. Too restless to sit down, even if there had been a seat free, she stood at the counter, making patterns in the whipped cream with her spoon, and keeping an eye on the crowds outside.

And now came the sound of a brass band approaching the piazza, and Jane put down her empty cup. She started towards the door when she was swept forward by the surge of others leaving the bar, and ended up outside with her back pressed against the plate-glass window. A little further along there was a step up to the building next door that no one had yet claimed as a vantage point. Sliding along the glass she took possession of the space, and now had an unobstructed view over the heads of the crowd.

First came the band, followed by high-stepping majorettes. And why is it that majorettes are so popular in Italy, she wondered. These ones came in all shapes and sizes, but were arranged by height, with the tallest ones in the middle and the smallest, many of them children, ranged along the side; there was much stamping and twirling of batons, greeted by cheers and applause from the crowd. Then came the first Tivoli float, which represented a jokey version of Hell with numerous imps and demons clinging to its sides, and a jolly-looking Satan howling and brandishing a pitchfork. The next group were on foot, bizarre figures with what looked like complete sheepskins drawn over their heads, horns projecting from the top, and they carried a placard with CROAZIA emblazoned on the front; they carried bells and noise-makers, which they employed to the full in a cacophony of sound that had people groaning and holding their ears in mock agony.

And as the grey afternoon deepened into dusk above the rooftops of the town, the merry and motley holiday continued, filling the streets with its kaleidoscope of colours that glowed ever brighter and richer against the approaching darkness.

The sound of cheering came from outside the piazza, signalling the arrival of King Carnival himself. In lumbered his carriage, heralded by a group of sumptuously-attired courtiers – NEW ORLEANS proclaimed their placard, five of them walking before, scattering sweets and confetti, one perched on the front of the carriage itself.

And *that* is King Carnival? thought Jane in almost comical dismay. What had she been expecting? Because for all her research and notes, immersed as she had been in the White Sibyl, Faunus Lupercus, the Vestal Virgins, and the whole month of February, after living with legends and prophesies, ancient conflicts and their modern re-enactment – and it seemed she had been living with it all forever – she had not looked at the Tivoli carnival itself.

Lo Zibaldone wore baggy white trousers splodged with huge red spots topped by a blue jacket and red belt stretched over a rotund belly. Bright yellow hair, a white face, big red nose and wide painted mouth were framed by a huge white ruff about his neck. The Carnival King was a circus clown.

The contrast with the courtiers who preceded him could not have been greater – while they were elegant, glittering and self-possessed, seeming to have strolled from some sophisticated decadent past, he erupted from the world of comedy, slapstick and childhood.

Jane's reaction to him was hers alone. The *Tiburtini* knew their *Zibaldone* – they cheered and laughed and held up small children to get a better look, the whole piazza in a ferment of enjoyment and fun. Life was about the banana skin, and the bucket of water in the face, a riotous knockabout affair with no rhyme or reason. *That* was Life, and *that* was Carnival; the king was a clown, the emperor had no clothes.

As the float drew nearer Jane froze. She had recognised the sixth courtier seated on the carriage. It was the woman who called herself Signora Zauli, sitting, almost lounging, at the feet of the *Zibaldone*. She was dressed in a black satin ball dress slashed with scarlet and scattered with sequins, the coils of her dark hair iridescent with – surely they could not be – diamond and pearls. She threw no sweets or confetti but gestured languidly to the on-lookers, her slow dark smile inviting them to mock the king, see his clownery for the ineffectual farce it was.

Jane shrank back, feeling the hardness of the door on her shoulder blades as she pressed against it, an instinctive revulsion stirring the hairs on the back of her neck. Unconsciously she clenched her hands into fists and stood straighter, all the while staring defiantly at the woman.

Signora Zauli's languid glance swept over her, paused

and then swung back. She smiled and raised one pale hand in greeting, the blood-red nails shining in the light spilling from the bar. The long fingers spread and gestured. "We'll see each other soon," said the gesture, "*very* soon", and then she was gone as the float trundled on its way.

For a moment Jane stood motionless, feeling weak and afraid. How she wished that Professor Caseman were there! How she wished that she had the professor's strength and calm. What had Lena written to her? "You always were kind, Jane, kind and imaginative and brave." But were those qualities enough? Would they be enough? Blindly she put one hand against the wall to steady herself, and stepped down onto the pavement, suddenly engulfed and jostled by the crowds who – now the parade had passed – were re-possessing the piazza as the council men began their work of dismantling the barriers.

She thought longingly of the year before. There had been not only the professor, who knew exactly what they should do, but her gallant friend Barbara, George of the heroic shorts (and would he still be in Siberia?), and – the name she had been avoiding – Gabriel, maddening but reassuring, annoying but strangely heartening. What would *he* have done now?

As if in answer, a voice said, "*Caffè corretto.*" For one heart-stopping moment she thought it was Gabriel himself, magically reappearing in answer to her thoughts. She choked back a cry, took a step backwards, bumping against the plate-glass window of the bar.

It was the stonemason, standing and regarding her

gravely, like a doctor assessing a patient. The light from the window illuminated the black slashing eyebrows, casting shadows over the slanting eyes and drawing a line down the strong jaw. His jacket was buttoned up to a clean-shaven chin, and he stood casually, hands deep in his pockets, now smiling and nodding towards the bar. And the problem of what to do next was solved.

They went in, he linking arms with her as if they were old friends. "*Ciao, Nico!*" trilled the girl at the counter. "*Buon carnevale!*" And now Jane knew his name. Just then she had no other questions, was content to sip at the *caffè corretto*, 'corrected' with grappa, with a teaspoon of more whipped cream on the top. A small dish of heart-shaped chocolates in red and blue foil appeared to go with the coffee, and they stood at the counter together in companionable silence.

"Everything will go well," he said after a while. "Trust me."

"Yes," agreed Jane, and she did. The noise of the carnival celebrations still sounded outside, and the bar itself was filled with the hum of conversation, but they seemed to be standing alone in some quiet protected place. When he took her hand, she curled her fingers inside the warm calloused palm and placed her other hand above his, suddenly feeling strong and alive and aroused. They smiled at each other, turned towards the door without another word and walked out into the evening. "*Nico!*" trilled the girl again, now laughing. "*Amore mio! Buon San Valentino!*"

And they remained in that quiet protected place. It stayed with them as they walked through the milling crowds, the smiling adults, the calling teenagers, the children in their colourful costumes. The onrush of events was suspended, time stilled, and the present existed entire and complete. As the noise from the piazza died and became a distant murmur, only the dark streets and squares of lighted windows chequering damp walls witnessed their silent passage.

Via Palatina, Via Ponte Gregoriano, Piazza Rivarola, and into Via della Sibilla, where they slipped through a narrow door beside the empty gift shop, and took possession of a hidden timeless world.

The short-hacked hair smelt of juniper and pine, the strong body held the heady scent of warm earth under spring rain, and as they came together in the giving and receiving of pleasure, that cold February night in the third millennium reached back through the years and decades and centuries to meld with other times, other ways, and other powers.

The sense of life and strength and arousal that Jane had felt also remained, and was transformed into a passionate tenderness. As he was alive, so was she, as he was strong, so was she, each separate and distinct but now forming another greater being. She caressed the injured foot, which was twisted and foreshortened, bulky with scar tissue, and rough and ridged to the touch. It held no memory of pain, if anything seemed part of some vast forest, the gnarled root of an ancient oak giving shade and shelter. And if too, the far-off howl of a wolf echoed faintly through the glades, it was the howl of exclusion and disappointment, thwarted hunger and impotent rage. The charm was set, the enchantment complete.

22

Tuesday 16th, the last day of carnival. Afterwards winter would return in full force, everyday life would resume its course, and all that remained was to keep one's head down, wait out the bad weather, and hope that Spring would not be far behind.

The programme for that day would begin in the afternoon with street events and performers, the official end being at seven in the evening: King Carnival would be consigned to the flames of a bonfire in Piazza Plebiscito, wine and biscuits distributed ("until supplies exhausted") and fireworks set off to burst over the town in a last glittering climax.

Back at her B&B Jane was sorting out the contents of her shoulder bag, mind free of speculation and fear. The small homely task became necessary every couple of weeks as the bag became cluttered with old receipts, fliers, pens, and loose change that had fallen from her purse. Slowly,

The White Sibyl

even dreamily, she went through the slips of paper, checking her diary as well, and then paused and went through them again. Was she throwing out something important? No. There was an out-of-date ticket for public transport in Rome, a glossy sheet advertising end-of-line trainers – and she never had got to the shop, several bar receipts, all showing cappuccino, and three sachets of sugar. Nothing else.

And now, she thought, I'm going to take myself out for a proper lunch – pasta, a big meaty chop with roast potatoes, a glass of red wine, and crème caramel. Then, back home, decide what to wear – something warm – and go out to keep the evening appointment. Whatever will happen, will happen.

The afternoon slipped away. In her vast dim apartment Signora Zauli was carefully lifting a blasphemous statue wrapped in black velvet from an oaken chest; in Tivoli Terme Mamie was still knitting the bright yellow jumper with green bobbles even though her first offering had been rejected, while Jedson was outside the hotel, smoking his second cigarette of the day; the Sibyl, her studies complete, was laying out her leather sandals and animal-skin cloak, and humming as she worked; the stone mason, face thoughtful, was watching the Hotel delle Sirene, where Mowenna was regarding her aunt, and remarking, "'Tis known I am a pretty piece of flesh." "Don't talk such filth," snapped back the good woman.

And Eric Moonday. Once again in the bar opposite the

corner of the hotel in Tivoli Terme, car parked at the ready outside, he watched and waited. Every so often he took out the piece of paper he had picked up in the cemetery car park, smoothed out the creases yet again, studied it, and put it carefully away again. He no longer knew why he was there, was only, in some dim way, aware of a dull pulsating excitement. He would wait, follow the people in the limousine, find out who they were, and why they were so important to him. That was it – once he knew, everything would be all right; he took out the piece of paper again.

It was about 8.30 when Jane left the B&B. She knew it wouldn't take half an hour to walk across the Ponte Gregoriano to the apartment in Via Platone Tiburtino but having spent as much time as she could, first over lunch, then lying on the bed, then choosing heavy trousers and trainers to wear, and then re-reading her notes, she had nothing left to do and could no longer wait.

As she walked down the road towards the arch, then under the arch and down the flight of steps to the road running past the supermarket, she was wondering about the statue. It had seemed such a major – such an integral – part of the ceremony, but the Sibyl had not even reacted to the news it had been stolen, had not seemed to care in the least. She quickened her steps. At least it wasn't raining; the air was still and heavy with moisture, suspended around the street lamps and shop signs in glistening whirls, the alien atmosphere of some watery half-world. She reached the road to the bridge, crossed over to the hotel and its tree-shadowed entrance. That was where the dinner had been, Mamie arriving to hail Jane as a long-lost friend and then talking to Barney in the private alcove with Jedson's black-suited figure guarding the entrance. And Carl, his face beaming and shiny, expansive and *so* debonair when he spoke Italian; she really should give him a ring – it was him who had got her the job after all.

Just past the hotel, before the bridge, there was a paved promenade overlooking the valley, with more trees and four or five benches in a line; it would be a pleasant busy spot in summer but was now empty, except …

There was a small brief glow, and the dark outline of a tree, larger than the others, split into two and began to walk forward. Jane paused in disbelief, mind alive with images of ancient oaks and gnarled roots, scents of juniper and pine, and then came the smell of cigarette smoke and a tall figure was suddenly standing beside her gripping her arm.

"Wha ..?" she managed to whisper.

"Hey, Jane, take it easy," came Jedson's wonderful voice. "Where're you going? Come in for a drink."

Now icy cold despite her layers of clothing, Jane pulled herself together. She looked down at the hand where he held a cigarette clenched between two knuckles. "You frightened the wits out of me," she said, and was amazed at the sound of her own voice; it was light and reproachful, even slightly flirtatious. "Grabbing me like that. How are you?"

"Good, great," he said, releasing her arm and taking a drag at the cigarette. Momentarily his face was lit in its glow:

the intense blue eyes, the blond hair drawn back in its ponytail, the diamond stud in one ear. "How about that drink then? Nice bar here."

She patted her jacket into place – it had been pulled from her shoulder by his grip, saying, "I can't, I'm afraid, I'm meeting one of the local guys. How about tomorrow?" And again she was amazed at herself – the real Jane, hidden, was baring her teeth in fear and anger, while this new Jane not only implied regret that she had other fish to fry but also the promise that tomorrow she would be more than available.

He took a step closer, leaning over her, and took another deep drag at the cigarette. She could feel its heat on her cheek, but held her ground, smiling, as if unaware of its proximity. For a moment they stood, and then voices and laughter sounded from the hotel as two couples came out and started towards them. He drew back, threw the cigarette away, and straightened his tie. Really CIA, thought the real Jane, as the new one smiled and said, "Well, how about tomorrow?"

He seemed baffled and at a loss, then returned the smile, and said softly, "Come on, Jane. We both know what's going on, but leave it, OK? Miss Mamie likes you, *I* like you, but you get in the way you'll get hurt."

"OK," agreed new Jane. "But maybe see you tomorrow anyway?" And she patted him on the arm, fell casually in behind the two couples who had just strolled past.

"Jane!"

Now some distance away with people in sight and

hearing, she looked back. "It's a private party," he called quietly. "No gate-crashers, so don't try. You'll see."

She waved, as if he had wished her a nice evening, and sped lightly after the two couples, while he gazed after her, frowning and lighting another cigarette.

Having been delayed by Jedson, Jane was now almost late, and, once over the bridge in the wake of the two couples, increased her pace so that she was now almost running. She was out of breath as she rang the doorbell outside the large street-door, stamping her feet to get some warmth into them as she waited.

There was no answer, nor was there to a second longer ring. Impatiently Jane – the new Jane it must have been – punched at another button, and was rewarded with a loud click as the door catch was released.

"*Chi è?*" called a woman's voice from upstairs.

"*Scusi, sono venuta a trovare la … signora con il negozio,*" Jane called back; 'the woman with the shop' was all she could come up with - she *still* didn't know the Sibyl's name. "*Ma non risponde …*"

"*Secondo piano,*" drifted back the reply, and there was the sound of a door closing as Jane slipped inside and took the stairs two at a time.

The Sibyl's door appeared closed, but when Jane knocked, it shifted slightly; it was not latched. With a quick look round, she pushed at the pitted wood with her palm, and when the door swung open, took a step into the room.

Two lamps were lit, one on the sideboard, the other on the large table by the window, and at first the room appeared to be empty. The first thing she saw was some kind of rough fur cloak laid carefully over the back of one of the armchairs, then, a large volume, cover-downwards and pages creased, on the floor by the wood-burning stove. It was only when she looked towards the spare room, the room where she had been nursed back to health, that she saw the body propped against the wall, the flowing skirt and frizzy hair giving it the appearance of a discarded doll.

With a deep shuddering breath, Jane pushed the door to behind her and walked softly across the room only to stop again when she caught sight of the body of one of the white cats, its lustrous fur now dull and dappled with red, its teeth bared in a rictus of pain or fury. Of the other two there was no sign.

Jedson, thought Jane, as clearly as though she had seen the black-suited figure stand there in the room. "It's a private party, Jane," he had said, "No gate-crashers, so don't try. You'll see."

Almost tip-toeing she went closer and knelt beside the still body. The vivid green eyes were reduced to filmy slits, the imperious mouth swollen and bitten, and the neck, forearms and hands disfigured with the raw craters of cigarette burns. Tears filled Jane's eyes. "My poor dear," she whispered, letting herself slide sideways to sit on the floor. The Sibyl's hands had been tied behind her with one of her own blue-green scarves, and Jane tore at the knots with her nails, feeling the trickle of tears on her hot cheeks, until finally the thin hands were free. "My poor poor dear," she said again, and gently stroked the cool skin, remembering the day at the Villa D'Este, the place of power, and the Sibyl in the pool, splashing and singing beneath cascading waters. It seemed so long ago now, so far in the past.

She did not know how long she remained there, sitting in her heavy outdoor clothes, stroking the hand she held, until gradually her pity and sadness gave way to anger and outrage. I'll make them pay, she vowed silently. I'll make them pay for this. And a cold hard resolve began to form. She would defeat Mamie and the Black Sibyl, she would kill Jedson, and destroy whoever else tried to stop her. No holds barred. No quarter asked or given.

The statue. They had taken the other part, but the Sibyl had been keeping the head. And had been tortured. Did they possess both parts now? With a final clasp she laid the limp hand on the worn carpet, only to start as she heard footsteps coming up the flagged stairs outside; the door was not completely closed.

She leapt upright, hands again clenched into fists, and faced the door. Slowly – horribly slowly – it swung noiselessly open.

It was the stonemason, the Sibyl's … He came into the room, paused to take in the scene, and there was a sudden flurry of white as the two remaining cats ran from their hiding place under a chair, and boiled about his feet. He bent down, stroked their fear-spiked fur, then picked them up, one cradled in each arm, and crossed the room.

"I am … so sorry," said Jane. "I …"

He nodded, eyes on the still figure, fingers smoothing the cats' fur. Bizarrely they started a low rhythmic purring, butting their heads against his heavy jacket. Thus they remained, the silence relieved only by the quiet crackling of the wood fire and the steady purr from the two cats, until he turned and placed them on one of the armchairs, briefly laying one hand on each of their heads; they settled and curled round each other, green eyes wide and unblinking.

He returned to Jane, took her hands between his, and again strength and life flowed into her from the calloused palms. "We must go," he said. "The time is about to finish."

"Do we need the statue?" asked Jane, looking into the dark slanted eyes. "Your ..." She looked down. "She had the head, they have the other part."

He tightened his clasp, and a brief smile, almost mischievous, curled his lips. "They have a copy," he said. "It is useless to them."

"So, we go to the temple ...?"

"Yes, but the gates are barred, the way is guarded." Again came the almost-mischievous smile. "We must go through the valley, approach the temple from below."

Jane nodded; the gates were barred, the way was guarded, they would go through the valley, approach the temple from below. Hand in hand they left the apartment, closing the door quietly behind them.

23

Tuesday 16th February, contd.

There was now no one on guard outside the apartment where Mowenna and her aunt were staying. It was unnecessary, for Mamie had skilfully appropriated their passports after the hotel had completed the check-in; well, there was just *no* reason to tie up the boys when they would be needed elsewhere that evening. To the aunt she said: "And knowing as I surely *do*, Doreen, that you are just not *used* to foreign travel, well, I don't want you to be *bothered* in any way with all those *boring* details!"

    The aunt, whose rationalisation mechanism was in full working order, had quickly assimilated the news into the scheme of things. The mechanism had clicked forward from "the adoption of a special needs child by a God-fearing American couple" to "who would be willing to recompense the aunt in recognition of her loss" to "Italy was where the intermediaries would be" to "obviously the aunt would accompany the child to settle her in", to this last, "No, she certainly didn't want to be bothered with the boring details". The one link that had refused to be assimilated and had thus been dismissed was Jedson's appearance in London and the fright she had had; if she had been reminded of it, she would have hurriedly filed it under "accompany the child" and "boring details". As for Mowenna herself, she showed no interest in where she was, apart from spending much of the time at the window, looking down into the gorge or gazing intently at the two temples on the opposite side. She would do that – fix on something and stare at it for no reason at all.

That Tuesday evening Eric Moonday had followed the people from the hotel in Tivoli Terme up the hill, and then, having parked the car in the large car park down by the river – he somehow knew they would be going to the Hotel delle Sirene, began an aimless ramble that began with the high railings around Villa Gregoriana, and took him past the hotel and the now-deserted promenade, over the bridge and down into the side streets below Via della Sibilla. He was tired and weak, and when he saw a flight of steps, leading up from a small cobbled piazza, he sat down, wrapping his arms around himself, and digging his hands – he had forgotten his gloves – into the inside pockets of the flimsy jacket. He found the remains of his baseball cap and put it on, found his piece of paper, smoothed it out and stowed it away again, all the while staring down into the piazza,

The White Sibyl

where a street lamp showed a stone parapet and the blackness of the valley below.

As if onto a stage, a small fantastic figure walked into the misty light of the lamp, paused and looked around. Slowly Eric focused on it with dull interest. It was a little girl. Her fine blond hair straggled from under a shapeless felt hat, and she was dressed in an odd array of garments: a pink sweater with bows was tucked into a woman's skirt clumsily held in place by a red belt high on the thin chest. The hem trailed over unlaced trainers – she wore no socks – and she was clutching a large thin book.

For a moment she paused, looked up and regarded Eric solemnly, then looked down at the book, before crossing to the steps, dirty laces trailing on the damp cobblestones. They regarded each other, the gaunt scarecrow of a man hunched on the worn stones and the fantastically-dressed child holding the slim volume. "Come on, my boy," she said, and her childish voice was clear and oddly comforting. "How doest, my boy? Art cold?"

Eric understood "boy" and "cold" and guessed the rest: "Yes, cold," he muttered, hugging his jacket closer with icy fingers and ducking his head in agreement. "Very cold, but they are evil and I must stop them."

"I will help you to't," said the child solemnly after a short pause, and she held up the book; it was a copy of the same guide book that Jane had bought in the gift shop, the one with the photograph of the two temples on the back. The child pointed at the photograph, as if it explained everything. "Give me your hand," she said. He heaved himself obediently to his feet, took the small warm fingers, and allowed himself to be led up the steps towards Via della Sibilla.

The stonemason's battered truck was parked in the space at the intersection. No one was around. The small bar where Murph had had coffee on the day of his departure was open but only two people were visible through the lighted window, the owner leaning on the counter and one man playing a slot machine. The streets too were almost empty, the only sound that of a car swishing down towards the large car park by the river.

They climbed into the truck, and set off towards the nearby entrance to Villa Gregoriana, the one Barney's group had used on the tour of the valley. It was only minutes away, and, leaving the truck parked in a side road, they walked towards the gate. He must have had a key (Where had he …?) for it swung open, and he carried two torches (How had he …?). Jane gave a last glance back towards the town of Tivoli. The orange glow of the street lighting was pierced by a fiercer yellow glow. The bonfire? To destroy the Carnival King, the pseudo-king who had to die for life to be reborn? No, it was too late surely.

Down the steps, past the small wooden ticket office, to the path leading into the valley. Their footsteps were noiseless on the sodden leaves, the way treacherous, and Jane, torch in one hand to guide her, the other hand clasped in his, emptied her mind, thought only of the next step, each taking her nearer to the temple on the other side. The muted rumbling of the cascades swelled somewhere to their right, and her torch briefly showed the sign pointing towards the viewing point. Down again, past the flat area in front of the remains of the villa of Manlius Vopiscus, and down again towards the valley floor.

As they descended it seemed to Jane that the valley became warmer, the night lighter, and the sounds of water became the placid gurgle of lazy rivers on summer days. While above them the Hotel delle Sirene stood like a fortress on its rocky ledge, lights blazing, and the two temples, the round and the rectangular, showed starkly white from the floodlights at their base, here in the deep cleft of the valley it was a world apart, a sanctuary and a refuge. If in the town, the *Mensa Ponderaria* hoarded its dark and ancient secrets, the valley, once the sacred grove of Faunus, lay quiet, dreaming of its own tutelary gods.

Jane had lost all sense of time, was walking as if in a dream herself, but was aware they had reached the central clearing, *Radura di Ponte Lupo*; the thin light from her torch briefly rested on one of the commemorative benches, "Donna Luisa Aldobrandini" read the plaque.

"Wait," he said. "Rest," and they sat down, hands still clasped, the summer evening (or so it seemed) hushed and tranquil around them. The clearing was not the lowest point of the valley. Over to the left was the narrow path down to the Valle dell'Inferno, the marshy corner beneath the Ponte Gregoriano, and lower still, the *Grotta delle Sirene*, the huge cavern roofed in a storm-tossed sea frozen in stone.

And it was in the cavern that the valley was silently coming to life, the waves and billows of the petrified sea becoming translucent, a blue-green light shot with gold rising from the stormy depths. The cavern gleamed, dimmed, gleamed again, then glowed with greater strength as the forces of the valley gathered. That night, as Signora Zauli had said, was the point when our old times briefly touch the new.

But now the climb was before them and they started up the first incline where a flight of steps became a wide track hugging the side of the valley in long zigzagging bends. Larger trees, first arching above the track, slowly dropped below, thinned and became dwarfs as the valley's rocky slopes gave less and less purchase to their roots. The temples could no longer be seen as a whole, for the path was directly beneath them, but their floodlit walls reared on the promontory of Tibur's ancient acropolis, white against the orange-tinted gloom.

And finally they reached the top, where the squat bulk of the tourist centre marked the very end of the journey. Jane was exhausted, hot and sweating in her heavy clothes, legs trembling and aching with the effort of toiling up the steep slope. They stopped. No one was in sight in the bright glare of the floodlights. Where were the enemy? It was late, at least two hours had passed, perhaps more, since they had stood in the Sibyl's apartment in Via Platone Tiburtino.

Abruptly the floodlights died. Now there was no light at all. Jane's fingers searched for the switch of the torch, but his closed over them, and she felt rather than saw him shake his head. He took her hand, and she felt the rough irregular surface of stone pressed into her palm; her fingers recognised the head of the statue and closed round it protectively. Then, he gestured that she should stay there, and trod softly to the damaged corner of the Sibyl's Temple, where the fissure would afford a glimpse of the bare interior. Jane stood motionless, eyes scanning the snack bar and the courtyard that gave onto Via della Sibilla; if it had been guarded, it was now empty and unwatched.

A soft sound made her head whirl round. From the side of the snack bar came two figures, one large and one small. Jane's eyes had now become used to the orange half-light, and the two could be seen like the people in a ghostly negative, a man in a tattered baseball cap and a small girl who looked as if she had been playing at dressing-up with her mother's clothes. They came closer, hand in hand, the child leading the man, who watched her with trusting eyes. The man was the wild young man who had accosted Jane in the car park, but nothing now could surprise her, and she held up one hand in greeting, then placed a finger to her lips; they could have nothing to do with the others. The man held out a piece of paper, as if it were a ticket that allowed him entrance, then seemed to want to continue forward but the child pulled him back. "If they do see thee, they will kill thee," she whispered, and he halted obediently. The child patted his arm, with her other hand plucked the battered felt hat from her head, and dropped it to the ground; lustrous pearls of moisture began to gather in her fine blond hair.

Jane had automatically taken the proffered paper, and

now looked down, straining to make out the words: **Years will be** .... The sound of raised voices distracted her – first, Mamie's, screeching and incomprehensible, then Jedson's, lower and defensive, then Signora Zauli's, a virulent poisonous hiss. Cautiously, Jane walked to the front corner of the temple, hearing the rustle of gravel as the man and the child followed her.

"So *why* doesn't the damn thing work?" howled Mamie, and at the sound of her voice Eric Moonday loosed his hold of the child's hand, evaded Jane's own warning hand, and started forward in a shambling lurching run. Jane instinctively moved to follow him, but felt the child's hand slide into her own. She looked down into the serious blue eyes, and saw the child shake her head; if she had previously stopped the man, she had obviously decided that now he had to go.

The abrupt silence from the interior of the temple signalled that they had seen him. Then,

"Jewish bitch!" shouted Eric, though his voice was a thin quaver. "I know you now! You're the one ... but not for long! I'll kill you, I'll ..."

There was a scuffle, a moan, a thud, and then Mamie's voice again, now sounding calm and satisfied, more than satisfied, replete: "Now, that was *nice*, Jedson. You surely are a *good* boy, and I declare that I *surely* couldn't have done it better my *very* own self." He murmured something, before she went on: "But for the *other* thing," her voice came nearer, "well, you ballsed up *good* time there, sweetie, and you've killed me *dead*, honey. Just stone *dead*!" Another murmur.

"Shush, honey," her voice further away; she had moved. "That's right, you're a *good* boy, sweetie. Just ..."

And now there was a cry of shock and pain, followed by a horrid gasping gurgling. "Tim-ber!" yelled Mamie, and then broke into a wheezing breathless giggle, joined by the silver chime of Signora Zauli's dark knowing laughter. The ghastly sounds – the gurgling and the giggling and the laughter – echoed around the walls, now nearer, now further away. Then, Mamie, still giggling and wheezing: "Oh, I just couldn't *help* myself, sweetie. And you *really* fucked up, you *know* you did!"

Jane now felt the child pulling her forward, and she obeyed the pressure of the small hand. They left the shelter of the corner of the temple, climbed the high steps to its platform, and she bent to help the child. Together they stood up.

Inside, two camping lamps coldly illuminated the interior, and the faces that turned towards Jane were drained of all colour, seeming the hollow faces of the dead. To the right, Mamie still held a knitting needle in a hand blotched and stained from her disease. To the left stood Signora Zauli, the smile frozen on her face, her long fingers curling and smoothing her sumptuous ball gown. By one wall lay the huddled body of Eric Moonday, his baseball cap lying beside him, while Jedson, blood spurting from the neat hole in his neck, he trying to clutch it close with both hands but weakening and dying fast, writhed on the ground. Jane walked forward, looked down at him. The once-immaculate black suit was crumpled and smeared with brown dust, the white shirt drenched with blood that also shone wet on the jacket shoulder. And before his eyelids drooped and his hands slowly lost their grip on his savaged neck, their gazes met. His held entreaty, hers a stony detachment. You have paid, said the gaze. Burn in hell.

It was Signora Zauli who was the first to speak: "Well, Miss Harrison. You managed to join us after all. And the child is here too," she murmured. "But to no avail, as you have probably guessed. The statue has no power. And without its power, my own cannot be awakened." She stepped to one side, gestured at a second statue set beside that of the White Sibyl on a small table behind them; incongruously it was a folding table, like those used by the make-up artists in the piazza, though it had been covered with a black velvet cloth embroidered with silver snakes in an endless writhing ball.

Jane looked at what the woman had called 'her' statue, a truncated crucifix around which a snake was coiled, its forked tail possessively holding the heavy base, its head rearing malignantly above the crossbar of the stunted upright.

"So, you *see*, sweetie," came Mamie's wheezing voice, now wheedling and querulous. "I am well and truly *fucked*." She had started to edge forward, the needle still held in one pudgy paw.

"The head you have is a copy," said Jane, and Mamie stopped in her tracks. "I have it." And she held up the fragment of stone. This was the new Jane, who was strong and fearless and free of doubt. "We will complete the ceremony – leave it to the awakened powers to decide who they will choose."

"No, I think we'll take it," murmured Signora Zauli, and she too started to advance, the long fingers lengthening into thin crooked talons.

"No." said a quiet voice. Now loosely clasping a short scythe in one hand, the stonemason limped forward to stand beside the child. He briefly touched her hair and its shining pearls of water, and she looked up, rubbed her head against it as the two cats had done; the pearls glowed and scattered. Jane smiled at him, ignored the two women, Mamie, swaying slightly but still clutching her needle, Signora Zauli, a still, dark figure, had also halted, and now stood looking at the newcomer, her brow creased like someone trying to remember a face and the time that was linked to the face. For the first time her assurance seemed to falter. For she was remembering her visions. And the three she had seen were there – the foreign woman and the crippled man and the mournful child. Only ... the visions had been incomplete, the outcome was hidden from her.

"Jane," he said calmly, "Continue. I will keep these bitches from you." And he moved towards them, scythe still hanging casually from one hand, and they flinched back. "Child," he went on, "Go with her."

They walked to the table. The fake head had not been glued to the body, merely balanced there, and Jane removed it, replaced it with the missing part, and then clasped the two together, cradling the completed statue in her hands. The child too approached, and placed her hands on Jane's.

Warmth began to rise from the cold stone.

In the valley below, the stone sea, blue-green shot with gold, became luminous water – but water that was also light. It swelled and swirled about the cavern, flowed to fill the marshy valley floor, rose to cover the dark trees, gilding each bare twig with golden droplets, then rose again relentless until the bowl of the valley brimmed with its presence and power. Its tides lapped the steep cliffs, drew near the ancient acropolis, and gathered waiting at the Temple of the Sibyl.

Inside, the four hands – the woman's and the child's – unclasped. The statue was whole again, healed, glowing in its turn with blue-green light shot with gold. They stepped back from the table, watched and waited.

And now a dull red light suffused the base of the other statute, and as it crept higher, the forked tail twitched and lashed, the coils pulsed and stirred, until finally the flat deadly head reared higher and swayed.

"Ah, my Lord ..." breathed Signora Zauli, gliding forward in her rich glittering gown and kneeling beside it in adoration; the satin folds billowed and pooled on the dusty ground, and as she raised her head, gazed up, her face became subtly different, the forehead more prominent, the jaw thinner and the neck longer and more sinuous.

The snake's flat head slowly uncoiled from the crossbar, stretched and extended to touch the sinuous neck, then suddenly darted to bite so that bright blood showed on her white skin and trickled down into the dark folds of her gown. "My Lord ...," she breathed again, her face an ecstasy of pleasure and worship.

The glow from the two statues – blue-green shot with gold, the dull red tinged with grey – rose and merged. And the bare walls of the temple were transfigured, became mirrors and pools and jewelled expanses that seemed to have no beginning and no end, the light endlessly reflected into infinity.

The centre of the merged glow – of no earthly colour – thickened and became dense, rose and thickened yet more, first a spiral, then a column, finally to resolve itself into the body of a huge black and gold snake. It towered above them, its enormous head swaying and questing from side to side. Signora Zauli cried out in full-throated triumph, Mamie whimpered and dropped her blood-stained needle, while the child entwined her fingers with Jane's and the stonemason quietly watched.

The snake continued its rhythmic questing sway, each sweep bringing its head closer and closer to the floor beneath, where glimmering marbles had replaced the dusty concrete. The final sweep dipped to encounter and then nuzzle – first the broken body of Eric Moonday, then Jedson's still form, and it nudged them together, opened the lipless mouth to reveal – not the flickering fork and sharp fangs of a reptile, but the fleshy wet tongue and blunt teeth of a human being. It licked hungrily at the bodies, still nudging them together, and then settled back to feed, the tearing of meat and crunching of bone loud in the still night. Again Signora Zauli cried out in triumphant pleasure.

Soon nothing of the two bodies remained, but the

snake's head dipped again, its tongue busily licking up the spilt blood until there was no trace on the glimmering marbles.

"*Godammit!*" screeched Mamie, shaking Signora Zauli's arm; the other was still rapt, in thrall to her god. "*Do* what you gotta *do*! Tell it to make me *better*!"

The snake's gold-black head swung, reared, then dipped again, now above the two women, and though no words were audible, all present heard the thought: *What do you desire?*

"Get *rid* of this fucking thing!" screeched Mamie again, "Make me *better!*" And in a hysterical frenzy of desperation she began pulling at her clothes, threw aside the shawl, ripped off her scarf, and struggled out of her jacket, tearing at her blouse to reveal the purplish welts and pustules covering her arms and body. The gold-black head came close, the tip of the fleshy tongue protruded, touched her on one mottled shoulder, and even as they watched the welts faded, the pustules disappeared, and she began to giggle and crow "That's my *boy*! That's the *ticket*! Oh, my …Oh, no, no …!" And then the screaming began.

It had not ended there. Now that the welts were gone, the skin too had begun to peel and fall; glistening flesh was stripped away, exposing white bone and diseased organs, 'getting rid of it', 'making her better', as she had demanded. The screaming stopped; the soft tissues were gone. What remained writhed, and then lay still. *Complete*, came the thought. *Is there another?*

Unafraid, Jane looked at Signora Zauli. She was

standing motionless, no longer smiling, no longer triumphant, and so deathly white the drying blood on her throat stood out in sharp relief. Something went wrong, thought Jane, and then, with sudden inspiration, the wish was taken literally. That was not supposed to happen. The statue of the Sibyl has changed the power of the other, made it ... unpredictable, dangerous. She glanced back at the stonemason. He nodded, as if to say, continue, you will know. She looked at the child, who seemed to ponder and then said: "If it t'were to be done, t'were best to be done quickly." But what? thought Jane. There's no time. If there were just more time, if time would just ...

It came to her. The paper from the sad young man, the last message from Elfriede Baader. Gently she freed her hand from Mowenna's clasp and stepped forward to confront the monstrous gold-black head. The hooded eyes narrowed, were waiting.

"Years will be shortened like months, months like weeks, weeks like days, days like hours, and an hour like a moment," she recited loudly and clearly, head erect, looking into the ancient eyes. The air quivered and moved, the eyes seemed to be considering. Was it enough, wondered Jane. Was it *right*?

It was then that the blue-green waves shot with gold, the luminous tides that were water and yet not water, light but yet not light, burst and rolled into the confines of the temple, crashed soundlessly against the mirrored walls, swirled over – but left dry – the glimmering marbles.

Jane, dazzled and enchanted, felt a calloused palm

against her own. Looked up to see the strong jaw, dark slanting eyes, and almost-mischievous smile. He had discarded the scythe, now held hers and the child's hand, the three linked as he pronounced the words: *"Breves ut menses fient anni, menses ut dies, dies ut horae et hora ut momentum."*

Time stopped – the moment, last particle of its blind relentless rush, was caught and stilled, held in the blue-green waves shot with gold, to become at one with eternity.

Jane stood gazing into the heart of the calm, eyes wide with awe and wonder. Of Signora Zauli nothing could be seen, but the huge black and gold snake, itself caught and stilled by the powers of the valley, was undergoing a sea-change. Even as she watched it shrank and dwindled, became slender and silver, rose and then dived beneath the bright waters with the joyous leap of a dolphin.

24

It was shortly after ten o'clock on Wednesday 17th February, the first day of Lent, and there were detectives from Scotland Yard together with their Roman counterparts at the Hotel delle Sirene – unheard-of. The Romans were terse and although they used the polite *Lei* form to the manager, they looked as if what they would really like to do was bang his head on his desk and force his arm up his back. The English on the other hand, their clothes rumpled and creased after their journey, their eyes tired, spoke quietly and were very polite; they were accompanied by a tall fair-haired woman with glasses, an Englishwoman, a social worker, they said. All of them – Italian and English – looked grim.

Briefly they explained, ignored the manager's obvious shock and dismay. They presumed the woman and child were in their room? Suite, corrected the manager mechanically. As far as he knew – he had not seen them himself, and would they like coffee? Yes, thank you, very welcome (this from the English), and we need an office, somewhere quiet where we can interrogate the woman (this from the Romans). No problem, still mechanically. Now, if he could just show them the way to the room (Suite, thought the manager; he was still grappling with the news), and bring his passkey as well?

It was the English who went down to the lower level, two men, one middle-aged and fatherly, the other younger but with burnt-out worldly eyes, with the social worker discreetly in the background; she would be taking care of the child. The manager's tentative knock, followed by louder, more imperious ones from the detectives, went unanswered, and the passkey had to be brought out. (They think of everything, thought the manager distractedly. Dear God!) "We can manage from here," they said, and were going into the room as the manager escaped upstairs.

They found the aunt crouched on the bed, fully clothed but with her limp bun in disarray, hair straggling greasily about her neck. When she had woken up to find Mowenna missing, she had panicked, first snatching open the door only to see an empty corridor, but then retreating inside, muttering, "Artful! Cunning! Wicked! Well, *they* can find her. She's not *my* problem now."

But it was her problem now. The detectives spoke the official phrases, and she gazed at them blankly as the rationalisation mechanism was smashed to pieces, and they had to haul her up by the arms to get her off the bed, not because she was resisting arrest but because her legs had folded as completely as structure of the mechanism. Where was the child? they kept repeating as they took her along to the lift. Where was the child?

As for the manager, he had gone back to his office, ordered the coffee, and sat down to shake his head and drum his fingers on the desk, meanwhile keeping an eye on the reception area. All this and breakfast still being served to the guests. Terrible, a scandal. A child! He was the father of three daughters and could not contemplate the reality behind the blank official phrase "child abuse and trafficking." Dear God!

He glanced at the clock, only five minutes had passed. Everything looked normal – a couple of guests, Germans, strolled past and wished him good morning; yes, they were going up to Rome today. Have a good day. Thank you, and they left – but what about that woman downstairs? Would they have to drag her upstairs kicking and screaming, dear God? Perhaps it could still be kept quiet. At least he had had the forethought to give them the office next to the service lift, and they would be able to come directly upstairs without coming through reception. He had explained that to the English detectives, but it had been the tall fair-haired woman who had nodded and thanked him. The fatherly and the burnt-out eyes were too intent on what had to be done.

He started the drumming again. What was going on, dear God? – and then glanced towards the hotel entrance – those glass doors needed cleaning – and saw the doors swinging open, affording a momentary reflection, just a flash, of the trees outside the entrance. Clients?

It was a woman holding a little blond-haired girl by the

hand, both looking tired and bedraggled but somehow serene. They came up to the desk, but even before they got there, the manager guessed who the child was; she was dressed so strangely.

"I found this little girl on her own," said the woman, "But she seemed to want to come here. Can you help?" She had spoken in Italian, and the manager, overwhelmed with relief, blurted. "*Sì! Sì! Un momento! Torno subito,*" and rushed from behind the desk to get the detectives.

"I was coming back from a party," Jane was explaining, sipping at a cappuccino. She was talking to the two English detectives in the hotel lounge area, while their Italian colleagues were guarding the aunt in the office. "I found her wandering around on the other side of the bridge. I don't know her name but she seemed to know her way here so I came with her to make sure."

"And you don't know the aunt?" asked the one with burnt-out eyes, leaning forward.

Jane shook her head. "No." She did not elaborate. "Is she all right?" she asked, looking round. "The little girl, I mean." A tall woman with large glasses and a kind face had taken charge of the child, and Jane had not seen her since.

The detectives exchanged a look: "We'll have to see," said the fatherly one slowly. He did not elaborate either.

"Can I ask what this is all about?" she asked timidly; she had reverted to English mode now.

The two exchanged another look. "Possible child abuse," replied the one with burnt-out eyes, watching her intently.

Jane had no need to simulate her shock and disgust, could only look at them wordlessly. "Oh, God ..." she whispered finally.

"But we've got her safe now," said the older man. They both seemed to have relaxed.

"Can I help with anything else?" asked Jane. She had finished her coffee and was suddenly deathly tired; she hoped they would understand the implied "Is it OK if I go now?" The two detectives went into silent communication again, and the fatherly one, said: "Yes, off you go. We've got your details and phone number. Thanks for your help."

With relief Jane left the lounge, and made her way towards the glass entrance doors. All she wanted to do was sleep. She had fulfilled the professor's request, completed the ceremony, and – so it seemed – also saved (but had she saved?) the little girl, the little girl who had somehow been part of it all.

The night before had come to a quiet, almost prosaic conclusion. The valley returned to its silent darkness, the temple was again an empty rectangle, and the three of them climbed down from its bare platform, went through the courtyard and out into Via della Sibilla. Nothing was guarded, nothing was locked.

They went to the narrow door next to the gift shop, slipped inside, and slept – at least Jane and child did, curled up together on the large bed. The stonemason had woken them in the morning; it was time to go.

He came to the door with them, clasped Jane's hand, and rested the other on the child's blond hair. Again, cat-like, she rubbed her head against his hand.

"It is complete," he said, smiling and holding out her shoulder bag. "Goodbye."

"Yes," agreed Jane, taking the bag and smiling back. "Goodbye."

And so it had ended. The door beside the gift shop had closed and there were no more answers, nor even questions; it was time to return to normal life and somehow assimilate the events of the past weeks.

Jane sighed as she continued on her way to the hotel entrance. The hotel doors were open and a porter was polishing the heavy plate glass. And sitting on a large couch to one side were the kind-faced woman and the little girl, now dressed in her own clothes, a neat plaid skirt and a brown jumper; she looked even younger, dangling her legs and fingering a collection of leaves and twigs that she clutched in one small fist. The woman smiled and beckoned, and Jane went over to sit on the chair next to the couch. "I'm so glad ..." She gestured at the child. "I never did know her name," she finished apologetically.

"Mowenna," said the woman, smiling; her tortoiseshell glasses supported thick lenses, though not so thick as to distort her wide-set eyes. "Her name's Mowenna – it's Welsh. And I'm Margery. Margery Maxwell."

"I'm so glad Mowenna's safe, Margery," said Jane, thinking, What a lovely voice she has; the woman reminded her of someone, though for the life of her she couldn't think who.

"Yes, we'll be going back to England later today."

There was a pause, then, "Jane – I hope you don't mind me calling you Jane?"

"No, of course not," said Jane, her tiredness forgotten in sudden surprise. How …?

Margery gave a quick understanding nod; her face was sympathetic. "Jane, I know you're tired, but you need to know that last night was not the end."

"Not the end," repeated Jane slowly, her exhaustion returning in full force. She looked at Mowenna, who regarded her gravely before going back to sorting through her leaves and twigs.

"There have been two battles," the other continued slowly.

"Yes."

"There is a third battle, the last and most decisive."

"When?" queried Jane numbly, thinking, there was last summer, this is February …

"In a few months. Springtime."

"So soon!"

"Yes, I'm sorry, but you have to start preparing for it now. I'll send you details of what I know when I get back to England."

Jane, once more back in the dream when she had thought she was done with it, fished a piece of paper out of her shoulder bag – the faithful shoulder bag – and wrote down her email address. "This is it," she told Margery, watching as the other folded the paper and put it carefully into her purse. The terrible tiredness had returned, and she got up from the chair with difficulty.

"Margery, I'm so sorry, I know I should ask you … I don't know … lots of things, but it's all too much … I can't take it in just now."

"Yes, I know," Margery said gently, and hearing the warm sympathy in her voice, Jane felt tears prick her eyelids. "I'll write to you, Jane."

Jane nodded, was about to go and then looked down at solemn little girl, "Goodbye, Mowenna. Take care."

The child looked up, clambered off the couch, and stood in front of her holding out a spiky twig from her collection: "There's rosemary," she said in her clear child's voice, "that's for remembrance. Pray you, love, remember."

"Mowenna knows," said Margery, as Jane gazed at the sprig of rosemary between her fingers, feeling tears in her eyes and a sudden painful clutch at her heart. "She's an exceptional child."

"Yes," said Jane slowly. "Thank you, Mowenna. I promise. I'll remember."

25

Epilogue

As regards Mowenna and her aunt, the affair went more or less unnoticed in Italy since the players were foreigners, and revelations of more government scandals at home occupied most of the space in national news. It was only later, when it formed part of a much larger police operation involving several European countries and the United States, that it became blaring front-page news. "Kittens at The Pussy Drive!" shouted one, "Child Pornography Ring Exposed", read a more sedate other, while an inside page of one of the middle-market papers got the exclusive "How I found out and *did* something", ghost-written for a senior secretary, who had seen confidential memos at Mamie's London lawyers' office, and taken photocopies to the police. Mowenna's name could not be published, but she featured as an anonymous 'special needs child', a genius, who would have been swallowed up by the underworld of abuse and exploitation.

Mamie and her chauffeur/bodyguard had disappeared, probably to Mexico, the feds thought, and since computers continued to be backed up "from here to Albuquerque," Mamie's other activities became history, the Spike Killer file sometimes being brought out as a case study in training courses.

Barney Highman reaped all the benefits of leaving the 'people stuff' to Mame, but he would spend several years and millions of dollars on lawyers, as district attorneys tried to prove he knew about The Pussy Drive's darker offerings. That Mame, he would think, hope she's rotting in some Mexican jail, the bitch. It was nothing to him that he could afford the millions he needed for lawyers. When *The Pope's Protocol* came out it was one of the year's top grossers, despite being booed by critics, banned in Israel and lambasted for its dreadful cliché-ridden script. And the wavy mark had appeared again on each and every copy, flitting across the screen as if on its way to more urgent business; the film was shown anyway.

In Tivoli nothing of the events in the Sibyl's Temple had been perceived by the town's inhabitants. For them, the burning of their *Zibaldone*, the Carnival King, was all that marked the 16th February. No one had seen the glowing valley, no one had heard Jedson's death throes or Mamie's enraged screams. It had been a normal winter evening like any other. And the good thing about winter, as Maria Grazia the travel agent confided to the film technician (who she called *Cetriolino* – gherkin – but only when they were alone), was that it was so nice to stay in bed.

It was a quite different affair when a man's body was found in the marshy Valle dell'Inferno of Villa Gregoriana on the 18th, then all hell broke loose, and the reporter for the local paper *Tiburno* had a field day. The body must have been there for a few days, and was only found because another group booked an out-of-season visit, and one of them, a bird-watcher, had been training his binoculars on a crow. When it flapped down to land, the binoculars following, its beak jabbed at a splayed fish-white hand, causing the birdwatcher to bang his nose; he would have a mark there for days. A shock for him ("But they *are* scavengers," he would keep telling himself afterwards), unpleasant for the others, but giving a macabre thrill to everyone else; the man was one of the film crew, it was said, just passing through, so nothing to do with Tivoli at all.

That was until a second body was found in a flat in Via Platone Tiburtino, a woman's, the eccentric owner of a gift shop, and she had been *tortured*, they whispered. "But she had *nothing!*" a neighbour wailed, and immediately arranged to have her own locks changed. But were the two murders connected? people asked; investigations were ongoing, and since the gift shop woman had no family and no one to mourn her, only the police retained an interest in developments.

Dott. Salmone, the mayor of Tivoli, was left a sadder and a wiser man. To his mind the murders and the scandal of child trafficking on his very doorstep, were the direct result of the film. In future he would only promote documentaries with their gently-spoken presenters and unobtrusive technical staff, and have no truck with anything that smacked of blockbusters or Hollywood. "They made everything here look so *squalid*!" he raged to his nephew after seeing the film. Enrico held his peace; he had learnt a few things too.

Down on the plain, Tivoli Terme, with its twin milky lakes and huge quarry, held its own secrets. The stonemason's warehouse with its clutter of blocks, panels, joists and off-cuts, was silent and empty, had been empty for as far back as anyone could remember. Across the dusty floor a sudden chill draught blew a scrap of paper, the words "... *an hour like a moment*" briefly visible in a band of sunlight as the scrap drifted into a corner. Its message had been conveyed and the commission was complete. Elfriede Baader too had fulfilled her part, and although no one would come to leave flowers on her quiet grave, clusters of violets would appear there every spring and a curving swathe of wild cyclamen every autumn.

And Signora Zauli? In the vast dim apartment above the Temple of Hercules, she was speaking quietly on the telephone and smiling her slow dark smile. The lamps were lit, and the air in the room was hot and heavy, just the way she liked it. As she spoke, her eyes lazily scanned the polished table, the velvet curtains and the serpentine carvings of the heavy door.

"Yes, your Eminence," she was saying. "No, events did not *quite* transpire as expected." She listened, gave her silvery laugh. "Well, as you know, Eminence, there is always an element of uncertainty in these matters." A pause: "No, it was not the definitive meeting, but, no, I shall not be staying." Another pause, another laugh, but now the silvery sound held grace notes of contempt and scorn. "Why ever should you have come to that conclusion?" she asked with mock incredulity. "My part was always ..."

The interruption was passionate, venomous and lengthy. Signora Zauli listened and yawned and then gently hung up, cutting off the poisonous flow. "How he shrieks like mandrakes torn out of the earth," she murmured to the hot still air. "What fools these mortals be!" She laughed the silvery laugh again but glanced with sudden disquiet at the sculpture of the dragon, large as a mastiff, standing sentinel in the shadows. An image had flashed before her: the pale face of a child, forehead furrowed but eyes blank, gazing from an ivy-framed window. And with that image had come the alien words, which were not – and could not have been – her own. The dragon's scales rippled in the shifting light and its eyes were knowing. Despite what Signora Zauli had said, she would be staying, she had another carnival to attend, and it was time she was on her way.

ABOUT THE AUTHOR

Joanna Leyland was born in South Wales but grew up in England. Leaving the UK in 1984, intending to work temporarily in Rome and then go on to Tokyo, she has lived in Italy ever since. She has made her home in the Monti Lepini, south of the Alban Hills, and her interest in this heartland of early Roman history and legend has given rise to her Goddess Trilogy. The first novel, *The Sacred Wood*, is now followed by *The White Sibyl*, while the third, *The Earth Mother*, will be available in 2014.

Printed in Great Britain
by Amazon